THE HEROBORN

MIKKO RAUHALA

Published by Water Dragon Publishing
waterdragonpublishing.com

ISBN 978-1-957146-79-9 (Trade Paperback)

FIRST EDITION

10 9 8 7 6 5 4 3 2 1

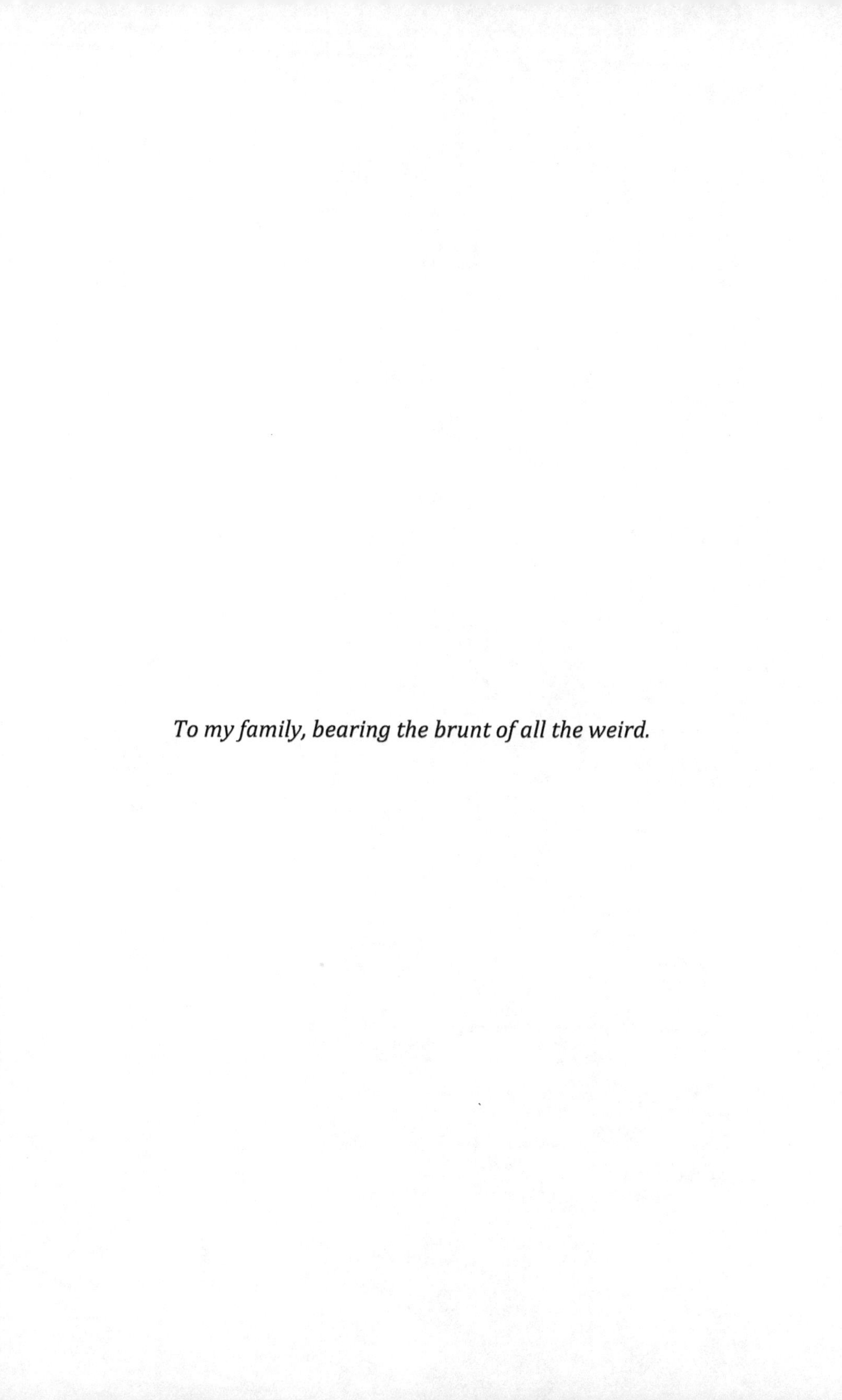

To my family, bearing the brunt of all the weird.

THE
HEROBORN

PART I

1

S ASHA CAST A NERVOUS LOOK around the cemetery. The grounds had been well-kept until a couple of weeks ago when the groundskeeper vanished into thin air. Still, the grass was green for an inner-city churchyard, and the trees made for a welcome change in scenery. Rows of gravestones spread out from the center, walkways between them leading straight to the central mausoleum.

Let's see, if I were a secret entrance to the catacombs, where would I be? The maps she'd seen had shown no corridors under the building, but that was neither here nor there.

Sasha traced a pattern on her staff. A brief green glow indicated readiness. She squeezed the weapon resolutely, her fingers settling into the well-designed grooves among the woodland themed decorations.

She opened the door to the mausoleum carefully, the staff at the ready. She didn't expect any trouble yet, but better safe than sorry. The room was indeed empty except for the central grave with the slab of stone on top. The walls were covered in simple pictographs representing the achievements of whoever was buried here.

The dust on the cover was disturbed. *Anybody could've found this by now if they'd only dared to look.* Sasha took hold of a corner and managed to lift it just enough to get the slab out of its groove. She pushed the cover aside, and it crashed onto the floor. She grimaced, hoping that she hadn't woken anyone up. As for the priests, if they'd try to give her trouble for messing with the grave, she could easily blame it on the undead.

Miraculously, the grave was empty. Sasha felt around the box, suppressing the queasy feeling of violating someone's purported resting place. The bottom seemed to wiggle a bit when pushed from one end. Her eyes turned towards the carvings. *There must be a trigger somewhere.*

Judging by the muck on the floor, the left side had seen more use recently than the right. She went to poke at the wall, especially at any round or otherwise enclosed pictographs. In the middle, something clicked: the moon among the stars that a stick figure was worshiping.

The bottom of the grave started pivoting slowly around a central axis. Sasha rushed to grab it lest it make more noise, then remembered caution and looked down, brandishing her staff. There was no movement.

Still, waiting quietly until somebody came down would be within the capabilities of the creatures that had terrorized the neighborhood for a week or so now. She awkwardly pulled an oval of Dust off her belt with her staff hand, pointed at it with her wand, and made the gestures for the Wardstone spell. The Dust lit up briefly, acknowledging her command. It would hiss quietly if it noticed any creatures larger than a mole aside from her.

Sasha dropped the stone into the darkness. Nothing in the immediate area. She cast the Light spell on another oval, dimmed it a bit, and tossed it in as well. Still no hissing, and the bottom was visible now, not very far down. There were steps dug into the wall for easy access.

It was time to make some of the riskier preparations. Sasha enchanted her ovals of incendiary Red Dust. They'd go off on impact after being thrown at least a few meters first. Merely dropping one on the floor wouldn't cost her a leg, in theory.

Sasha stashed her wand under her belt and clambered down the shaft. The staff made it awkward to climb, but she managed. She got to the bottom and picked up both of the ovals she'd dropped.

The corridor was dark and dank. There was no ornamentation on the walls or evidence of burial use. The church catacombs would commonly be used to house the earthly remains of noteworthy people who were not quite close enough to the top of the ladder. This must have been just a side tunnel.

Opposite the tunnel there stood a large black obelisk, embedded just far enough into the rock that she'd missed it from above. Sasha'd seen a couple of them before. They were spread here and there around the realm, but usually in secluded places in nature. The smooth columns were more than two meters high and more than a meter wide. They seemed to be made of black stone, but somehow treated with a strong, glossy finish, not unlike her elven staff. They were widely suspected to be magical and to have some grand purpose aside from being imposing, but they never did anything nor reacted to any investigation, be it with a wand or with a pickaxe. They were also stuck to the bedrock with fierce insistence. It'd probably require a mineful of dwarves to get one unstuck, but what then? People just left them alone these days.

Sasha drew her focus back to the task at hand. She kept the dim light and the wardstone in front of her while carefully proceeding forward. Soon she came upon a wooden door. The corridor itself turned and continued to the left, toward the mapped regions of the catacomb. If there were zombies lying in wait behind the corner, they'd certainly have seen the light. Sasha carefully rolled the wardstone toward the bend while holding the staff ready for attackers.

There was a light hiss. Her heart jumped. She edged slowly along the wall towards the bend. Strangely soft breathing began to register. Then she saw it: a human figure in dirty, ragged clothing slumped on the floor. As if on cue, it snorted and turned. She could see its face now. There was the telltale green-hued discoloration, but not much of it. It was probably a recent acquisition.

She had, of course, known that zombies slept. That was part of the reason why she was here at high noon. The news was that they'd sleep while on duty as well, if indeed this one had been ordered to guard their lair as seemed likely. Zombies clearly made lousy substitutes for wardstones. Luckily for her, necromancers had a limited repertoire.

She approached the corner with great care, but there were no more guards. The side corridor was shorter than the one she'd come through and ended in a large wooden door, as wide as the corridor itself. The door was closed with a bolt. She was pretty sure the mapped areas were right behind it. Maybe the other side was camouflaged somehow, concealing the lair.

Now there was the question of what to do with the poor zombie. The obvious answer seemed a bit harsh and unheroic now, the thing being fast asleep. But a zombie was a zombie, and the horde had already wreaked havoc on the city. It needed to be stopped.

Sasha comforted herself with the thought that the zombie had never been a proper person to start with. Necromancers could only turn neople into thralls, and neople lives were cheap, to be sure. This very church was just preparing to sacrifice a few, in fact. Not that Sasha much liked the sacrifices either, and not only because of their doubtful utility. The practice just seemed … uncivilized, somehow.

Regardless, she could hardly leave the zombie be, and she'd be doing the poor thing a favor, really. Even if she let it live, if she somehow subdued it instead, the clergy would still destroy it as unclean. Probably more painfully than she would.

Gathering her resolve, she pointed the staff at the creature's head. It would be clean, quick, and hopefully quiet. Her fingers moved hesitantly along the grooves of the staff, but move they did. A bolt shot out from the hollow end, and with a thud and a whimper, the breathing was gone. Averting her eyes from the mess, she touched the top of her staff with a fresh oval from her belt. The Dust shed its shape and flowed inside.

Before trying the first door, Sasha thought it better to check the end of the corridor. She unbarred the large door there, slowly opened it, and then tossed the wardstone through the crack. Nothing, as she expected. The necromancer barring his own zombies out into the public areas while he rested wouldn't have made much sense. He'd want them handy in case of an attack.

Stepping through the opening, Sasha found more traditional catacombs. There were rows upon rows of small doors, just large enough to fit a casket. The door itself was disguised as a wooden shelf. There were some urns on it, placed in depressions and behind small railings that kept them in place as the door opened and closed. Sasha picked up her wardstone and closed the secret passage. It occurred to her that it was probably not the only one. There might be other secret escape routes in the catacombs proper. She could block this one, make it only traversable by her.

She took a couple of ovals of Dust off her belt, pressed them on the latch, and flicked her wand at them. The ovals melted together and flowed to envelop the latch.

She then backtracked to the door that the zombie had been guarding. It would probably be bolted shut from the other side, maybe even trapped. She double-checked that her red ovals were handy and tried the door softly from the side with her staff. It didn't budge.

Sasha took a white oval, charmed it into a thin stick, and probed the small crack on the side of the door. Moving the stick up and down, she could feel the bolt, but it wouldn't move an inch before the stick started to give. Perhaps it was of a sliding type, too heavy for the instrument, or otherwise locked down.

If everything remained quiet for a while longer, this was a mere inconvenience. Sasha placed the stick on top of the bolt, sent more Dust from another oval to flow through the crack to the other side, and cast the Burrowing charm. Then she settled to wait with a red oval and the staff at the ready.

Soon she tried the door again, and it slowly pushed open. There was a faint light on the inside. She couldn't see the source, but the shadows fluttered like from a candle's flame. There were some bags by the wall, a small hole in the roof—likely a hidden ventilation shaft—and yes, shadowy forms lying on the floor. She'd gone unnoticed so far, she thought. Then the door, still slowly opening, gave out a loud creak. The forms on the floor stirred, and a sleepy voice from further in muttered something unintelligible. *No time to lose.* She tossed the red oval in and spun to the side.

The reaction was milder than she'd hoped, but the bang did indicate some damage. It had been a while since she'd used Red Dust. The voice, quite awake now, shouted clearly: "Attack, minions! Protect your master!"

Leaving her light near the door to illuminate her targets better, Sasha ran into the graveyard corridor which would give her more room to operate in. Slightly banged up human forms emerged shambling from the room. The discoloration was more pronounced in this group. Sasha shot a couple of bolts towards the first zombies. Neither target fell or even appreciably slowed down their steady walk. *Damn.* Sasha would have to make the shots count. The staff should have had ten bolts in it to start with. Another volley took the first ones down. What, six bolts left, only a bit more Dust in her belt, and she might need that for something else.

More enemies were incoming. She shot at them both, this time aiming a bit higher. The head was a smaller target, but her magic would help guide the bolts. One took a good hit to the throat and fell. The other was hit on the side of the head. It looked bad, but the minion was still shambling toward her, as did others. Sasha glanced at her Red Dust ovals but it was too dangerous to use them now. *Shit.* She should have opened with a larger volley of them, but Master Aaron's teachings had made her overly conservative in her dealings with the red stuff.

Sasha kept thinning the herd until there were only two left. She'd hit both of them, but the shots hadn't been lethal. *Not immediately …* She quickly pointed her wand at the zombies and made a gesture. The first one's gait grew slightly more awkward. Sasha scrambled to feed her staff from the ovals left on her belt. Just as the Dust was flowing into the staff, her opponent bellowed from the shadows: "Lunge at her, you fools! Grab and disarm her!"

The thralls did as they were told, taking Sasha by surprise. Fast zombies were unprecedented in the lore. They were supposed to be strong and resilient, but shambling and slow in their movement.

Desperately, Sasha went for an oval of Red Dust, but the zombies seized her arms and forced her hands open, making her drop her weapons. There was a thud as the oval fell onto the ground. Sasha grimaced, bracing herself, but there was no explosion. The safety had worked.

Sasha struggled to pull herself out of the zombies' grasp, but the lore was right about their strength. As the stench of death surrounded her, she had to concede that she was well and truly stuck. The necromancer stepped out of the shadows and through the door, dusting off his black robes smugly. He was a little taller than Sasha and had perhaps ten or twenty years on her.

"So. They sent a little girl after me. A Heroborn, surely? Too few explosions for a fire mage," he mused, stroking his beard. He was calm and collected now, holding the upper hand.

"I'll have you know I'm here because all the big boys were too scared," Sasha said with a snarl.

"The common folk do scare easily when confronted with arcana. That's why these places make such good bases, for a while at least," the necromancer said, furrowing his eyebrows in thought. "I guess I should be taking my leave now that you've discovered the mausoleum entrance."

Sasha felt the hold over her left arm weaken. She might still have a chance if she could stall the man for a moment. "How did you make them move so fast?" she asked.

The necromancer chuckled. "They're shambling when left on their own but seem perfectly capable of moving quickly when explicitly told to do so."

"I've never heard of it." Sasha said, raising a quizzical eyebrow.

"No, I suppose not," he said with a scoff. "My colleagues don't tend to be very creative. But you, you seem different. I think I'll take you with me, keep you around for a while. You can teach me your kind of magic. If you'll prove yourself useful, I might show a measure of mercy."

Sasha's eyes widened in surprise. This wasn't how necromancers usually operated. She wasn't about to complain about the opportunity to stall further, however.

"You must know that your kind cannot use Heroborn magic," Sasha reminded him. The hold on her right arm weakened as well. She smiled inwardly. Soon she could make her move.

"As with the case of the shambling zombies, I suspect it's less about ability and more about being stuck in their ways. I'm willing to give it a try."

"Order your thralls to let me go and I'll consider it," Sasha tried.

The necromancer shook his head, smiling deviously. "I'm afraid that's not a part of the deal. However, if you can be made to see the merits of my way of thinking, in time, who knows?"

Sasha drew a long breath, nodding slightly, as if considering the necromancer's proposal. Then the zombie on her left let go and fell onto the ground. The bolt that had failed to kill the thrall was still made of her Dust, and while its power was mostly depleted on firing, there was some left for the sake of magical guidance. The power would not have been fully drained during the bolt's brief flight. That's what she had called upon, casting the Burrowing charm to churn away at the body's soft tissues.

Sasha yanked herself free of the other zombie and dove to grab her staff and the red oval, which she threw at the necromancer. He deftly jumped back through the door and to the side while Sasha lay flat on the ground, fingers in her ears, hoping that the bodies strewn on the floor would shield her.

The boom left Sasha reeling, but she picked up her wand and got onto her feet as quickly as she could. The other zombie had fallen in the commotion and was twitching on the ground. Sasha slammed the end of her staff against its head and it quieted down.

Then she pointed her wand at the oval of Dust giving off light near the door and turned it up a notch. The light revealed the necromancer, not much worse for wear, pointing a light crossbow in her general direction.

Sasha immediately traced a groove on her staff, and dozens of tendrils of Dust burst forth from its surface in all directions, coalescing into a shell as round as the corridor would allow. Several sturdier strands of Dust remained, keeping the shell attached to the staff.

The necromancer stared at the semi-transparent barrier, his mouth agape, then let loose his bolt. Sasha heard three sounds in rapid succession: soft ones in front of her and at her back, and finally a metallic clank as the bolt struck the obelisk. The shield wasn't sturdy enough to stop anything, but it could deflect bolts and arrows away from the staff's wielder. It would take a powerful and well-aimed shot to even graze her.

The necromancer bolted out the door and towards the side entrance. Bad move, but he couldn't have known that the shield was powerless against touch. Sasha wasn't sure how much of her Dust she'd managed to get into the staff when the zombies had grabbed her, if she still had anything to shoot with. He might've still had a chance if he'd rushed her.

Sasha quickly loaded one of the remaining three ovals on her belt into the staff and approached the bend. The strands holding the shield moved in tune with her, sometimes snapping away only to be replaced with new ones. She heard some banging and cursing from the other end. The necromancer had found her block. Her eyes darted between the room and the side corridor. Satisfied that there was nobody coming for her from either direction, she stepped to confront her opponent.

The flurry of attackers gone and her quarry being an actual person, Sasha grew more hesitant again. She pointed the staff squarely at him. "That's far enough," she said, in a not at all satisfyingly Heroic voice.

The necromancer froze, raised his hands slowly and turned to look at her, dark determination in his eyes. "Impressive. Now you've really caught my interest. Don't think the commoners aren't afraid of you as well, even as they use you to do what they dare not."

Sasha startled. The necromancer had struck home, though not in the way he'd meant it. Those who knew her to be Heroborn were wary enough of her already, but if they knew what else she carried in her blood, they'd hang her in a heartbeat.

The necromancer took advantage of her reaction and continued: "We're better than any of them. I'll do you one better than my last offer: let us work together, share our secrets. I know the Heroborn are just itching to get their hands on necromantic magic."

Sasha didn't have aspirations toward necromancy, but the complex magic that made thralls out of neople would be extremely valuable all the same. In the past, necromancers had kept their secrets just as well as the druids had, even under torture.

But no. She could trust the man about as far as she could throw him. Besides, she strove to follow in the footsteps of the ancient Heroes. Taking the deal would betray all they'd stood for. "Drop the dagger and the wand on your belt slowly. In fact, drop the belt," Sasha commanded.

He complied, but not silently. "Is that a no, then? I'd much rather have done this the easy way."

Sasha tossed her final ovals at his feet. "Hard way it is. Pick those up, slowly. Good. Stay still." The man flinched but stayed still as the Dust crawled up to his wrists, forming solid restraints.

"You may want to know that if you try to run or attack me, you forfeit your hands," she said coldly. It was no idle threat.

The man nodded with a grimace. He seemed to take her seriously enough after all the neople blood spilled. The thought made her slightly faint for a second, but she focused on the man instead of the battleground and regained her composure. *Just a little while longer ...*

She backtracked towards the cemetery exit with the man following her at a respectful distance. At the hole, she stopped him far enough to quickly dart up herself without having to worry too much about him grabbing at her feet. After being reminded of the nature of his shackles, the man grudgingly followed.

The aftermath got a bit blurred in Sasha's mind. She took the man to the church first, since they were conveniently on its grounds already. With news of this magnitude, she managed to get the attention of the head priest easily enough even amidst the sacrificial preparations. The City Guard were sent for. Descriptions and locations of the secret passage and room were given. The Church would of course take care of the cleanup, she was assured. It occurred to her that she could still retrieve some of her Dust from the corpses for re-empowerment, but quickly pushed that idea aside. *Let the Church handle it.*

Once the Guard arrived, money, praise, and the prisoner were exchanged. The restraints were swapped for mundane ones, and the prisoner hauled off to rot somewhere until they could decide what to do with him. She cared little, but was glad she'd managed to capture him alive, at least. No people blood on her hands today.

She was asked to stay for the day's sacrificial service as an honored guest. She excused herself as needing to rest after the trials of the day, barely managing not to vomit right there. Everybody understood, of course. She got the impression they were even relieved. It would probably have just seemed ungrateful not to offer.

A vacant stare in her eyes, Sasha returned to her inn on the outskirts of the city. She lay on the bed, reminding herself she'd done a Hero's deed today.

2

THE NEXT DAY, just after Sasha had had some porridge and fruit for breakfast in the common room and gone back to her quarters, there was a polite but firm knock on her door. Sasha cracked it open. There was a jovially smiling uniformed man on the other side.

"Yes?" she asked through the crack.

"Ah, you must be Sasha of the Heroborn. Captain Perell, at your service. We've heard a lot of good things about you at the Mage Corps."

After her heroics, it was just a matter of time before the king's recruitment officers took a shot at her, she supposed.

"I'm not particularly interested," she replied. When Master Aaron had taken her in, he'd raised her to abhor violence. Later, the stories about the Heroes of old had captured her imagination and she'd gotten aspirations to fight on the side of righteousness, thus reducing the sum total of violence in the world. But Aaron had not relented, telling her about why her parents had died so early on, why she in particular would be likely to be consumed in an ever-escalating maelstrom of bloodshed if she took one single step down that road.

Well, she was on that road now, but having to wreak destruction on command didn't appeal to her. Besides, if they ever found out about her lineage, they'd string her up to avoid her taking them down with her.

"Come now, hear me out. Seeing as you've already proven yourself resourceful and brave, we have a special offer just for you," the captain beckoned.

Yeah, right. Master Aaron had warned her about these guys. They'd be just slightly less persistent and annoying than it would take for their mark to go off on a rampage—or so he had said. They must really have managed to irk the peaceful old man.

Sasha opened the door slightly further. "Fine, I have a bit of time. Give me the short version." If she heard the man out, maybe he'd leave her be for a while.

Perell took it as an invitation and pushed the door the rest of the way open, barging into her room. As Sasha closed the door again, the captain started his speech: "Well, first of all, our mages all get large, comfortable rooms. No cramped quarters like this for our elite, no sir." *Except when they were sent out to battle*, Sasha mentally filled in. To be fair, it didn't happen a lot. The Corps were the greatest military concentration of mages this side of the elven forests. Not many dared to mount an offense worth sending the Mage Corps to counter.

"It's a life of privilege, it is," Perell carried on. "At first, you'd be stationed in a training facility, but with your evident aptitude, I'm sure you'd be able to move to a research garrison in no time. There you'd be able to live among like-minded professionals. You'd even have funding to do your own research. Subject matter is negotiable, as long as it can be applied to national defense."

And offense, no doubt. "Where would I be posted, geographically speaking?" Sasha cut in.

"Good question! They're both near the capital, up north along the coast. A great place to live." But not where Sasha was headed. *So much for that backup plan.* The pitch continued: "King Galen himself sometimes hosts banquets for all of his mages. Speaking of, after a few years of service you'd be eligible to apply for a position in his elite guard. The post comes with a lot of responsibility, but it has its own perks."

"Right. Thank you for the information. I'll mull it over for a while and get back to you," Sasha said, trying to appear as enthusiastic as possible while showing the man the door.

"Certainly!" Perell exclaimed. "In fact, I must firmly request you to stop by our offices by the end of the week after you've thought it over. We can commission you then or talk further if you need more information. And, of course, if you have any existing obligations, we'll be more than happy to help you get out of those."

"Oh. Well, that's a load off my chest," Sasha deadpanned.

"One more thing before I leave. Not on behalf of the Corps. I promised to relay a message." The captain twisted his mouth, reluctant. "I hate to be the bearer of bad news, but the man you apprehended has managed to escape."

Sasha winced and her eyes went wide. "How? And what's it got to do with me?" Was the man coming after her? Did they except her to chase him?

"Oh, nothing. You did a fine job, very fine, and it's not your problem in any way. As best we can tell, he's skipped town. It appears that the jail uses neople for bringing food to their prisoners, and, well, one thing led to another. I'd like to stress that the Mage Corps had nothing to do with this debacle."

Sasha palmed her face. She should've emphasized that the necromancer be kept away from neople, but she'd not been at her sharpest at the time. The man would have needed a wand and Dust, but if they'd also neglected to search him properly, she had some guesses as to where a resourceful and paranoid mage might have hidden those while his thralls kept an attacker busy. Necromancy needed very little Dust, and you could get by with a short wand if aim was not your greatest concern.

"Okay, fine. Have word sent if he's seen. I'm not saying I'll go after him, again, but I'd like to know to watch my back."

"Certainly, and I think it's only fair that the City Guard clean up their own mess if he returns. Shameful, how they shirked their responsibility the first time around, resorting to Roderic to find someone braver. A proper Heroborn has more important things to do, greatness to strive for—at the Mage Corps." The man visibly suppressed a chuckle at his own rhyme. Luckily Sasha was already exasperated, so her opinion of it didn't show.

After giving her directions to the local Mage Corps recruitment office, Captain Perell left, bidding her good day. Sasha wished him likewise and decided to get new accommodations. The man had been too insistent. The Corps didn't always forcibly draft mages. Master Aaron had managed to stay out, after all, though possibly only by making his home deep in the countryside and only ever involving himself in local matters. Still, the good captain had pointedly neglected to mention the option of her refusing their gracious offer. She wouldn't put it past the Corps to put a tail on her, to make sure she wouldn't skip town. They liked to act nice at first, Master Aaron had warned her. Drafting a mage would be easier if their mark thought it was voluntary.

Maybe Roderic could help.

• • •

The innkeeper nodded her a quiet farewell as Sasha left for the street, staff in hand. Outside, it was quieter than yesterday. *Good.* A country girl at heart, she was still unaccustomed to the bustle of the big city. So many unfamiliar faces around her made her nervous. She glanced down at her belt and moved her purse from the side to the front, to better keep an eye on it. Then she was off.

Her inn was situated on the outskirts of the city, outside the original city wall. Deep inside the Middle Kingdom where monsters were rare and border skirmishes unheard of, they hadn't bothered to fortify the new settlements. Sasha quietly wondered when it would come back to bite them.

To avoid the crowded city streets as much as possible, Sasha circled around to the northern gate, where there was no urban sprawl. Those in power had perhaps wanted to keep at least one gate clear of the rabble.

The detour would also help her to spot if anyone was following her. She tried to be nonchalant about it, fixing her gaze at particular buildings while walking past them, allowing her eyes to linger to the point of looking backward.

By the time she was closing in on the gate, she was pretty sure she had a shadow. A young man dressed in unremarkable gray had been popping up in her peripheral vision. Could be just a pickpocket eying her valuables, of course, but if he was, he was very persistent about it.

There was a guard on either side of the open gate. Sasha dug out Roderic's token to flash at them should they give her any trouble. It seemed he had a hand in many things in this city even though he held no office. His independence was a blessing, now. She was pretty sure he wouldn't flinch from hiding her from the authorities. But would he be inclined to?

The guard on the left was sitting down on a thinly protruding foundational stone, and the other one was leaning against the wall on the right. He looked at her direction, and involuntarily her eyes darted to meet his. He winked at her with a mild lopsided grin.

Sasha blushed and she moved her gaze forward. She heard a muffled laugh from the direction of the other guardsman. She sped up her steps and kept her ears peeled in case the guard would actually approach her, but she got away clean.

The north gate road took her towards the marketplace, near her destination. The inner city was bustling with people, and the tall two- and three-story buildings seemed to squeeze her in with them. She held tightly onto her belongings and concentrated on moving briskly onward. On occasion she glanced back to see if the earlier man was still following, but couldn't be sure. Anxious with the crowd, she was more obvious about it than before, but it couldn't be helped. Perhaps her tail, if he was there, would just think she was nervously checking for pickpockets, which was also true.

When she got to the marketplace her mood improved. The crowds hadn't thinned, but the familiar context of the market made it easier to take in. The plaza was bustling with sellers peddling everything from foodstuffs and simple clothing to tools and ornaments. Prospective customers were eyeing wares with exaggerated suspicion, haggling away. Scattered about were what could only be neople, lugging around weightier articles of trade and boxes thereof for their masters.

Sasha stuck to the sidelines, making her way towards the inn she hoped Roderic still conducted his business in. Soon she reached the large stone building and entered. The common room was full of people eating, drinking, and making merry. As she walked past the tables towards the stairs, she heard someone describe, in great detail, the gushes of blood in yesterday's ritual. Sasha shivered as visions of yesterday's battle flashed in her mind. She shook her head to clear it and tuned out the talk.

A guard was standing by the stairs, protecting the better folk upstairs from the rabble. Sasha flashed Roderic's token at him and confidently walked up the stairs like she belonged. The man let her pass in peace.

Upstairs was markedly more peaceful, with only a couple of parties of people. Velvet curtains partitioned off private tables by the right wall. She recognized Roderic's personal guard in front of one of them. Sasha approached him, token in hand. The guard hesitated, allowing her to part the curtain with her staff.

"Sasha! What a surprise!" Roderic exclaimed from his table, successfully hiding the annoyance that Sasha suspected was hiding behind his sharp eyes. Then he turned them back toward whoever was behind the other curtain. "Sorry, an urgent matter with the hero of the week, it seems. I trust you'll take care of what we discussed?"

"It will be done," a voice said, and the other curtain rose to reveal a young man. He was dressed well and had some ink blots on his fingers. A scribe, perhaps, or an accountant. Sasha slipped in through the curtain as he left.

"I thought I'd see you at the ritual, considering you'd already solved our little necromancer problem by then. Figured you'd be a guest of honor, even," Roderic pondered.

"They did offer, but I'd seen enough neople blood for the day. Besides, I don't think the sacrifices do any good."

Roderic pursed his lips. "Surely you've seen the brightened star? Angered gods are not to be trifled with," he said with just the slightest hint of sarcasm in his voice, daring her to go on.

"Master Aaron used to study Church history. They first came up with the ritual after a couple of Church neople had died in an accident when the first star had flared for a week or so. But he thought it was a coincidence that it died out soon after. Later sacrifices didn't placate the stars so quickly, the timings seem more random than anything. The priests are just doing it to be seen doing something."

"You don't say?" Roderic prodded with a hint of a smile on his lips.

"Besides, if the gods were just placated by the sacrifice as they say, why do they fade out afterwards? Sure, maybe gods sleep for a long time, but it's been the better part of a century since the first disappearance." *Not that they've been up to much lately in any case, their envoys long gone.* At the back of her mind, Sasha couldn't help but wonder if she couldn't find out the why of that as well on her ... quest, as it were. In her grandest moments of hubris, she'd fantasize about attracting the gods' attention somehow. She'd make them notice the sorry state of the world they'd created, make them bring the Heroes back.

"You're not the first one to think that the flareups are death throes rather than anger," Roderic said sympathetically. "Best to keep any speculation about divine wars to yourself, though. The Church is quite fond of its doctrine. Now, what was it you wanted to talk to me about?"

"Someone from the Mage Corps visited me," Sasha said.

"Did they? Well, you've proven to be a formidable mage in spite of your age. I'm sure they'd give you a good position in their ranks. I can still get you out of the trade caravan job if that's what you want."

"No. It's just the opposite. I need to get to Kilnkeep and they don't seem particularly inclined to let me go. I was ordered to report to their headquarters by the end of the week. I'm concerned about what might happen if I do that, or if I don't and they catch up with me. I'm not sure, but I may have a shadow."

Roderic frowned. "The Corps are none of my business. I've arranged your placement in the caravan as we discussed."

Sasha stood up, slammed her hands on the table, and leaned forward. "You promised to get me *on* a caravan within a fortnight if I handled the necromancer problem that both the priests and the City Guard were too scared to touch. Well, I handled it, and a deal's a deal." She could feel her heart pounding faster and faster.

"And you're seriously holding me to the literal phrasing of our agreement?" Roderic asked, holding a hand on his chest and looking affronted.

"You'd do the same to me and you know it," Sasha said with a snarl.

A tense moment passed. Then Roderic's stern expression suddenly melted and he gave out a hearty laugh. "Right you are, lass. Right you are. Looks like I'll have to be more careful making contracts with magical creatures in the future. Let's see ... I have a safehouse in the woods well outside the city. You can hide there until the caravan leaves and join them on the road. How's that?"

Sasha backed down. "That'll do. I'll need the ingredients we talked about with me, to replenish my Dust."

Roderic nodded. "My people are acquiring them as we speak." He paused for a moment and seemed to consider whether to open his mouth again. He did. "Mind, you could probably do worse for yourself than by enlisting. The Corps are demanding, but they don't skimp on rewards either. What's so important about Kilnkeep anyway?"

Sasha looked down, drawing a long breath. *That way lies the long-lost Hall of Heroes, where I hope to find a way to shed the curse carried by my bloodline.*

She furrowed her brow and gave Roderic a stern look. "You just take care of your business and I'll take care of mine. How are we going to do this?"

3

EARLY NEXT MORNING, a carriage made a delivery at Sasha's inn. As she'd arranged with Roderick, she slipped onto the back and lay down on the side, cradling her backpack. The driver nonchalantly covered her with a cloth and put some of his lighter sacks on top of her for good measure.

Sasha waited nervously for the carriage to leave. Whenever she heard footsteps, she braced herself and squeezed on her staff. fearful that it was a recruitment enforcer. She'd caught a glimpse of the man that had followed her last night near the inn, further compounding her concerns.

After an excruciatingly long few minutes, the driver hopped on and they were off. The ride was uncomfortable, every bump adding to her aches. The carriage made one more stop where the driver dropped off some of his merchandise before they left for the fields.

After a good while of creaking, shaking, and bumping, the driver said in a low voice: "All's clear. I've a good enough view here. We're not being followed."

"Thanks," Sasha said quietly. "If it's all the same to you, I'll stay down until we're there. Just to be sure."

The driver snorted. "Have it your way, kid. We're pretty close now, anyway."

"You have my stuff?" Sasha asked.

"It's all in the middle sack there next to you."

Sasha grimaced. Putting all of the materials necessary for the creation of Red Dust together in one sack was not quite foolhardy, but not the safest way to travel either. Not a problem if the bottles stayed intact. Otherwise, well, she'd prefer not to spontaneously combust.

She considered the risks for a moment, then decided to trust the driver's judgment on the pursuer situation more than his packing. Carefully she sat up and opened the ingredients sack. It was full of pouches and bottles, all intact. You could make Dust out of most anything varied enough, but since Roderic was paying for her expenses, these were a prime selection of ingredients. It would make the process much faster than it would otherwise have been.

Sasha identified the bottles with the most volatile substances and verified that they were well sealed. Then she moved them on the opposite sides of the sack. *Good enough for now.*

Then she had a look around. They were just entering a forest, leaving fields of wheat behind them. The driver had been right; there was no pursuit. That's not to say they wouldn't try to find her when she wouldn't show, but hopefully she'd be beyond their grasp soon. She didn't quite trust Roderic, but the man had a reputation to uphold. If he'd start selling out people he'd made a deal with, it would be the end of him. That afforded her a measure of confidence in the man.

The bumpy ride was only a touch more comfortable sitting than lying down, but she'd manage. She looked around the thick forest. "The caravan will probably not take this path?" she ventured.

"Indeed, they'll take big road north from here. I'll come back for you in five days and take you where you need to be, a bit further along. Meanwhile, we're just about there." The horse neighed as the man signaled him to stop.

"The house is over there, behind the thick patch," the man said, pointing into the forest on their left. "Grab that other bag as well, it has some food and drink in it. There should also be a barrel for rain water at the cabin, probably decently full."

Sasha carefully hoisted the sacks onto the ground, hopped off herself, and grabbed her backpack and staff from the cart.

The driver nodded and started to turn the carriage around. "Be seeing you."

Sasha looked at him, then the sacks. The man didn't seem to be about to help her with them, and she wasn't about to ask. She put on her backpack and grabbed one sack in each hand, squeezing her staff under her arm. Then she started to make her way through the thick foliage toward the cabin she'd been promised.

After a while of walking, she started to make out a small building in the forest. Its mossy roof did a decent job at camouflaging it when viewed from further away. The sacks started to weigh heavily on her, but she was determined to show the long-gone driver that she could manage by herself just fine.

With great effort, she made it to the shack before her hands gave out. She let the sacks rest on the ground while she gathered her strength and surveyed her surroundings.

The forest was thick, but from this side of the trees, the road was just visible. The barrel was by the door, and there was, indeed, some water in it under all the leaves and other droppings. The shack itself was small and shoddily built, but would serve its purpose. Good thing winter had come and gone, though. She'd hate to have to stay here when it was cold.

Sasha looked at the door and cursed. In her exhaustion, she'd neglected to check if someone had taken residence. She readied her staff, still good for a bolt or two, and pried the door open with it. The barren room was empty with only a hard wooden bed for furniture. Her lack of vigilance had not come back to bite her. *Not this time ...*

Sasha dragged her things inside and sat on the bed for a moment. She'd be here for almost a week. She'd better prepare for tonight and make a quick batch of Dust from what she'd brought. Maybe another slow one from what she could forage later. *Except ...* She cringed. She'd neglected to arrange for a suitable vat for the Dust. The brewing would take ages in her soup bowl. She quickly scanned the hut, but found nothing suitable.

Her gaze darted to the barrel of rainwater. Quickly she checked the amount of drinks in the sack, rummaged through her backpack, took her waterskin, filled it from the barrel, and drank her fill before pushing it over. She could probably find more water, and even if not, she could eke it out for five days. What she wouldn't risk was any more time than she had to without ample Dust. Besides, she'd sold her expertise as a mage to the caravan. They'd rely on her to be equipped for the part.

Sasha rummaged through her backpack for the cube of Dust she'd held in reserve and commanded it to feel the limits of the barrel. She visually verified the reach of the Dust to be appropriate. Wouldn't want it to start eating up the house, or the forest.

Not that it would get very far, the Catalyst limiting its growth. She gathered the various materials, biomass and inert matter alike, into the prepared barrel, and poured a measured bit of the concoction over the whole thing. Alchemists frowned upon the naming of the substance. While quite little of it did go a long way, the Catalyst was actually used up in the process rather than merely aiding it along. But that's what the Heroes of old had called it, and that was the end of it.

Nothing left but to start the reaction. With a few gestures, the Dust already in the barrel gave off a faint glow, its intensity highest where the Catalyst had splashed. The glow would soon fade, but the process was underway. In a few hours she'd have the first batch ready.

Meanwhile, there was not much to do but sit and wait. Sasha's mind started twitching. Perhaps she could use the time for spellcrafting. The trick she'd used in the catacombs came to mind. She could, perhaps, make a dedicated spell of it.

The concept would work a lot better with a Red Dust propelled missile. With those, the normal Dust used for the bolt didn't deplete much at all before impact. Unless one were to use already drained material, there would be a lot of unused power left at the point of impact. Just that nobody had harnessed it—that she knew of. King Galen's forces would have done a lot of research on offensive spells, but they'd likely keep such a missile secret. Master Aaron and his ilk, on the other hand, had never been focused on combat spells, so the oversight was understandable.

Sasha dug her papers out of the backpack and told the staff to eject what Dust it had left onto the wooden bed. A small pile of gray Dust appeared, half-spent from the shield. She separated it into two small cubes with her wand. *This would do.* She made a wardstone out of one of the cubes and went outside to attach it on the corner of the roof to keep watch over the hovel. Aside from the mundane uses of the staff, she only had a few ovals of Red Dust left to defend herself with, and she'd like a bit of warning if anyone approached.

The other cube she'd use for spellcrafting. Sasha made the gestures for the Scribing spell and the Burrowing spell in succession with a sheet of paper next to the Dust cube. Tendrils extended from the cube and touched the paper delicately here and there, rendering the highest layer of the incantations for the Burrowing spell onto it. Sasha repeated the process with the Red Dust missile spell, shaped the Dust into a pen suitable for her own hand, and set to thinking.

The crafting turned out to be relatively easy, the new spell being a straightforward combination of existing spells. It almost sufficed to imprint the incantations back on the wand as a single spell, but she ended up having to insert some glue incantations in between. She also decided to make an adjustment to the burrowing portion. The bolt would break up into fragments and separate strands of the spell would proceed in all six cardinal directions.

Stranded spells required advanced crafting techniques, so Sasha was very careful about it. She didn't want to have to do too many series of tests. She had procured excess amounts of the concoctions required for making Red Dust, but it would not do to be wasteful. Once ignited, it couldn't be reused like normal Dust. Luckily the explosive part of the spell was well-tested already. She hadn't needed to tamper with that. Mistakes there could be fatal.

After she was satisfied that she'd integrated the spells properly, she pointed at her papers with her wand, cast the Imprinting spell, and made the gesture she'd decided on for the new spell. The wand gave out a brief green glow. There were no overt errors in her incantations, and the wand had accepted the spell. It remained to be seen if it actually worked as intended.

Sasha went outside to check the barrel. Its bottom was covered in white, powdery substance; the native form of Dust. With a gesture from her wand the powder coalesced into a number of ovals, revealing some leftover refuse beneath. Sasha filled her belt with the ovals and took those that wouldn't fit inside.

She'd want to have some more Dust of the red kind in reserve, particularly if she was going to use some of it for testing. The conversion wouldn't take much time given the ingredients she now had. She placed a few of her new Dust ovals in her soup bowl, flicked her wand at them, and very carefully started to measure and pour. Soon enough, the ovals had acquired some more mass and volume, as well as that familiar red tint.

Sasha placed a few of the remaining white ovals in the same bowl and made a stirring gesture. The pieces of Dust flowed into each other, making several ovals of half normal, half Red Dust ideal for missile spells. The normal Dust would provide the structural integrity and the Red Dust would provide the thrust—and, if you played it a bit risky, an explosive head. Her new spell would potentially provide much the same benefit with less use of the volatile substance.

Sasha pulled some of the single-color ovals out of her belt and left them on the bed, replacing them with the mixed ones. Then she fed her staff as much white Dust as it would swallow. Preparations done, it was time to venture into the woods in search of test subjects.

It being a cloudy day, she eventually chanced upon a rabbit. She cast her spell on a mixed Dust oval, which took on a pointed shape with the Red Dust at the back. Then she pointed at her quarry with the wand and tossed the missile to her side to protect herself from the flash. The rabbit jumped at the sound of the igniting Dust, but not fast enough to evade the magical bolt. It corrected its flight path, struck true, and ate into the rabbit with mechanical abandon.

Sasha felt queasy at the sight. This did not turn out to be a spell suitable for hunting small game. Still, the bolts worked, and would be a useful option in her arsenal

4

AFTER SEVERAL DAYS of further spell refinement and study as well as foraging and hunting for more Dust ingredients to fill up her backpack, the day came. Now that Sasha had ample material, she'd set a wardstone on each corner of the roof for greater coverage. Two of the stones started hooting alarm.

Sasha was in the middle of proceeding with her review of the spells her master had passed to her and startled at the sound, but soon remembered she was expecting the driver back. A quick glance out of the small window verified that everything was as it should be. She could just make out a carriage on the road and a familiar large frame of a man. The latter was walking towards the cabin. She readied her staff and waited until she could properly identify him.

Once the man was near, he said just loudly enough to be heard: "Come on, lass. Pack your bags and let's go. We'll need to be on time."

The voice was familiar, so Sasha got out of the shack. "Just a moment. I've got most of it ready." She put her papers back into their carrying case, stuffed that in her backpack, and dragged the pack outside. Then she went around the building, pocketing the light gray wardstones at the corners. Finally, she waved her wand at the thin sheet of white Dust she'd spread on the far side of the roof where it got some sun through the leaves but couldn't be seen from the road. The Dust flowed into a cube which she stuffed on the top of her backpack. She'd hesitated to re-empower her Dust at all during her stay, but she wanted to be well-prepared for her journey.

Suddenly, Sasha became aware of the driver being next to her, and glanced at him. He remained nonplussed. She guessed he'd seen more than enough in his time working for Roderic not to let a little Dust flowing around bother him. *Good.* She hoisted the backpack onto her back and grabbed hold of the sack with her leftovers in it.

Sasha went through her mental checklist and took a final look inside the cabin to make sure she'd remembered everything. Then she nodded to the driver. "Let's go."

•   •   •

The driver stopped their cart at the edge of the forest near an intersection. "We have some margin, so make yourself comfortable," he said. "Your fellow guards have been informed that there will be a proven warrior to join them on the road. The grunts don't know you're Heroborn—or a young woman—so expect some surprise there. Roderic thought it best to keep them in the dark. We don't want a bunch of recruitment enforcers tailing the convoy."

Sasha shook her head affirmatively and leaned on the backrest. "Somebody there knows who I am, though?" she asked.

"The convoy master is Jaime Solsworth, who's trying to impress his father with his business acumen. He knows, as does the captain of the guard. They don't know your exact circumstances, nor should they."

You don't know the half of it. "Don't worry, I know better than to expose them."

The man laughed and nodded. "I bet you do. You're all right."

Sasha barely registered the compliment. She *should* know better than to expose the convoy to herself, but she couldn't risk the long journey alone, not in her condition. The road to Merfort had been hard enough, her having to ... deal with a bandit with his neople lackeys. She shivered and shook off the memories of red, but others took their place. The necromancer's bloody thralls strewn on the catacomb floor. The goblin knife in Master Aaron's back. The ...

No. She couldn't get lost in it all now. All of her fighting, all of the blood had been *necessary*. The goblins to try to save Aaron and to help save the village. The bandit to save herself—and undoubtedly others who would follow on the road. The necromancer's lackeys to prove herself battleworthy, to gain a convoy's protection on her long journey—though perhaps she'd also done it to prove to herself that she could be a force for good, a true Hero, if only she could clear her blood of the curse. If only Master Aaron had been right about there being a chance for her at the Hall. If only he hadn't used his last words to send her on a wild goose chase into the wilderness lest she bring death to all those around her.

Such as the convoy ... Sasha shook her head. The curse wasn't very advanced yet. During her time in the safehouse she'd only attracted a few predators, easily noticed and dispatched with her magic. She could still find safety in numbers, and she could fight well enough to offset the risk she posed to them.

Her conscience soothed for the moment, Sasha glanced around the forest out of habit while they waited in silence. It occurred to Sasha that she'd never caught the driver's name, but that was probably how he liked it, so she didn't ask.

Eventually, two horsemen came around the bend. Sasha's driver took the carriage up to the main road and waved at them. They galloped to the cart.

"Did Roderic send you?" one of the horsemen asked Sasha's driver.

"Yes. I'm your new guard," Sasha said and produced her token.

The other horseman muffled a laugh. The men glanced at each other, then shrugged. "The captain's on the first wagon. He'll make the call."

Sasha frowned. This was going to be a long couple of weeks, but needs must. Hopefully she could win them over once they knew what she was capable of.

Wagons started appearing one by one from where the horsemen had come. One of the horsemen continued forward to scout, and the other rode back to give his report. Then he rode past Sasha again after his mate.

As the caravan arrived at the intersection, the wagons came to a halt. A man dressed in leather armor sat next to the driver. He raised his hand. "So, you're the mage?"

"Sasha of the Heroborn, at your service until Kilnkeep."

The man nodded, measuring her with his eyes. "I'm Urich, but you can call me captain. You can take the front now. I'll be at the back of the wagon. We'll talk more when we stop to rest. I trust you can manage until then?"

"Yes, sir," Sasha said, jumped off the cart, and hauled her belongings onto the larger wagon. She took a seat next to its driver, staff ready for trouble, and created a quick wardstone. The spell would recognize those present at the time of casting, so it wouldn't bother her about the driver. Then she looked back at the man who'd brought her here. He was already turning away. "Thanks!" she hollered at him. The man waved slowly at her and nodded. Then they were on their way.

•   •   •

When they next stopped to feed and water the horses, Captain Urich gathered his forces. There were twelve of them in total, though only ten traveled with the wagons while the two that Sasha had seen earlier scouted ahead. The two centermost carts traveled with one guard each while the others had two, the better to react to attackers from the front or from the rear.

As Sasha had expected, she ended up at the receiving end of incredulous stares from the group of hardened soldiers. She forced her chin up, defiant. There were two other women in the mix, but their eyes were just as skeptical as the others'. It probably didn't help that all of her fellow guards were markedly her senior.

"Enough gawking, people. This is Sasha of the Heroborn. You may have heard that a necromancer had taken residence in Merfort," Urich said, and paused for effect. A few of the others nodded acknowledgment. "Well, she took care of that, alone, so we're all fighting men and women here." The incredulous stares turned into something else. Awe here, amusement there, suspicion of another kind almost everywhere. They took her seriously now, but as what?

"A mage ..." whispered someone as Sasha was looking another way. The whisper was full of suspicion, reminding her of the necromancer's words. She'd never truly be a part of this troupe. No matter. They'd use her, and she'd use them in turn for the duration this journey. Then they'd be done.

"Yes, a mage, and she comes highly recommended, so you'd all better get used to it. She'll be very useful. As I hear, your magic can guard our camp? Warn of approaching enemies? Take down attackers from afar, far more accurately than a bow and arrow?"

All things she'd told Roderic to convince him that she'd be an asset. Sasha nodded. "All that, and more. I can also help in more mundane matters, if need be. If you need a spare part for a wagon on the fly, I can probably shape one."

Someone at her back laughed, but amiably. Sasha turned around. A man stood apart from the rest, dressed well but suitably for travel. This must have been Jaime Solsworth.

"I'll keep that in mind. It hadn't occurred to me that magic might have such practical applications," the merchant said.

Sasha's forced, sternly confident expression melted into a half-smile. Many people laughed at magic's more blasé uses, accustomed as they were to the traditional crafts, but here was a man who appreciated the art of rapid forging.

When she turned back, she could see that most of her fellow guards' faces were shifting towards approval.

•　　　•　　　•

Sasha made a habit of having a wardstone on the roofs of the first and last wagon, as well as all around them when they rounded the wagons up for the night. The roofs of the wagons provided a large, mostly sunny place to whiten the used Dust on the road. She was able to spread it very thinly, so the re-empowerment cycle didn't take long at all.

The trip started uneventfully. Once a stone went off in the night, but the resulting commotion drove off the interlopers. The guards on duty only saw a human form scurrying into the woods. Perhaps it had been a scout to gauge their alertness, or just a lone thief trying to sneak in for a quick grab and run. The guards might well have noticed the intruder anyway, but Sasha's contribution could not be denied. The suspicion she still felt from her peers lessened somewhat.

They stayed at increased readiness for the night at the cost of some sleep, but nothing more came of that. The stones alerted them the next night as well, though that time it was a lone wolf peering curiously at their circle. He bolted when a guard approached to investigate, perhaps to rejoin his pack. The next day Sasha modified the warding spell to exclude animal alerts. Their group was big enough to be safe from local wildlife in any case, and there was no need for extraneous alarms.

The convoy fell into a steady routine. On occasion they'd reach a village or a small town and exchange some goods for coin. While their main destinations were still further inland, it was wise to stay on good terms with the people along your route. Thus also the smaller villages got some attention, even if Jaime said they were not strictly worth their while.

In a few weeks' time, they arrived at their final destination—the edge of human civilization—unscathed. Sasha was almost surprised. Possibly her curse was not strong enough yet to attract foes in sufficient numbers to take on her entourage—not quickly enough, anyway, considering that she'd been on the move the entire time. She wondered if she had been overly pessimistic about just living her life, taking care she'd always be in well-guarded company, but she'd heard enough stories where it'd been tried before. Even surrounded by guards, sooner or later a large enough force would gather—or the cursed one would fall to internal strife. By this time the road expected the caravan back, and if there wasn't anyone lying in wait for her, not all of the company liked mages.

Onwards it was then, having come this far. She'd take a couple of days to rest and gather supplies for the wilderness tour. Being properly prepared was only prudent, even if she wouldn't have to resort only to carried goods. No beast of the forest was a match for her, and she knew how to set up simple traps for small game in lieu of blowing them to smithereens.

According to the map there would be a river between Kilnkeep and her destination. The roads would likely have fallen into disrepair long ago, and she held little hope that there would be a bridge to help her cross, but she'd manage. More importantly, the river would provide easy replenishment of her water reserves, though in a pinch she knew what plants would be the best sources of liquids.

But duty came first. She'd keep watch over the caravan for the rest of the day, and give them an opportunity to find new guards for the trip back. Though Roderic had made a point of the inconvenience of replacing one-way guards, it wasn't as unusual as he'd implied. Two others had also opted for a one-way trip in pursuit of other opportunities inland. It was easier to find people willing to work for modest pay when they had their own interests involved as well, no doubt.

The caravan stopped at the gates of Kilnkeep's wooden but hefty fortifications. This time the wall covered the whole of the town. Three guards came out to welcome and vet the convoy. Jaime was there to greet them and present his credentials. After a short exchange, the town guard came to inspect the wagons. Perhaps for an attacking force, Sasha thought.

As the only force present was also out in the open, the gates were open for business. The wagons just barely fit the street ahead as they headed for the local marketplace. Next to that lay the local church, quite a bit more modest than the cathedral she'd visited earlier but recognizable by the familiar four-pronged star symbols. On the other side of the street there was a small stone garrison for the local defense troops.

As the convoy settled in, trade partners started coming and going. The wagons lightened their loads, if only temporarily. They would be filled by local merchandise to be taken back—or if not, they would be left behind. The convoy back was likely to need less wagons. The mines' riches tended to be compact.

Sasha took a guard position away from the horses, a habit she'd picked up along the way. She couldn't be quite certain, but the animals seemed wary of her. Not enough to hinder their journey, but perhaps the curse affected them, too. There was no reason to risk spooking them when there was no need.

She maintained a facade of some vigilance while her thoughts were already on the trip ahead. Then she suddenly noticed one of the customers approaching her. Spooked, she turned to gape at the middle-aged man. He was well-dressed but not overdoing it. His were working hands that immediately started to move to the sides in a placating gesture. The movement revealed what appeared to be short rods of Dust peeking out of protrusions on his belt.

"Eh, sorry if I startled you. I was just conducting my business here and heard there was a fellow arcanist among you. Saying hello seemed like the thing to do," the mage explained calmly.

Sasha composed herself, embarrassed. "Oh, right. Hello, I'm Sasha of the Heroborn. I didn't actually know there would be mages here."

The man smiled sociably. "I'm Gibli, an elementalist and a dabbler in alchemy. There is plenty of work in and around the mines for one adept with explosives." He left his expression inquisitive, though not actively prying into her affairs.

Sasha decided some reciprocation was in order. "Ah, I see. Well, you won't have to worry about me encroaching on your business. I'm just passing through here on research. Elementalist, you say? What of those?" She pointed at the Dust rods on his belt. It was a curious limitation of fire mages that they could not control magic that wasn't predominantly red. Some White Dust could be intermixed in their spells for support, but it needed to be in the minority. It was theorized that somehow, the elementalists' magic flowed from their wand only to the Red Dust, through which their limited control of the normal variety would then be channeled. It made some degree of sense.

"Oh, these? I see, yes, they actually have red cores. I find that encasing it within a layer of White Dust makes for a longer life in my profession. If you do use the stuff, I heartily recommend doing the same."

That makes sense. "I might just take your recommendation, thank you."

"You've actually been lugging a whole bunch of materials for Red Dust and other explosives for me. There's enough demand here that it pays to order materials from the coast," Gibli said, and quickly continued as alarm rose to Sasha's face, "though of course I provided specific instructions on which materials to carry in separate wagons."

Sasha sighed in relief. "Thanks for that. By the way, you'd probably know. Is there any Mage Corps presence here?"

Gibli shook his head. "The crown knows better than to gather a concentration of mages here in this place. Not many mages want to tempt themselves by coming to live here, either, so the recruiters don't bother," he said, raising an eyebrow.

"Why's that, then?" Sasha asked, feigning ignorance.

"The elven woods to the west, of course. Everybody knows about them, though not many have dared venture there in recent memory.

No sense in wobbling the present peaceful coexistence. We don't bother them, they don't slaughter us. You don't know the story?"

Sasha had an inkling of how it would go, but shook her head. She'd want to be sure that she was properly informed.

"Well, some eighty years ago the governance wanted to get their hands on the resources of the deeper woods, disregarding the elven dominion as fairy tales. To be fair, nobody had seen them since the time of the Heroes, and even then they had been reclusive. But when the woodsmen were sent exploring, they never came back. When soldiers were sent to see what happened, they never came back. Finally, plenty of woodcutters were sent in with orders to start thinning the forest around the edges, accompanied by a small army for support. And that's when the elves came out into the open and slaughtered the bunch of them with overwhelming magical force. Some managed to flee to tell their tale, probably by the elves' design. We've been content with the current borders since, and if somebody starts thinking otherwise, I'm packing my bags and leaving. So, if this research project of yours concerns the elves or the deeper west, I'd recommend doing it from afar," Gibli finished with a measuring look.

Sasha found herself fidgeting a bit. "Oh, no, not to worry, I'll be doing my work strictly on our side of the border," she lied, feeling like she wasn't fooling anyone. *One wayward person wouldn't be enough to start any wars, right?*

"I did also hear that you can take care of yourself," Gibli granted. "Good job on the necromancer. They can give us mages of less noble ancestry a bad name. Too bad about the escape, but they can be slippery."

Huh. Her fame, if not quite preceded, then at least traveled alongside her. "Thank you. That was nothing, really."

"Don't sell yourself short. I'd love to compare notes, if you're in town for a couple of days. The day after tomorrow perhaps? I have business at the mines tomorrow."

"Certainly," Sasha said, and to her surprise meant it. Meeting with a magical peer without any pressure for a change would be just wonderful. Maybe she could get some more pointers from the resident Red Dust expert, swap some tricks of the trade.

Gibli gave her instructions to his lab, and they bid each other farewell as he continued about his business.

•   •   •

Alas, the meeting was not to be. Sasha had settled in an inn and paid for room and board for three days. For the first day, she managed to shop and rest as intended. Deciding to fully take in the calm before the storm, she slept in that night. That was just in time, too, for as she was having a late breakfast, she was greeted by an official-looking woman with a guard by her side.

"Good morning. I am Vera, with the Warden of the Peace. Heroborn Sasha, if I'm not mistaken?" the woman inquired.

Sasha almost choked on her milk, but managed to put up only a moderately alarmed front. "Yes. What is it?"

"May I suggest we talk in private, in your room?"

That seemed like one of the better options for private conversation that the Warden's office might offer.

"Yes, sure," Sasha said and led the way. She'd eaten most of her breakfast anyway.

As they made it to the room, the guard was mercifully left outside. Vera started to explain: "I am asking around regarding the disappearance of one mister Gibli. Jaime Solsworth said he'd seen you talking to him at the market yesterday."

Sasha's eyes went wide. She hoped she projected innocent surprise rather than guilty alarm for her personal safety. With some effort, she managed to avoid blabbering about not having anything to do with it. "Yes, he came to talk to me," she said instead. "I was planning on seeing him today, professionally, as he said he'd be busy yesterday. He's not around then?"

Vera shook her head. "He didn't show at the mines yesterday. When people were sent to look for him, they found nothing. He wasn't home or at his laboratory, but nothing looks amiss. Did he mention anything to you that might give a clue as to where he is? Or ... might you have said something inspiring him to take off somewhere?"

Sasha certainly didn't like the implications in her tone, but then ... A strange mage arrives, has a chat with the resident one, and the latter vanishes into thin air. That didn't exactly sound like a coincidence. But surely, it must have been. It's not like Gibli was itching to join her in her quest through the elven lands.

Regardless, the guy must've been important indeed to the local mining business to warrant such attention after being missing for a day. They'd hardly send out search parties in most such cases.

Her hesitation was growing long. *Better answer something quick.* "Umm, no, I can't think of anything. I said I didn't intend to stay long or bring him any competition. He gave me a tip on Red Dust storage and invited me to see his lab where we could talk shop. We didn't actually have a chance to get into any major exchange of ideas that might've distracted him from his obligations." Better not mention the part about the elves. Though she really doubted he'd have ventured into elven woods to, what, warn them that she was coming, and apologize on behalf of the city in advance? Or would he have fled the hypothetical elven onslaught? If he thought one trespasser could actually start a war, he'd have rather mentioned her intent to city officials. Or at least he wouldn't have left all his possessions behind, if indeed nothing looked amiss in his dwellings.

The official frowned. "Well. You were going to stay one more night, I understand. If you remember anything else, please come by the city hall. And if you see him, of course ..."

"I'll tell him to come see you, of course," Sasha blurted out.

Vera nodded curtly and started to make her way to the door. "Thank you for your cooperation. Oh, and I heard about you taking out a necromancer back in Merfort. Impressive," she said before closing it behind her.

Sasha was left wondering if that was the extent of their interest in her. First the whole necromancer quest was thrust upon her at Merfort, and now this. Things seemed to revolve around her to an uncomfortable extent. That she wasn't in custody right now didn't mean much. The locals probably had some respect for magic users, being well familiar with one who had a penchant for explosions. Thus, they wouldn't necessarily dare apprehend her even if they had some suspicions of foul play. Not before they had something more concrete, or before she forced their hand. And about the necromancer, had she actually congratulated her or noted that she'd taken down a mage before?

Maybe that was a tad paranoid already. Regardless, she should follow through with her original plan with renewed haste. Gibli could fend for himself if he was in trouble. She could not afford more than her fair share. Besides any possible suspicions the Warden's office might have towards her, who or what Gibli had run into might be generally interested in harassing mages. It had happened before, groups suspicious of the arcane arts taking direct action.

Sasha was recently fed and had most of the supplies she'd need. Well, all of what she'd absolutely need, but she could still visit the marketplace to grab some dried foods and fill her new waterskin while pondering how to make her departure. She'd best prepare for the possibility that the guards at the gates would have instructions to dissuade her should she try to leave in the midst of the investigation.

After waiting for a small while to not fly out right in the official's footsteps, Sasha switched into her spare outfit, gathered her belongings into the backpack, and left for the market. Frequently glancing around and behind her, she noticed no suspicious followers. Certainly no more suspicious than she was being.

Finding the final supplies was easy, and she didn't bother haggling. There'd probably be little use for money where she was going. Not that she'd be throwing the rest away; maybe the elves still used something similar for currency. And, thinking positively, it might even be possible that she'd need it when she got back.

First she'd have to get going, though. Some further rudimentary disguise might be warranted. Simple clothing was available from a few sellers, and after browsing a bit, she settled for a light greenish gray cloak. It wasn't very stylish, especially on top of the backpack, but wouldn't be very out of place in the forest.

Everything bought, she ducked into an alley. She pulled an oval of Dust from her pouch and transformed a pair of Dust scissors. Dust blades never were very sharp, but they were good enough to trim her hair with. The resulting hairdo probably wasn't pretty, but that mattered little. She put the cloak on, leaving the hood off for now. No need to look too shady. The staff was a problem, but she tried to hold it low for now. If she managed to get transportation, she could hide the weapon in the back.

With no local allies to call upon, Sasha couldn't very well trust anyone to hide her. Traveling openly, even with her precautions, she'd need something to fall back on. A diversion. She dug one of the larger cubes of Dust from her backpack, tagged it with her wand, and hid it under some trash that looked like it wasn't going anywhere any time soon.

She stopped for a moment. Maybe the cube would be enough. Maybe not. She looked at the walls. They seemed relatively sturdy. Surely enough to take a small explosion. Nervously, she took a small mixed Dust oval with a red core off her belt. Gibli's suggestion had been easy to implement. She dropped the explosive in the muck at the other end of the alley and tagged that as well. Then she was off to the market again.

Sasha made inquiries with a few traders who had not much left to sell and succeeded in finding a couple of peasants leaving town soon. They happily gave her a ride for a modest price. She asked where they were going, of course, though just for show. "I'm going that way, too," would've been the response whatever the destination. Still, in a stroke of luck their general direction happened to work for her as well.

She settled herself at the back of the small wagon, nonchalantly hiding the staff under some sacks while the peasants weren't looking. The backpack she used as a makeshift seat after likewise covering it. Her travel gear thus camouflaged, she hoped to evade notice as her brief travel companions joined her on the wagon, one in front, one at the back with her. Under her cloak, she held her wand at the ready along with a mixed Dust oval in her right hand.

She tried to look tired and bored as the gates approached. Guards didn't seem to be on high alert. Maybe there was nothing to worry about. One did appear to be peering at the cart, though. She let some of her changed outfit show from beneath the cloak and turned her head a bit so that the guard could see her short hair. The guard was satisfied. They went through. Sasha kept her eye on the gate, just to be safe.

After only fifty meters, the guard peeked from the open gate at their direction. Then he started a rapid walk toward her, kicking some stones as he went. *If I was told to check the cart again but thought it was a waste of time, that's how I might go about it.*

There was no time to waste. Hopefully the alley was still in range, what with the fortifications. At least they were made of wood and not stone. Within her cloak, Sasha discreetly pointed her wand and made a few gestures, calling upon the tagged cube of Dust. In the alley, the Dust would rise up along the wall in a large sheet, increasing its surface area to better fulfill its function. The spell was called *Dragon's Roar*, though mercifully enough, Sasha had no idea how accurate it was. Dragons, giants, lich kings, and the like had not been seen since the sudden disappearance of the Heroes. They'd managed to eradicate the greater monsters before leaving, at least.

A terrible roar pierced the air. The guard startled and looked back. Sasha's traveling companions went pale as well. The driver wasted no time, hurrying his horses to go as fast as they could. The guard glanced back toward Sasha but decided against pursuit of the speeding cart. Rather, he ran back through the gate, presumably to defend his city against a dragon attack. Sasha found herself admiring the man. He'd have made a good Hero.

Sasha kept her wand ready in case she'd have to resort to the other diversion, but she wasn't followed. And if she was? Perhaps the brave guard found his way into the alley. Perhaps he'd find her sheet of Dust, putting him right next to the explosive when she'd trigger it. She grimaced and called upon its tag, commanding the Dust to disperse safely. It would still burn if exposed to flame, but spread thinly enough into the muddy ground, it'd be fine.

Little by little they got out of earshot. The peasants were scared silent and concentrated on getting far away from the city. That was fine with her. She'd travel with them a few kilometers until jumping off on her own. There would possibly be remains of an old road west thereabouts, though her map wasn't very exact, and the road might well have grown over by now.

She'd find her way regardless.

PART II

5

MASTER AARON HAD WARNED Sasha of the ruthlessness of the elves, and he should know. Diedre, his grandmother, had felt it first hand, having ventured into the elven lands in her old age to see if she could still make a grand discovery or two. Fully knowing that she might be going to her death, she'd left the heirloom staff with Aaron's mother before setting off, lest it be lost along with her.

Diedre had hoped that being able to trace her Heroborn bloodline to the elven warrior mage Valarin would make her a palatable visitor for the elves, even if she was mostly human. Valarin's bloodline was even hypothesized to be charmed, pacifying monsters, and deterring attacks. The effect was subtler than the curse, but anecdote after anecdote supported the theory.

Of course, if one purposefully put oneself in harm's way, even a charmed life could be undone. *Like Diedre, braving the elven lands. Like Master Aaron, courageously defending the village.*

Sasha grimaced, shook off her memories, and made haste into the woods. She probably wouldn't be breaching the elven borders on the first day. After all, there had been human activity around these parts for a long time, mostly without incident. Little was certain, though, and as she made her way through the thickening forest, Sasha wondered if traveling at night would be the prudent choice once she'd put some distance between the town and herself. At least she was fairly sure that nobody there wanted to follow her where she was going even if they found her tracks.

She eyed the environment as she walked briskly onward, wondering what would be a logical place for the old road. If there was even a trace of it left, it could make travel more convenient. Less bumps and roots to stumble on. She'd started a bit north from where she figured the road should be, so veering slightly to the south should bring her to it. Not that she should rely on noticing the old road.

Now and then Sasha conjured up a compass needle on a string to ascertain that she wasn't veering overmuch southwards. The needle took a while to settle each time, though, and she'd have to be still for it. She couldn't check it all the time. Instead, she'd choose a faraway target in the correct direction, make her way there, and repeat the process. This allowed for both accuracy and decent speed.

After an hour or so of travel, a slightly less grown streak of forest became visible on the left. Sasha made note of her current target and veered further south to check it out. The streak was squiggling between the larger trees, the trees in it younger and smaller. It certainly seemed laid out like a road, and the overall direction was good, though she'd be sure to check the needle once in a while too. Sasha allowed herself a smile. *Some good news for a change.* Not only would the travel be easier, this was evidence of her being on the right track. Things were going according to plan again.

As for changing her plans towards night travel, she thought better of it as the day turned darker. Progress became tedious, her footing uncertain. The forest cover would have to be enough. The elves couldn't be everywhere at once. She could hope to slip through. And if they had magical detection, the lack of light probably wouldn't make much of a difference.

She spread her bedding in the shade of a few large trees, set a couple of wardstones—more for the wildlife than anything else at this point—and huddled up with the new cloak for extra warmth. The purchase had clearly been worth it. Not overly worried about elves yet, and sufficiently far from her fellow humans for them to dare follow, Sasha quickly drifted off to sleep.

A peaceful night's sleep was too much to ask, however. In the middle of the night, Sasha woke up to the sound of barking. A wardstone had gone off. She reached for her staff, and her eyes darted around the area covered by the activated stone. The moon was bright in the sky, but the wood cover made it difficult to see all the same. Nothing was moving very fast, that was for sure.

After a moment that felt like minutes, she spotted it: a shadow of a canine creature looking towards her, head slightly tilted as if curious, unfazed by the wardstone's sound. She readied her staff in case the animal would try something.

Her observer was likely to be a wolf, though she couldn't see any others anywhere. Would the pack come if she attacked this one? Would it fetch reinforcements if she didn't? Wolves didn't generally attack humans. Even cursed, maybe she'd better put her trust in that.

Sure enough, the animal soon turned from her and bolted away. Sasha quieted the tripped wardstone and put a couple more in good vantage points in case he'd come back with friends. In the end though, she decided that any danger was unlikely enough, and went back to sleep. She'd need her rest.

The morning arrived without further incident. Sasha allowed herself a bit of a sleep-in. The area was as safe as it was going to get in the days to follow. She managed to have good dreams, even, of reaching a glimmering city marked by the nearby double peak, as on the map, with her trusty canine companion by her side. It was a hopeful image, even though the real city would certainly not be in such a pristine condition.

Long ago, before the elves had closed their borders, expeditions had confirmed the city abandoned, and looting was pretty much a given. Her hope lay in the mentions that the central Hall of Heroes had remained impregnable. Hope as well as fear. Perhaps it would remain closed for her as well. But she was a Heroborn mage, with the rediscovered ancient arts at her fingertips. If anyone could get in, it would be her.

Her resolve thus strengthened, she plowed through her morning routine, and pressed onward. The goal now was to make haste through the elven territories. Though it was uncertain how far safety lay, her working theory was that at this point the elven lands were blessedly narrow, the river making a bend towards human dominion. The mountainous areas beyond the river would likely belong to the dwarves instead. These particular dwarves, if they still lived there, would probably not have had human contact in quite a while, but there were other colonies who had retained contact and good relations with humans. Hopefully racial stereotypes would work to her advantage there.

Hurrying aside, she would naturally have to try to keep a low profile. She pulled the cloak's hood over her head. It would narrow her field of vision, but also make her all too human head less noteworthy to any local passersby. What with the elven staff, maybe a faraway glance wouldn't attract further scrutiny. As for her own awareness, she could augment that with a wardstone tiara placed on top of the hood.

Walking onwards, by midday she'd lost the track of the old road. It simply wasn't distinguishable from the environment anymore. At least the thicker elven woods provided ample cover, even if the going was slower than before.

After two or three hours of traveling in the woods, the trees made way for a sudden clearing. Sasha approached with caution and could see that the clearing stretched far and wide in both directions. The clearing was about a hundred meters wide and seemed blessedly empty of elves as well as trees. She'd make a nonchalant break for it, walking briskly with her eyes forward, as she imagined the locals might do.

When she ventured out into the open, Sasha saw a black or dark gray strand passing into the distance from left to right. A road of some kind, perhaps. Crossing it didn't seem to be optional, so she pressed on.

Walking over the dark gray surface, Sasha marveled at the material. Very smooth, though not slippery. Must make for a comfortable ride. There was no time to stop and examine it further, but she wondered how cumbersome it had been to make. There was no telling how long the road was, but covering the visible portions alone seemed like it would have been a large undertaking. On the other hand, she had little knowledge of the progress of elven magics. Perhaps it was just all in a day's work to them, though the Dust costs would be enormous by her standards.

After she got back into denser woods, Sasha dared glance around again. Nothing. That was a relief. Her tiara would have probably warned of approaching elves, of course, but they might have ways around it. Onwards as usual, then.

The next hour or so went smoothly, but then the wardstone tiara buzzed softly on her head. She resorted to her default stalling action: having a drink while eyeing around. The brightest part of the day had passed, but there was plenty of light. Still, she couldn't see any cause for the alarm. *Wait.* There was some movement in the corner of her eye. Glancing towards it, she could see nothing but some bushes, not dense enough for hiding.

Still, something was off. She squinted a bit. Suddenly, it dawned on her. There was someone, or something there. A blurred figure hidden in plain sight, but for depth. The color escaped her face. Panicked, she made the gesture for shielding, preparing to bolt the other way.

The staff remained inert. She froze as she heard a graceful but cold voice from behind. The accent was unfamiliar and some words were pronounced strangely. Still, the speech was understandable if somewhat archaic Human. "You can praise the Stars above it was the shield you tried. Now, refrain from any sudden moves, and do explain your presence here," the voice said.

Heart pounding, Sasha slowly turned around. Where there had been nothing, there was now a tall elven woman in a long, forest green cloak. She drew off her sizable hood, revealing a long, egg-shaped head with the point towards the back. Pointed ears held the blond hair on the sides, with a long ponytail at the back. If elven facial expressions matched those of humans, her stare would probably be one of disdain. That seemed fairly likely to be the case.

At least Sasha would get a chance to say something. She was surprised but happy enough at the elves still speaking her language. They had been known to do so back in the day, but she'd thought their skill at it to have been lost for lack of contact. She herself had learned some rudimentary Elven from Aaron, but he had been the first to admit that his skill with the ancient tongue was sketchy at best. His family had not had any community of elves around to try it on for generations.

Caught off balance, the first thing to say that came to mind was, to her immediate regret, "How..?"

The elf sneered. "If you are referring to the staff, did you honestly think a weapon of our ancestors could be used against us? Or did you mean this?" She gave a small nod to her side. A green-cloaked figure materialized behind her, a few meters away and to the right. The hood, at first covering the whole face, came off. It was another elf, probably male, dirty blond, long hair braided on both sides. His expression seemed more curious than hostile, though with a dash of suspicion.

Remembering the form that had spooked her first, Sasha turned her head back towards the bush. There was a blur in the air, and a hovering, darkly amused elven face appeared from beneath an invisible hood. This one was bald, and the face seemed somewhat older than the others, though gracefully aged at that. The head shape was unnerving without the cover of hair. The rest of the barely visible form blurred into a now familiar green cloak, which parted to reveal a wand at the ready. *Right, no sudden moves.*

Sasha turned her head back, thinking it best to address the elf that had talked to her. Telling the truth seemed like the best solution. Well, mostly. Part of it. She gathered her courage, but stumbled regardless. "I, um, mean you no disrespect, I am just passing through to ... study the City of Heroes firsthand, see if there's some answers to be found to their history and disappearance."

Ponytail snorted. "A fool's errand, so I might even believe you. But what is a human child doing with her hands on an elven staff?" The word "human" had left her lips especially chilled.

What I wouldn't give for a smidgen of elven blood right now. On the other hand, who was to say she didn't have it? She forced her chin up and faced the taller woman.

"I am mage Sasha of the Heroborn, and the staff is my heirloom, given to me by my father Aaron, who received it from his mother Kestrel, who ..." she rattled off her master's lineage right up to Valarin, hoping they'd buy the lie. It was a small one. Aaron was in essence her adoptive father, after all.

At least she'd gotten enough of their attention to get to finish. Master had been right when he'd said that names had power, even if they weren't magic. Braid's suspiciousness had faded, and mostly curiosity remained. Ponytail was still looking down on her but was more reserved with her disdain. "You certainly do not look the part you claim, but we have our ways of verifying your heritage."

"Can we be sure if she is as far removed as she—" Bald started from behind, but was cut off by an annoyed glance from Ponytail.

A bluff, then. At the very least they had some doubt over their ability to disprove her story. *Good, cancel impending panic attack.*

Braid closed in. "She did try to use the staff. It may be that it has been voluntarily passed to her. Shall I check?"

Ponytail nodded. Braid pointed at her with the wand, which was unnerving even if he did appear to be the closest thing to an ally she had right now. Sasha glanced back at her own elven artifact, and the staff glowed a faint green where she held it in her hand. Ponytail seemed disappointed, somehow. Braid continued: "So, it is probably not a deception. Her story would be a reasonable explanation for having properly bonded with the staff. We should take her in, let the Council decide what to do."

Ponytail considered this for a moment. "Fine, but you take responsibility for her." Braid flashed the briefest shadow of a smile, and Ponytail flinched ever so slightly, as if regretting her words. She did not take them back, however.

When Braid came in for her belongings, she surrendered her wand, Dust, and backpack to him without protest. It wasn't like she could take on three elves with magic so advanced they had bloody *invisibility cloaks* anyway. The veracity of the stories featuring such artifacts had been under some doubt, but she'd take this as evidence for them.

Next, Braid let his Dust flow around her neck, forming a collar. Sasha shivered, but didn't resist. There was no instruction, but she recalled the shackles she herself had used on the necromancer. There was little doubt in her mind that the collar would have uses besides decoration, if need be.

Appropriately restrained, Braid directed her to walk towards the northwest, somewhat off her original direction. Ponytail went ahead, clearly confident that Sasha posed no threat to her back. Arrogant perhaps, but correct. The others walked behind, wands in hand, and no doubt ready for action if required.

It seemed strange to Sasha that the elves had not relieved her of the staff. Perhaps they thought the possibility of mere physical assault to be beneath their notice. On the other hand, they did keep distance enough to allow for a magical counter to any attempted bludgeoning, so they didn't seem blind or overconfident on that count. And they had made a point about the binding. Maybe it was something they respected.

While walking, Sasha studied the material of the cloak on the lead elf's shoulders. It was reminiscent of her master's experiments into magical clothing, but it was much smoother and flowed much more naturally. Dust, somehow woven into or onto fabric. Precision work. They'd also colored it green somehow instead of the usual black and white scale. Then again, that was quite a small wonder after witnessing the cloak's ability to seamlessly blend into the environment.

Wondrous though it was, the cloak's workings were not of immediate concern. Other practical questions rose to the forefront of her mind. Where were they going? How far was it? What was the Council, and what were the most likely conclusions they could reach? Would it be at all a good idea to open her mouth without being spoken to?

She could hazard a good guess on the latter. She was lucky enough to have survived the initial encounter, and Braid's words and attitude certainly suggested that her fate wasn't quite sealed. Better not give them any reason to get more annoyed at her than they were.

Soon they arrived on a small dirt road, on which they made their way northwards. In a while the woods gave way to fields, crops on the right, and something rather more shocking on the left. It was only logical, of course, for a highly magical society. It was just the sheer scale of it that made her jaw drop.

Before her spread entire fields of Dust. Workers with wands were magically sheeting the land with the dark gray variety, while others manually spread around fully depleted black Dust. A white spot was being harvested by a single elven mage, the Dust gathering onto a horse carriage. She wondered why they'd bother with the horse at this point. Surely, they could arrange for magical transportation. Perhaps they still needed to conserve the magic for more important matters, making beasts of burden a more economical option for hauling the product long distances.

Her wondering eyes caught Braid behind her. His grin was subtle, but definitely there. He was clearly enjoying her wonderment.

Not in a completely hostile, downwards looking manner either. It dawned on her: she was as novel to him as all this was to her. Some of the elves might be bored with the isolation. It was unlikely she'd run into the only one.

The bad news, of course, was that she had no idea how fast her novelty would fade. It could be that the interest was genuine and lasting, but she couldn't overlook the possibility of her shine wearing off. She'd have to strive to be entertaining to retain whatever edge she had over the previous generations of explorers.

She wondered if master Aaron's grandmother would have been able to get a word in edgewise if she'd just kept the staff as a conversation starter. It was doubtful the elves would've thought twice about offing Sasha as well if it weren't for wanting to question her about the artifact. Going by drawing and description, Diedre's subtle elven features would have been easy to miss on a cursory glance from afar.

Without breaking her stride or turning her head backwards, the lead elf suddenly started muttering in a voice too low to be directed at her apparent subordinates. The elf didn't make any actual attempt to conceal her words, just that she was addressing someone else entirely. She couldn't make out any telltale signs of invisible companions around, though that didn't necessarily mean much. She did manage to get a glimpse of something the elf was holding in her hand, talking to it. Recording spell? No, she was having a conversation. Yet more elven magic.

She could just make out the words. Her captor requested an audience from the Council of Elders, explaining that she had a captive human claiming heritage. The staff bore mention as well. It wasn't until after the elf had gone silent again that Sasha realized that she was still talking Human. Strange, unless she'd specifically wanted her to eavesdrop. That didn't seem likely, but Sasha was still too wary of opening her mouth to ask.

There were scattered farmhouses on the fields, and Sasha could see more housing in the distance. It was already evident that the settlement was quite wide in area, and much less dense than a human city. No walls either, despite the large population. They clearly relied on their magical superiority over other races. From what she'd seen already, it did not reek of complacency in their case. They probably had some wide area warding too. Luck was a tad too convenient an explanation for the group of elves having surrounded her so readily. There probably wasn't much she could've done about it.

The lack of defenses lent some support to the historical anecdotes about elven infighting being rare or even nonexistent. If they'd have to defend against foes of roughly equal strength, they'd likely want fortifications of some sort in their population centers. Though for all she knew, they might just pull something up from the ground if necessary. It was better to not assume too much when these creatures were involved.

As the group escorted Sasha into town, passersby inevitably started to gawk at her. She tried to maintain a confident half-smile with only partial success. Some of the onlookers seemed overtly hostile but did not approach. She was clearly handled already, after all. Others did seem more curious, some even excited. It was the best that she could hope for: a notable lack of consensus about killing her outright.

Still, this Council she was being taken to could quite conceivably be more conservative. The leadership of her own race often was. If they took after humans there, it could prove fatal.

Ahead loomed a large, white, and circular two-story building that seemed likely to be their destination. Otherwise, the architecture was quite varied. There were large buildings of up to three floors, many seemingly with apartments, such as what one might expect in a city. However, private dwellings were also scattered about, more like what one might expect from the countryside. There were even yards, though those tended to be rather small. She'd seen a few larger green areas as well. Those seemed to be in communal use. Space was at less of a premium when you had no real need to fortify the area.

As Sasha had expected, they went into the round building. A wide corridor ran along the outside wall of the hall, seemingly around the whole building. There were clusters of seats at regular intervals along the outer wall. She could also see two other doors leading outside at the edge of visibility. Where doors were absent, large glass windows lit up the room inside. The glass was of rather good quality, too. Little distortion, quite transparent.

The inner wall was punctuated by doors and desks, some of them manned. Ponytail gestured for Sasha to stop and proceeded to one such desk. Bald and Braid approached from behind. They weren't so careful with keeping their distance here in their place of power.

Ponytail returned from the desk as the clerk disappeared through a nearby double door, larger than most on the inner wall. Pointedly looking at only the other elves, she said that it'd be half an hour or so. The others nodded and remained standing. Sasha glanced at the seats longingly, but maintained her policy of speaking only when spoken to for the time being. No invitations to sit were forthcoming, nor did the elves make moves to do so themselves.

As the minutes crawled by, Braid and Bald got somewhat fidgety but remained in their places. Not Ponytail, though. She was all about intense glower without direct eye contact. That would've been too courteous, Sasha supposed.

After a while, the clerk returned, but only to take a drop of Sasha's blood for "analysis". The process was surprisingly painless, and the elf was polite if firm about it. He then swiftly disappeared back towards the Council chambers. She supposed they'd somehow check it for her heritage, but she reassured herself with what Bald had let slip. Her claim to elven blood was sufficiently weak that the sample couldn't conclusively betray her lie. She just hoped they didn't have more exotic forms of magic that could take advantage of having her blood around, but everything she knew of the theory said no. Then again, she'd thought all of blood magic to be mere superstition.

Finally, after the promised half an hour, the uncomfortable wait was over. The clerk returned through the double door, holding one half open. "The Council will see you now," he stated matter-of-factly. Ponytail took the lead again, and Sasha assumed she was meant to follow. Nobody admonished her when she did.

The door led into another corridor towards the center of the building, with other doors on the sides. She ignored those, guessing they were heading towards the open double doors at the end.

The doors opened onto an inner yard of sorts, even with a few trees around the wall. The yard was covered by a dome-shaped ceiling made of glass panels within a metal framework. A couple of the panels had been slid open for ventilation. She wondered about the indoor trees, but they appeared to thrive.

A group of seven distinguished-looking elves in slightly and variedly off-white robes were sitting in the center along a half circle of a table. They seemed Elders indeed, though aged as gracefully as she'd have expected of the creatures of legend. Only one of them was bald like one of her captors. A few gray heads were in attendance, but also some dark brown and black.

She noted an absence of guards, but also the presence of various decorative pieces on the table. Their color and texture was the telltale white of Dust. Besides papers and writing implements, the Elders also had wands on their side of the table. Not in their hands, but ready to be used. The arrangement signaled wary confidence rather than alarm. The Council was undoubtedly quite capable of defending itself against most threats, especially if they came with warning and escorts.

One younger servant by the door announced them: "Patrol chief Jarin with Alion and Erian, and captive." That would be her. Jarin was undoubtedly the woman. If they went with seniority otherwise, Bald's was maybe the second name mentioned, but that remained to be verified.

Jarin went ahead of them again and bowed to the Council. Braid gently took her shoulder for a moment, so she remained where she was.

The elf in the middle, a gray-haired man, spoke: "The Council welcomes you, Jarin. We understand that you have caught a trespassing human that claims lineage, if in a slight measure."

"Yes, sire. Otherwise, we would have dealt with the situation as usual, but since she had a bound ancestral staff in her possession, we thought it best to bring the matter to you." Some eyebrows rose at that, and Sasha silently thanked master Aaron for the artifact once more. Jarin continued hastily: "The staff has, of course, been rendered inert."

"Of course," the speaker replied. "Given the unusual circumstance, you did well." Jarin relaxed slightly. The speaker continued: "We would have the captive repeat her claim to the Council. Sasha, was it?" The elf gestured for her to come forward, so she did, up to Jarin's side. She bowed as well, just as deep as Jarin had, but no deeper.

Her voice shook but only a little, as she hazarded a respectful greeting in Elven to bolster her story. Now all of the Council projected surprise, a few even delight. The speaker returned her greeting, still respectful though somewhat adapted to her admittedly lesser social standing. He added an introduction, as far as she could tell. His name was probably Faran.

Sasha wasn't confident enough in her language skills to go beyond the rote greeting. She'd made her point, and everybody else was speaking Human, accented though it may have been, so she also reverted to it. As in the forest, she repeated her master's lineage along with the small addition of herself to the Council.

"Heroborn mage, you say?" commented the bald councilman from the right side. He seemed somewhat disdainful, but not as much as Jarin. There was an undercurrent of amusement to his scorn. "That may be impressive among humans, but do not expect it to make you anyone of note here."

A grayed woman from the left countered: "Should it not speak to her advantage, that she is not of particular note among us?" That earned a chuckle from a couple of the Elders, the bald one included. They didn't seem quite as bad as Sasha might have feared.

"Be that as it may," the middle one interrupted the nascent conversation, "let us hear her answer to the other pertinent question. What were you doing trespassing on elven lands?"

"No trespassing intended, sire. I was following my master's map on an expedition towards the Hall of Heroes, and stumbled on your territory on the way," Sasha explained.

The brunette woman next to the speaker on the left frowned. "Should you not be aware of our presence here, a learned young woman? Surely you knew what lands you would be passing."

Inconveniently true. Sasha tried a diversion: "We know these lands are dangerous, to be sure. Your presence is more of a matter of myth and legend, with little verifiable contact in ages. As a woman of learning, I tend to work more with what I know than old folks' tales." It was a gamble, but mostly based on truth, and relied on the elves valuing knowledge. They would almost have to for having built this society that she'd seen glimpses of.

A few faces at the table seemed lightly amused again, and she could spot no appreciable increases in hostility in the rest. Jarin by her side let out a slight derisive puff, however. Sasha wondered if elven ears could hear it from across the table. Maybe not, or Jarin would have reined it in better.

The middle one spoke again: "We will clearly have to consider the situation carefully before any meaningful consensus is likely. Meanwhile, we might as well get an inside update on the human society. I assume you will not object to questioning?"

Sasha's predicament did not exactly call for insubordination. She shook her head, then belatedly thought that a verbal answer might be not only appropriate, but important to avoid cultural confusion: "No, sire."

"Whoever is in charge of our guest here will arrange for appropriate interviews, and post timely reports to the Council," decreed the Elder. Careful footsteps approached from behind.

A glance sideways showed Braid—possibly Erian—closing in with a bow: "That would be me, sire. I will see it done." Jarin tensed, but didn't challenge the claim. She wasn't one to go back on her words, it seemed. A couple of the more conservative Council members gave slightly exasperated looks but refrained from commenting. *Encouraging.*

With that, they were dismissed from the Council chamber. Sasha took to following Braid's lead, evidently being in his custody now. Again, lack of negative feedback confirmed it as the appropriate thing to do. At the front desk, the clerk handed Braid her backpack and a separate sack of items on the side. She hadn't noticed going in, but clearly the pack had been quietly passed to him for inspection. Going by the bulges in the sack, there'd be her Dust cubes, probably the spare wand as well. Braid grabbed the contraband and gestured for the backpack to be given back to Sasha, now.

The trio of elves split up outside after a few words about tomorrow's patrols and how they'd get someone to cover for Braid. He gestured for her to proceed by his side down a particular side street, and promptly let out a merry sigh of relief once the others were out of earshot.

He turned to her and, paying little regard to the occasional passersby, opened the floodgates: "Jarin can be a bit of a stickler for protocol, but I wager she could get used to you, if they decide your story rings true. What a stroke of luck that I managed to goad her into making me responsible for you, though. I'm Erian, by the way, in case you missed that. You chose a good time to visit. Mind you, later still might have been better from your point of view, but just a few decades ago you would have been dead by now for sure.

Oh, sorry, what I mean to say is that these days you stand a decent chance of being allowed … in. The consensus on isolation has steadily weakened and is flimsier than ever since the time of the Heroes, and us being cousins, if rather far removed, and you having the staff—brilliant, I would not have guessed there were any left outside our realm—make rather good excuses for treating you well. Speaking of, would you like for me to take you to a holding cell or our place? You can have a private room either way."

That was a bit much, but it didn't sound like a trap—that a sane person would set. Sasha wasn't quite sure how the concept of sanity applied in her present environment, but a cell wasn't appealing in any case. Any guards there might pose more of a threat than the seemingly jovial Erian.

She decided to risk taking the offer at face value. "Umm, your place, please, if that's an option."

Erian flashed a bright smile. "Good. We are headed the wrong way for the cells, anyway. Mind you, I am going to have to take some measures to avoid you disappearing on my watch, and I would rather you did not try anything that we might regret."

He was being rather matter-of-fact about it, didn't seem to be meant as threatening. "Okay," Sasha offered.

"Excellent. Del and Allain will be pleased to have a guest. I might also invite some people over at some point, if it is all right with you? Strictly of the more open-minded variety," Erian suggested.

It seemed like a genuine question. At least the direction of the conversation was increasingly incompatible with threats. Instead, it looked like she was to be a status piece. She could live with that, for a while. "That's fine, though not right this instant, please. Umm, how long are the Council likely to deliberate, anyway?"

Erian made a shaky, noncommittal gesture with his hand. "Not a lot of precedent. Best guess, weeks, maybe longer. They do have other things to do, and they are not ones to jump to conclusions. I suspect they will want time to mull this over in between discussions, and probably consult with other Councils."

Not jumping to conclusions? Well, the elves' evident fervor in enforcing conclusions they'd already come to was, in fact, a slightly different matter. Out loud, it seemed safer to concentrate on more innocuous details: "Other Councils?"

Erian nodded. "Oh yes, each town has one. They coordinate on important matters. Do yours not?"

Sasha frowned, confused. "No, if there is such a thing, they handle local matters. Country-wide policies are set by the King's court. Isn't there a higher authority to govern the Councils?"

The elf grinned, clearly amused by her idiosyncrasies: "Why would there be? Is that not rather rigid?"

"How would you avoid conflicts between the towns then? Surely, they can't agree all the time?" she pressed.

Erian smile smugly. "Evidently we are better at it than human society. Disputes can be resolved by discussion until a mutually agreeable consensus is reached among the Councils. Being composed of the wisest among us, they will formulate an argument that is invariably difficult to disagree with for the rest of us. We pride ourselves on being a reasonable people."

Sasha mulled that one over for a while. Reasonable when it came to other elves, perhaps. From the outside their approach seemed less so. Yet best not provoke them, even the tamer ones. She went along with him, not having to be entirely deceptive. "I suppose so. Humans are not the best at keeping things civil without a solid hierarchy."

Erian was lapping it up. "Yes, that fits the tales we have. I wasn't sure if you—or should I say they?—had gotten past that yet. At least us normal folk hear little news from the east. There are special units to keep an eye on the humans from afar, but it is quite unexpected to be able to learn all this first hand."

All of which would no doubt be on record in his report. The questioning had already begun. It was more pleasant than she'd thought it would be, Sasha had to admit. There was little in the way of complaints from her conscience, either. It wasn't like she had any state secrets to divulge.

"Ah, here we are," said Erian suddenly. Spilling the beans on humanity was put on hold, as he waved at the near end of a long two-story building. The many doors, all equidistant from each other, suggested smaller apartments within, perhaps two-story ones if none shared a front door. There were also some glass windows in view, not as big as the Council building's but respectable.

"It is a bit extravagant, but between the three of us it works out. And," he winked, "we need the room for one more." Erian took in her bewildered expression, and hastily proceeded to add: "Oh, not you. I mean, you too for now, but you will be staying in the room allotted to our children. It will be a while yet before they need it."

Huh. Erian inviting her into his home was one thing but said home containing his unsuspecting pregnant wife was another. Either he really didn't take her seriously as a potential threat, or didn't much care about his family. Probably the former, foolhardy though it was. Sasha wasn't sure whether to be offended or flattered. She wouldn't do anything to hurt them if she could help it, of course, but this kind of trust simply wasn't called for at this time. He had to have a rather low opinion of her capabilities.

Erian opened the door into an alcove that led into an open living space. A large sofa dominated the far left corner with a low table in front. The far right corner was occupied by a kitchen area, equipped with a stove and a counter for preparing food. The dining table was nearby, close to the side wall.

In the alcove, there were doors on either side into walk-in closets, perhaps. The back wall had another door set into it, along with medium-sized windows. Behind them was a small backyard. The side walls were decorated with a few woodland-themed paintings, and opposite the kitchen table were the stairs up.

"Get your boots off, if you please. Dear! Are you in? We have company," Erian hollered. Sasha removed her shoes as prompted and noted that the floor was very clean. Her socks would probably dirty the room rather than the other way around.

"Who is it?" asked a melodic voice from upstairs.

"Surprise," he countered with a grin.

The sound of footsteps approached, and a lithe elven woman came down the stairs, blond hair flowing free. Her figure was thin—sickly so, were she human—except for the notable abdominal bulge. Sasha's thoughts quickly wandered into the issues that the elves might have with childbirth, what with those large heads but delicate forms of theirs. Advanced healing magics? But there was no time for that line of thinking.

As the elf's eyes found Sasha, she froze, taken aback. "A ... human?" she said, puzzled.

Erian giddily made introductions: "Sasha, this is my darling Del. Del, this is Sasha, a rather distant cousin from the east, but yes, mostly human. The Council, in its wisdom, has left her in my care while they ponder on the implications."

Sasha noted the lack of mention of any potential executions that still loomed over her head. On the other hand, at least in this household her little lie just became official fact. It wasn't inconceivable that she might benefit from more introductions of this kind, if indeed Erian would invite people over to gawk at her.

"Hi," Sasha hazarded with a hesitant wave of her hand.

Slowly, as the shock faded, Del's face brightened and eyes widened. She stepped the rest of the way down with her arms wide for a hug, perhaps a little overly eager to seem welcoming.

"Welcome to Greenhold, cousin Sasha, our home is yours," she recited as Sasha positioned herself to be overrun. She managed to respond to the tense hug with her free arm, the other still holding the staff.

"Oh, what might this be?" went Del as she got a look at the elven artifact up close.

"Fine, is it not?" Erian interjected. "Bound to her, too, though of course we had to disable it for the time being. The staff is her heirloom, rather bolstering her claim to heritage." Del retreated from the hug but not far. She looked ever so slightly relieved by the now fortified lie.

Feeling a bit like dirty laundry, handled out of some household duty, Sasha kept up her awkward smile. A comment seemed appropriate. "I thought my father's heirloom would help keep me safe on my trip, but I didn't realize how right I was." Erian responded with a lighthearted chuckle. There was less on the line for him.

Nobody chimed in, so Sasha kept the initiative: "Sorry, but would you mind showing me where I can put my things?"

Erian raised a hand, explaining to them both: "Ah, yes. Come upstairs. Del, I thought she could stay in the empty room for now. Until the Council makes their decision unless it takes overly long. If it does, we can make other plans. Is that agreeable?"

Del just nodded. After the initial shock, nothing much seemed to faze her. Perhaps she was used to him, and not having opinions to speak of. They'd already been approaching the stairs before the nod came through.

"Did the Council really approve of this, though?" Del managed to wonder when they were already on the stairs.

"Oh, good old Jarin gave me custody of her rather easily before the Council even got involved and overruling that would be terribly impolite. Not to worry, I am just going to have to take care that she is safe and do some interr ... views," he quickly corrected.

Meanwhile, both Jarin and the more grumpy Council members were, what? Busy categorically denying that any misjudgment had occurred because elves didn't do that? How long could that last? Maybe quite long enough. Things clearly didn't work the same west of Kilnkeep.

Erian showed Sasha upstairs, where a small hallway led into three smaller rooms. "That right there is our master bedroom, that is Del's workshop and tinkering room, and you will be staying here. It is conveniently equipped to accommodate guests at this time. Nothing fancy, as we are already planning on turning it into a nursery."

He opened the door, revealing a cozy room with a small window and a bed with a small bedside table. That was the extent of the clutter, though the room would have been just big enough for a closet and a desk too. Going by geometry, the workspace would probably be around the same size, and the master bedroom would naturally be the largest. All in all, her hosts seemed to live quite luxuriously as far as town homes were concerned, though that was just by her human measure. Going by Erian's comment, this was at the limit of what they could afford, so at least the gap in living standards was only as wide as it seemed.

She laid her backpack and staff by the empty wall while Erian stopped by the window. Raising her eyes, she caught a glimpse of some wandwork. A lining of Dust slowly crawled up the window frame.

"Though I would like to think of you as a guest, we still have to take precautions, you understand. This will, well, react if the window is broken or opened," Erian explained, with just a dash of apology within the barely diminished cheer.

Sasha nodded. She hadn't expected to go totally unguarded—though at this point it wouldn't have fazed her one bit either.

His use of magic reminded her that her preconceptions on elven magic seemed somewhat off. The man seemed forthcoming enough, so she decided to put it out there: "I was always taught that your magic had more to do with crafting Dust-blended artifacts and less about wanded magic. There seems to be a lot of wands about, though." She left the question implicit, to seem slightly less prying.

Erian took the hint with enthusiasm. "They say that, do they? I suppose it is understandable, that being the way things worked in the days of old, before the Isolation. Nowadays we are more versatile than that. As you heard, being a Heroborn mage is not unusual here, though it sounded like it might be where you come from. See, we are all Heroborn here. I'm not sure why you would not be. It just makes sense."

Sasha frowned and retorted: "But you can't just choose to be Heroborn. You have to be born into it. It's not exactly fair, but that's how it goes."

Erian replied with a leading question: "You are correct. So, when you find out Heroborn have additional magical powers, which could help your society immensely if widely available, what do you do?" He was talking much as one would to a child, intonation and all. At least he was giving her the chance to come up with the answer herself.

Erian seemed to expect it to be an obvious one. And of course, there was one such candidate, though Sasha had difficulty imagining it to be the correct one. Then again, the elves were big on consensus.

She hazarded a guess, borrowing the animal husbandry terms that seemed appropriate: "You ... make sure that all breeding pairs include a Heroborn? Well, maybe not all at first, but as many as you can."

Erian's smile was that of a proud teacher: "Obviously. And yes, full coverage took a few generations to achieve, but now we all start from a level playing field as far as magic is concerned. I wonder why you humans have not done so as well."

In measured tones, trying to distance herself from the preposterousness of it all, she explained: "It seems as though elven society is more coordinated than human. It wouldn't even cross the minds of most humans to try large-scale reproductive management. I doubt the populace would go along with that if they did. Is it really that easy for you to arrange? Don't people frown on being told who to pair with?"

Erian shrugged. "Romantic pairings weren't interfered with. Just the breeding stock, though of course some romance resulted.

And it is not like there was much force needed. Who would not want the best for their children? In the first few generations, where we could not reasonably supply everyone without risking inbreeding issues, there was much competition for the services—personal or otherwise—of Heroborn males by mundane couples. At the time, it would have been a distinct advantage for the child as well as a boon for elvenkind. Female Heroborn could not practically participate as much, but they too were encouraged to take many lovers, or at least accept a wide variety of semen. Most were quite willing to do their part, with child-rearing help provided. Some of the children were also raised mostly in the families of the fathers, though with the option to stay in touch for the mother as well."

Sasha suppressed a chill and tried not to dwell on the implications. Instead, she moved forward: "Since you aren't all cursed, I suppose you filtered that out as well?"

"Oh yes, of course. There was an unfortunate incident with that, actually. I do not mind sharing a bit of our history with a cousin," he winked, "but if you could agree to not spread the word if you end up going back, that would be nice." Erian paused, so she nodded.

Trusting as ever of her elven blood, or confident that if she was untrustworthy, the Council would know and have her put to death anyway, the elf continued: "Right, so a few cursed bloodlines did make it into the pool without us noticing. With the breeding records, it was easy enough to catch when the problems multiplied, so to speak. Nevertheless, things ended up rather ugly. We had to sequester the affected offspring into their own community. It is not a source of any pride for us, but they were too much of a threat otherwise. After a few dragon attacks and other assorted raids, they dwindled out. We did try to defend them, fellow elves as they were, but having a few triggered individuals invited more trigger situations, and eventually the combined power of the cascading curses drew in too many powerful monsters." Erian seemed almost somber for a moment before shaking it off. If Sasha had needed more motivation to keep her bloodline status secret, this would have been it.

Sasha wondered about the other side of this story that was missing. That should be safe to digress into: "What about the charmed, then?"

"The what now?" Erian inquired, with a raised eyebrow.

Seemed as though the elves didn't hold the upper hand in all knowledge. Though with the implications … maybe it wasn't as safe a subject as she'd thought.

"Oh, never mind," she tried, fidgeting a bit.

His eyebrow stayed raised, and he spoke with a hint of seriousness layered on top of the usual levity: "I am quite sure I would be negligent if I left that alone."

Sasha sighed. "Sure, well, let's sit down first. I'm just hoping us elves aren't the kind to kill the messenger."

"That is not our custom," Erian assured her as he sat down on the bed, leaving a respectful distance between them. Then she told him all about what the human scholars, having had more time to observe various Heroborn lines, had learned.

"So, you see, if you didn't notice the subtler charmed bloodlines and thus didn't work to preserve them, they're likely to be diluted out by the other Heroborn blood. There are still a few charmed lines among humans, just because Heroborn lines aren't as widespread. Mundane blood doesn't have the same diluting effect as cursed or merely uncharmed Heroborn blood does."

Erian seemed serious, contemplative for a moment. Then he spoke quietly: "Interesting. Some might think your story a ruse intended to destabilize our society, but I believe you. I will put this in my report, but do not repeat it to others for now. Even if the Council judges your information to be true, they may not want to make this public. At the very least they will want to manage how the knowledge is spread. We have done well enough for ourselves without the benefit of having these so-called charmed lives. Though we get the occasional monster raid on smaller settlements or traveling parties, we are well able to counter them. Still, that there exist such bloodlines but that the way is closed to us now might be … unsettling for some. But perhaps we can yet turn it around. You might have missed something, after all."

He was reaching and they both knew it, but anything was possible. Sasha just nodded and filed the information away in case it would become useful to upset the elves. It seemed unlikely to suddenly emerge on top of the pile of smart things to do, but having options was good.

Erian switched gears and gave a shout downstairs, all chipper again: "Honey, did you listen in?"

"No, I was starting to set up dinner. You are welcome to join in, by the way. Was it important?" hollered the voice from the kitchen.

"No. Well, some potential Council secrets. Better not knowing for now," he replied. There was an accepting murmur from below. At least their relationship was an honest one.

He turned to Sasha and suggested that she get comfortable while waiting for dinner. Then he dashed off to the other upstairs rooms for a short moment each, no doubt securing the rest of the windows. That done, he headed down the stairs.

Sasha lay down for a bit and traced the front of the collar with her finger. It could easily be set up to kill her with a trigger. The windowpane could well be one, though there were other, less lethal possibilities. She wouldn't put it to the test unless absolutely necessary.

Down below, the elves were chattering on while preparing their meal. She caught a word here, another there. Still Human, even among themselves. She'd forgotten to ask about that. She would have to work it in somewhere. Meanwhile, she was as alone as she was going to get any time soon. Time to take stock of the backpack, see if they'd missed anything.

Her Dust was all obviously gone, but the strictly mundane items were still in there. She wouldn't have to go without a change of clothing or her bedroll. Even her papers had been left alone, maps, spellwork, and all. They would have had time to magically read in the documents for reproduction and later more careful inspection if they'd had a mind to. She didn't doubt their capability, as that was something even human mages could manage.

If they had gone through the papers, it could actually work in her favor. The map with its markings would support her story on where she was going. The spellcrafting experiments would hopefully speak well of her magical potential, just as long as they wouldn't mind her having crafted a combat spell.

Not that she'd be able to use it against them. The spare wand was gone. She still had hidden spare cores, but getting her hands onto a blank wand could be difficult, if it came to that.

For now, Sasha had no concrete plans aside from gathering information while playing nice and hoping for the best. She'd go help with the dinner if there was still something to do. Improving her standing with the host family could only be good for her.

As she stepped out of the door, she glanced at the small window at the end of the upper floor corridor. There it was, the Dust frame. She supposed it was warded. She could otherwise technically fit through the narrow window, but not without badly scraping herself on whatever shards of glass that would remain on the sides. The door to the workspace further down was closed, and she decided against actively prying.

The bedroom door, however, was ajar. She took the opportunity to glance in. The room was less spartan than hers with a large closet in one corner and a wide desk with drawers and a mirror in another. The window, sides obscured by heavy dark curtains designed to keep the light out if need be, was secured like the others.

What really dominated the room, though, was the huge, sturdy bed made of dark wood. The bedposts were adorned with simple but elegant carvings reminiscent of her staff. The bed was fit for a king or three.

The stairs creaked only slightly as she descended towards the main living area, where Erian had slipped into the meal preparation routine in a practiced manner. Cooking was clearly a team effort in this house. A larger team, even, but she resolved to let that unfold as it would.

"Can I help?" she inquired, for the sake of politeness. She presumed and preferred that she couldn't.

"No thanks, we will be finished with the preparations shortly, we just have to let it cook for a while afterwards. In the meanwhile, you can freshen up a bit in there. There is a big bowl of water, a guest towel, and all." Erian pointed at a door to one of the closets in the alcove.

Suddenly self-conscious, Sasha took the hint. "I'll just go get my change of clothes, then."

Her hosts seemed particularly pleased at that. She wasn't too scruffy yet after cleaning herself up back in Kilnkeep, she thought, but the house and the elves were pristine in comparison. Their standards probably differed.

She glanced at the windows before getting back to her room. They were dealt with here as well, including the one that was open near the stove. It made sense for them to have a way of opening the windows safely, or for the enchantment to recognize them somehow. Or perhaps the windowsills only interacted with the collar.

A quick trip upstairs later, her light green shirt and skirt in hand, she made her way to the washing room. "Oh, feel free to splash around in there, the surfaces can take the water," Erian commented from behind, as if she wasn't familiar with how to conduct herself. Though there was a kernel of truth in that, she was confident she could have worked out how to use a washroom, elven or not.

The walls and floor of the closet were all covered with a smooth but not slippery light brown surface. The floor was slanted towards a drain in the corner. There stood what could only be a white toilet seat by the back wall, and near it was a sizable barrel of water with a round bowl scoop hanging from the side. Over the barrel, a thin pipe came down from the ceiling, proceeding to wherever they got their refills from. Next to it on the side wall was a sink that fed into the corner drain. Evening light was provided by thin strips of windows discreetly along the ceiling.

Sasha proceeded to strip, using the hooks across from the sink to hang her clothes. As advised, she then started scooping up water and washing herself thoroughly, taking the liberty of using the soap she found lying on the sink. She'd want to give a good impression to her new acquaintances here.

After she was satisfied with her cleanliness, she sat to relieve herself on the toilet. As she got up, she pondered if she'd been wrong about not needing guidance with her business. The waste was just laying there in what she realized was a shallow, solid toilet bowl. She'd thought there to be a hinge or something to admit the material further in. As she stood there wondering how thoroughly she'd just embarrassed herself, the sudden movement spooked her. The bottom of the toilet bowl opened to admit the waste, and ripples around the edges left it pristine as its maw closed up again.

The toilet was magic.

The elves had magical toilets.

Sasha took a moment to sit down again and compose herself before finishing up and rejoining the others.

Partially recovered from the banal uses elves put magic to, Sasha returned from the restroom. Her hosts' quiet conversation came to an abrupt halt, but Erian quickly recovered: "You can put the dirty clothes in the bin over there in the corner. We will have them cleaned up along with ours."

She did as she was told, murmuring thanks, and joined the elves at the other end of the table. What she presumed was their meal was still bubbling on the stove. So much for that excuse to be quiet.

Luckily Erian was still on top of the situation, guiding the conversation. "So, how do you like our little apartment so far?"

"It's … quite nice, though … Excuse me, but I just have to ask about your toilet seat. Is that sort of thing common around here?"

The elves chuckled lightheartedly at her wonderment. Erian fielded this question as well, as she had expected. "Oh yes, relatively so. We put some stock in cleanliness, and though there are cheaper options available, the Dust bowls are gaining in popularity. It feeds into a reservoir that is regularly emptied and taken to the fields."

Sasha nodded once, and followed up: "Sounds reasonable. Makes me wonder, though. Should I expect to run into any other magical furniture here?"

Both of the hosts let out a small laugh at that. She noted that Del seemed to be getting more comfortable with her around as well. Indeed, it was she who spoke this time: "Sadly, not much. We do have the skills to make many magical luxuries, but at this time, they are just that. Maybe you saw the Dust fields while coming into town? While vast, there is only so much power we can get from them. Further expansion would carry practical costs limiting its marginal utility, and razing the whole forest in the pursuit of more magical power would not sit well. Now, the toilet bowl is low in energy usage and really quite convenient, so it is something of a priority."

Erian jumped in, seizing the opportunity to brag: "We do make use of some little things: magical locks, hand tools, and such. Dust itself is not scarce, and we could get a set of Dust furniture easily enough if we wanted, but the more interesting uses tend to be power hungry. We could scarcely afford the upkeep if we used them much. Given that, it is better to keep things modest."

Sasha pondered that for a bit. "How about replacing the old Dust with new brews?"

Del's face twisted slightly before she responded: "Yes, well. Aside from the material requirements which would become heavy with significantly increased consumption, there are several dumping grounds full of old, black Dust from when we did make a lot more of it. The Councils deemed that unsustainable long ago, hence the fields. We have not had to make new Dust in decades, really, since most is recycled and we can peel off the empowered top layer of the old dumps every now and then. Students sometimes make small batches just to keep the skill alive, of course."

Meanwhile, Erian stood to check on the food. "It is ready," he judged and brought the pot to the table with the aid of some thick oven mitts. "Bean stew with assorted vegetables and spices. Simple food, I hope you do not mind. We make something a bit more elaborate on our days off," he explained apologetically.

She got the impression the regretful tone was mostly for show, as were many things with him. "I'm sure it's quite fine," she played her part.

As it turned out, it was. She was quite sure there were some spices there that she hadn't even heard of, though the overall impression was still mild. Had it been otherwise, she would have been surprised. The elves seemed to favor subtlety in their tastes in general.

They ate a plateful of the dish each in silence. Even Erian, who was otherwise prone to filling gaps in chatter seemed quite content to let it be for a while. He did, however, open his mouth again when Sasha was done: "You can have seconds, if you like. We will have to save some for Allain who will be toiling in the fields for a while yet, but we made plenty enough."

"No thanks, but, uh. Toiling? Don't you have neople for that? Or is he..?" Sasha felt like she'd dug her hole deep enough and abruptly stopped. Del was taken aback, but Erian took it in stride, having already had some more exposure to her cultural eccentricities.

"Oh, Stars, no," he went while Del took the pot back to the still warm stove, "we did away with them at around the same time we started to breed for Heroborn blood."

It was, again, Sasha's turn to go wide-eyed: "Did away? What do you mean?"

"Oh, worry not, of course we merely restricted reproduction and phased them out. We are not savages. Quite the contrary, we would hardly wish on anyone the fate of neople. Poor creatures of limited potential, but still elvenkind. Their line had a dignified end while they were still useful to society."

Sasha spent a moment taking it in. She had a nagging feeling like she should have an opinion about the elves' solution to the neople issue, but she couldn't quite pin it. Out loud, she pondered: "Okay, I guess I wouldn't want to be neople either. But surely they could still make useful contributions. Do you really mean to say that you have Heroborn doing all of your manual labor? Doesn't that get tedious with their potential?"

This time it was Del who answered: "We take pride in whatever part we play to advance our society. Most will prefer some variety over their lifetimes, and usually it can be arranged. Besides, anyone with a basic spellcrafting education will carry that into their work, whatever it may be. Many a new spell has come from the trenches. We may not be able to splurge magical power on just any luxury, but even simple, inexpensive tricks may make a big difference in basic production and services."

Sasha was beginning to grasp how it was that the elves had progressed in magic as far as they had. With everyone a potential source of magical innovation, even if a rare few of them made any significant discoveries on their own, it would add up over time. And indeed having mages all over the social landscape would expose them to varied opportunities for creative magic use.

Erian took the opportunity to inquire, in turn, more about how the human society was arranged caste-wise. Though she didn't volunteer much, she didn't resist his curiosity either, so few stones were left unturned in the barrage of questions. She explained what kind of work the neople did among humans, how much supervision was required.

Selective breeding having been the topic of the day, Erian also inquired how the humans went about that. Sasha explained how they had a strong cultural taboo against human people and neople interbreeding, not that such errant couplings were very fertile anyway. She also mentioned how since the time of the Heroes there was more need for independent problem solving, and thus the ratio of actual people to neople had been steadily on the rise. Neople were discouraged from breeding overly much, to not overwhelm the demand or the ability of their keepers to take care of them. Their use in dangerous occupations such as mining also helped keep their numbers in check, along with the occasional sacrifice.

The elves both frowned at that. She hadn't thought much of mentioning it, but Sasha was quick to repudiate the practice for her part, explaining her putative father's reasoning on the matter.

"You did mention the Stars, earlier," she segued away from the sacrificial details, "I didn't see anything I'd recognize as a church in the town. Do you have one?"

Erian chuckled: "Not as such. We do recognize the celestials, as the Heroes did, but we also recognize that they're not doing a whole lot down here. It seems like they might have their own problems these days. Swearing by the Stars is mostly just a saying."

Sasha took the opportunity to slightly awkwardly approach the topic of languages: "Speaking of sayings, it seems like you have a surprising number of those in common with us. Like, the entire language's worth. I'm glad, don't get me wrong, since my family's Elven is not very good these days, but how come you're all speaking Human here?"

The elves glanced at each other, as if silently negotiating who was going to have the dubious pleasure of fielding this one. Erian defaulted in. "Do not knock your old Elven, you made a real impression on the Council with that ancient greeting. But yes, the change. It goes back to your Hero-ancestor Valarin, actually. He is reputed to have made an off-handed remark that having separate languages for the three main races was silly and inconvenient."

Sasha blinked, but as she remained otherwise silent, Erian proceeded to elaborate: "Whatever the Heroes said was taken with all due gravitas, of course, and at that time the trend was towards greater mixing and co-operation between our peoples. So, after much deliberation and discussion with several dwarf colonies, the Elders decided that standardizing on a single language would indeed be proper. Humans clearly lacking sufficient cohesion for a collective change, it was deemed our noble duty as the more adaptable civilizations to bring about this brave new era of the Common language."

Sasha caught her mouth gaping open, so she made use of it: "And after you'd taught all your children to speak Human, changed your entire civilization over to it, you just cut all ties with everyone else anyway and got stuck with the language?"

Erian cringed. "Well, it had seemed like a good idea at the time. But the Heroes' fall was eventually taken as a sign of their mixed society not working out. We wanted to avoid their mistakes. But the consensus shifted slowly, and the process was already well underway."

The fall of the Heroes seemed too much like a convenient excuse to withdraw away from other peoples again, Sasha thought while remaining silent. Erian took the opportunity to continue: "At that point changing back to our ancestral language would only have been more effort for what was seen as little gain. The transition was instead lauded as a great achievement of elvenkind, and left to stand."

And it would not have done to have gone to all that effort for nothing.

Del chimed in from the side: "It does leave the door open for our civilizations to more easily get closer again, if the consensus continues to shift as it has. Even if your society has apparently drifted a ways from Common, we can still understand you with little difficulty."

Sasha was getting irritated by the elven attitudes, and found a chance to vent in a small way: "Just us? I'm sure your Common has changed over time as well, just differently."

"No," both replied instantly. Del elaborated: "Even if it weren't for the fact that the human society has seen more generations than we have, we are very precise in our use of language. Old writings and Dust-stored speech recordings agree: Common is as Common was."

That figures. Of course it wasn't the elves who had developed new, weird accents, it was her primitive Human speech. There was not much time for an inferiority complex to develop, however. The door opened, admitting a somewhat more dirty specimen of an elven male than she'd been accustomed to. Field work was the great racial equalizer, it seemed.

The elves exchanged fond greetings and introductions. It was indeed Allain, returning from the day's chores. His reaction to her appearance was the most indifferent of the bunch, though being tired from manual labor may have been a factor. At least he didn't seem to mind the situation either.

Allain proceeded to grab a change of clothes from the walk-in closet across the washroom, and rushed to wash himself off. Couldn't let a rare breed of creature not seen in town for ages being at the table disturb one from cleanliness. Meanwhile, Sasha got filled in that they'd expected him a bit later still, so the day's work must've gone quickly. Erian went to the stove to fill a clean plate for Allain, then took it back to the empty spot at the table. It wasn't steaming, but probably remained at least lukewarm.

By way of extended introduction, Erian mentioned that Allain was a bit younger than the others, still studying architecture. Doing part-time grunt work while studying was usual for their kind. Something about letting the brain rest while the body worked and vice versa.

Sasha was a bit dubious of the methodology—it sounded like a ruse to get a society of Heroborn to handle menial jobs. She hadn't meaningfully tried if it worked, though. She'd had some chores, sure, but nothing that'd leave her exhausted. And then again, these were elves. Maybe it did work for them.

It was a short while later that a moist elf with towel-wrapped hair re-emerged, thankfully fully dressed. He seemed refreshed by the wash, and readily dug into his meal while the others gave him the highlights of what was happening and what they'd talked about.

"So, I thought I might invite some friends over for tomorrow night, celebrate the weekend, share the experience of meeting a real live mostly human and her strange tales of humankind, give Sasha here a chance to spread her side of the story, have some good fun while at it. How about it? I will be free of patrol duty, so I can make most of the arrangements. If you have some free moments you can help here, but do not overexert yourself," Erian put forth, the last part directed at Del.

Allain, mouth still full, grunted assent with a nod. Del responded more verbally: "Fine by me. I have not taken on a lot of work lately, what with the pregnancy. I can take the time to cook something festive if you go get the ingredients. Any heavy lifting I shall leave to your capable hands."

"Of course, darling. Great, it is settled then," finished Erian with a smile.

The evening continued on, but Sasha was getting tired after the filling meal. Allain wanted to field a question or two about humanity himself. Rather mundane affairs about their daily lives, social and courtship customs, and yes, architecture. Erian was listening keenly on the side, no doubt mentally preparing to report even on the banalities. She wondered if her words were being magically plucked out of the air into storage, like the words of the elves of old that Del had alluded to. Would Erian mind his family's friendly talks with a potential enemy of the state being stored for posterity? She honestly had no idea about that part and wasn't about to ask.

Instead, she started projecting even more weariness than her condition warranted, angling for a chance to recuperate and think in peace. This soon began to sink in to her hosts, and she was bid good night. Sasha went through the bathroom again, rinsed her mouth, and retired for the night.

Though her room was a cell of sorts, the bed, at least, was inviting. She stripped and slipped under the blanket. The soft fabric was cool to the touch but quick to warm up.

Now having as much privacy as she could hope for, Sasha proceeded to take mental stock of the situation. Her magic tools were gone. The sack containing them had been brought here, but come to think of it, it had disappeared somewhere when Erian had been securing the windows. It was likely to be locked tight where she couldn't easily burrow, lacking the very tools within. Erian might have been cavalier and overconfident, but he didn't seem downright stupid.

Tomorrow evening she'd have a chance to act nice, innocent, and most of all like she was in some small way a part of this race of people literally bred for magical as well as intellectual potential. No problem. She was better equipped for the task than … any human she knew. With proper tools and training, someone with actual elven blood and features would have been able to do better, but there were scarce few of those in the human lands. The elves hadn't as a rule interbred with humans much, and even Aaron had died without children of his own. While there was a history of Heroborn bloodlines being forgotten, many unknowingly carrying the blood, that did not apply to elven blood. The distinguishing features would have kept such lineages from falling into obscurity until recent generations.

She fell into pondering different approaches for making a good impression, fully aware that most of the planning would be for naught when actually immersed into a crowd of curious pointy-eared spectators. Eventually, the comfort of her prison bed and the tiring challenges of the past day overrode her anxiety, and she slept.

6

MORNING CAME. Occasional passing steps could be heard from the outside, along with distant birdsong. And a strange, faint buzzing from the corridor. Not ready to enter reality yet, Sasha drew the blanket over her, hiding from the faint morning light. The dreams had been uncomfortable and did not entice her to try to fall asleep again. There had been elves offering her food, drink, and inane questions, all the while critiquing her answers as mundane and human. Master Aaron had been there, only with more pointedly elven features. He'd been among the worst.

She made an effort not to dwell on the dream, knowing it'd slowly fade then. Concentrating more on the snugness of the bed, she lay there for a moment. The buzz, varying in intensity now, penetrated her consciousness again. It was getting annoying.

She fished her clothes off the floor while still under the covers, dressed up, rose with a stretch, and proceeded to peek into the corridor. The sound was undoubtedly coming from the master bedroom. The door wasn't properly closed, though there was no crack to see through either. Her curiosity got the better of her, and Sasha pushed the door ever so slightly open.

Right, of course. It was one of those tools that Erian had mentioned before. Its exact nature was surprising, but she had known the elves to use magic in the most profane of manners. That she hadn't guessed at this all along had simply been a gross failure of imagination on her part.

Stunned, she gaped slightly too long. "Oh sorry, did I wake you? I tried to be quiet, and I did not suppose this would be that loud," Del said apologetically after shutting the thing down.

"N-no, I just wondered what the buzzing was. Never mind me," Sasha managed, then shut the door properly, and turned mechanically away.

"Did you want to join in?" Del asked, her voice muffled by the door. Sasha may have not been completely devoid of curiosity, but she was pretty sure the answer right this instant was a resounding but very quiet "no".

She retreated back to her own bedroom and sat down on the bed to recover from the surprise. It didn't help that the buzzing resumed shortly after, but it didn't shock her further either. It was just her comment being taken at face value.

She directed her thoughts to the device she'd been using. The basic shape was obvious enough, though she was unsure how to achieve the vibration. Maybe a suitably imbalanced rotational element ... And then her mind twisted.

Master Aaron had taught her to be respectful of magic. Conservative. Experiment with small variations of existing spells, treating them as masterwork and herself as a dabbler.

The elves did no such thing. They had no reverence for magic at all. It was a tool to be used as one saw fit, for whatever purpose, in whatever way. Maybe Aaron would have encouraged her to be more independent in later training, but going by himself and Jamal, not to this extent.

The basic missile spells being pointlessly tame had been just one example of the lack of inventiveness in human mage culture. Wardstones should be able to point at the danger. The shackles were somewhat better, though the options for punishment could stand to be more varied. That thought made images of torture devices of various shapes flood all over her mental landscape. She shook those off. Maybe there was a time and place for being conservative.

Even the elves had not been immune to making their magical weapons all too fair. The old staff's missiles were all but depleted when shot, so not burrowing was more understandable. The shield, however, should be able to tear into incoming flesh on close contact, if not very effectively at that density. Still, delivering pain if not much actual damage would serve to distract an assailant. Or, you could concentrate on the eyes. So obvious, and probably doable if you had the skill for the shield itself. She wondered if the elves had improved on their spells since then. They seemed like that sort of folk now. Still, asking if their modern weapons would eat into the eyeballs of their enemies might not be prudent.

A torrent of ideas flooded within, but Sasha had precious little tools to put them in practice. She could start on something from scratch, but it would be slower and more error-prone, especially as she could only work on paper for the time being. Even novel projects could often take advantage of some parts of earlier work. She then recalled the burrowing missile spell she'd worked on earlier. She still had that one on paper. There was no obvious problem with the spell now—other than being limited to taking down just one target at a time. She could work on that.

She dug into the backpack for her papers, spread the previous spellwork on the bedsheets, and took the tiny bedside table for her writing desk. She first made a rough schematic. There'd be some need for experimentation, if she'd ever have the chance, but the basic shape was clear. She tried to remember what she'd learned of the Red Dust, of how to channel its force. She had little experience in tinkering with the parts of spells that concerned explosions, but she didn't let that bother her now. She'd just have to be careful in the experimental fine-tuning.

The basic form started to take shape. She scaled it down a notch, sacrificing range for multidirectionality. Now the objects could be conveniently carried and tossed. Perhaps give them a manual trigger so that they could be primed beforehand, obviating the need for delicate wandwork while in a tight spot. A simple switch, with a safety, wouldn't drain the object's power unless it had no light exposure at all, and even then it would remain usable for a good while. There would be risks, master Aaron had warned, in making magical weapons capable of being used by anyone. Here, though, among a population of mages, that concern felt pointless. Besides, the device would be strictly single use.

Balance and aim would be tricky while tumbling through the air, but the missile part had guidance built in, and she could remember how to get the orientation of a Dust object, hopefully creating a safe zone below while maximizing spread. She'd really need to be careful in that testing ...

"Oh, you are spellcrafting," said Del, suddenly behind her.

Sasha blinked, then turned around, trying futilely to cover the papers. Del merely continued: "Apologies, I knocked but it appears you were preoccupied. Can I have a look?"

Sasha nodded, unsure if the question was rhetorical, and took a step to the side. It wasn't like the other elves hadn't already seen her weapons research.

Del's eyes gleamed with curiosity as she started to read. "Oh, I recognize this, and the combination, ouch, not very sophisticated but clever. Just one will not do, eh? Well, I can sympathize," she spoke in a teasing tone. "This is your work?"

"Yes, I combined the missile and burrowing charms earlier and ... just had to work on something to relax, I guess, and this is all I had handy to start with. You can read this, then?" Sasha asked in turn, and immediately blushed in embarrassment. Of course the elf could, Sasha just hadn't properly internalized it.

Del, unfazed, answered while further perusing Sasha's work: "Yes, of course. I do spellcrafting work myself. Usually of the more civilian kind, mind you, but the patterns you used are basically familiar, if detailed somewhat differently from the ones we commonly teach."

Sasha felt doubly stupid. With what had she expected Del to busy herself in her workshop, embroidery?

Del continued to eye the papers absent-mindedly for a while, then startled as if shaken back to reality. She put on a mild smile, relaxing Sasha. "Yes, interesting. We have a testing hall not far from here, if you would like me to run some trials for you at some point. Not today. Enough stress with the party."

Sasha's eyes lit up. She hadn't been promised her wand, but at least she'd be able to try to accomplish something. She'd already been twice outed as a combat mage, there was little harm that being good at it could do. Maybe it'd win her some respect if she could get the spell to work. Certainly, it seemed, from Del.

"Yes, that'd be lovely," she replied with a genuine smile.

Del smiled back with a nod: "I have not gone there as often these days due to the belly, but I can manage if you will do the running around with target placements and such. I have mostly done a little maintenance on my previous projects here at home and made do with minor testing in the cage. The Council supports childrearing, so we get by even if I take a pass on new larger projects."

One detail had caught Sasha's ear. "Cage?"

"Oh, excuse me, local term of the trade. Let me show you," Del said and took flight towards her workspace, gesturing for Sasha to follow. Intrigued, she did.

The workspace seemed simple, but effective. On the near right, a sturdy wooden shelf stacked with volumes and binders. By the window on the left, a large desk with drawers, cluttered with papers with drawings and incantations on them. In the far-left corner, shelves sat stacked with cubes of Dust, with a series of small metallic boxes that might be used to house red ones securely. In the far-right corner was what she could only surmise was the cage: a large box constructed from thick double glass and metallic edges.

Del went in, demonstrating as she explained: "These walls open up and lock back down like so, with the rubbery edges here closing the gaps tight. The stand there can be used to place test material. The cage is suitable for small scale low risk testing; the redundant glass walls will slow down most things enough to get a counterspell in. Though you would not want to test any red spells in there," she concluded, raising an eyebrow at Sasha in acknowledgment of her more dangerous ambitions.

She nodded, stretching her neck left and right to get a better idea about the inner structure. The concept was not worlds above what she'd heard of, but greatly refined. This would have been quite handy in her studies. She said as much to Del, who was pleased at her appreciation.

Del nonchalantly cleaned up her current work in short order, but was happy to give Sasha a look at some of her more basic magical tomes. As Sasha browsed through the books, the elf chimed in with pointers for curious details she thought might be new to human-raised mages, or that might be useful in crafting her new spell. Sasha's eyes wandered towards the more advanced books, but she decided not to push it for now. She likely wouldn't get much out of them without the background of the local basic volumes anyway.

Before Sasha could properly bury herself in the books, Del suggested they carry a few of them, along with some extra paper, into Sasha's room. Del would start preparing for the party downstairs. She took the cue to leave the workspace, acutely aware that the elven lore in her hands would be the envy of all mages back home, and more so the rest that was left behind. She didn't notice Del locking the door or any obvious alarms, but she wasn't about to risk the sympathies of her hosts. The shelf was alluring, but extracting her hide would have to take priority to extracting knowledge.

Having browsed through the volumes enough to get an outline of their contents, Sasha returned to developing her spell. Couldn't let Del's offer of getting to properly test it go to waste, even though the books beckoned to peruse them properly. For now, she'd settle for a more thorough view of the portions most obviously relevant for her current work. In the name of efficient experimentation, she'd make several variations on the exact shape and on the control incantations. Those could be mixed and matched on the fly by reading in the sheets in appropriate groupings. The incantations could only be meaningfully varied so far without feedback from testing, but there were some timing options, and one of the elven books sported a stabilization method she'd want to try.

Engrossed in her work, she lost track of time. Before she knew it, she had a few variants stacked and ready and another in progress. This time, she heard the knock. Self-consciously she turned the paper over, as she'd done to the other ones, to reduce casual snooping. She was almost sure everyone living here would know what she and Del would be up to anyway, but only almost. Besides, showing such raw work was embarrassing.

"Yes?" she prompted whoever had come knocking.

Erian opened the door and flashed a smile at Sasha, though there were a couple of wrinkles on his forehead. The elf greeted her: "Hey. People will be coming over within the hour, you should probably get down and make yourself comfortable. But first, would you happen to know anything about two human neople tripping the road wards last night not far from where you crossed?"

That did seem like a bit of a coincidence, but at least she could honestly deny it. "No idea. I even made an extra effort to slip out of town unnoticed when I left. I've seen some around, obviously, but I haven't had direct dealings with neople since …" she trailed off.

Erian raised a questioning eyebrow. Right, out with it. "Well, I sort of destroyed a necromancer's lair back in Merfort on the coast in order to get on a trade convoy going this way. He got away, though … You sure your neople weren't zombies?" She had a bad feeling about this.

Erian's second eyebrow joined the first one at the revelation. "Going by the report, no, they looked quite normal. They did act strangely, but then, neople are not something we're used to any more in any case, and they might have just been scared. A necromancer, huh? We know them from history, of course, but we have not had any among us since our race was purified of neople and other non-Heroborn blood. Should not be a surprise that they still exist where you hail from. You have not had any contact with druids, have you?"

The seeming non sequitur didn't manage to faze Sasha by this point. "No. I've been taught the basics, but they're recluses. I haven't seen any that I know of. I did have a short conversation with an elementalist in Kilnkeep on the border," she decided to volunteer.

Erian nodded, apparently satisfied. "I believe you. There are sometimes strays in our territories, just that the timing was curious. Also, these ones might be involved with a druid, though we have not found one so far. One of the neople attacked our patrol with a pack of wild animals by his side. The other managed to slip away in the commotion, though lightly wounded. He left a smear of blood so we know what he was."

Something occurred to Sasha, and forthrightness in most things seemed to have been the best strategy so far. "I did see a wolf or something on my way here, at night, watching me for a while before it continued on its way. I didn't think much of it. Could've been a druid's way of checking me out, I suppose."

Erian smiled again, happy at the disclosure. "Possible. Druids have, on occasion, braved our borders before, lured in by our majestic forests. Seems as though this one has not ventured close enough to be directly detected, but has sent accomplices for some reason. Unusual for them, I gather. We haven't had our own druids either for generations, of course, so I cannot speak from experience."

Sasha nodded. "It does sound strange, though Master Aaron always said not to generalize too much. Not all druids are the same."

There was a sharp glint in Erian's eye: "Master, is it?"

Sasha reigned in her fluster. "He filled that role in my life as well. It took precedence as my training progressed."

The elf didn't pursue, to Sasha's relief. "We usually get our teachers from outside the family. Keeps things tidier."

Sasha took the chance to move forward. "Not much choice of masters in my village. Was that all for now? Should we be joining Del?"

Erian settled for an uncharacteristically terse reply: "Indeed."

They left for downstairs, where Del was laying out some pastries on the table. Already present were bowls of salad, some fruit, and slices of meat. A pile of empty plates was awaiting the guests. Self-service seemed to be the name of the game.

"Welcome back," Del beamed, as if she'd been away somewhere. "Did you have a good session? I hope we did not interrupt anything too savagely."

Come to think of it like that, she had been rather absent, writing away the hours. She nodded curtly: "Yes, it's fine, I'm close to having a suitable first batch of tests ready. Just some fine tuning."

Del grinned giddily. Maybe she'd enjoy getting to experiment with explosive spellcraft more than Sasha'd realized. Or being the first to work with a foreign mage in ages.

Part of it may have even been that Del actually seemed to like her now, having bonded somewhat over their common interest. Not that she'd been overly apprehensive earlier in the morning either, but Sasha tried her best not to think about that. Instead, she recalled the original wary welcome, and the contrast was quite striking.

Nevertheless, theirs was a budding friendship based on a lie. The deception about her elven blood had been instrumental in improving the first impression. Sasha felt an uncomfortable twinge in the back of her mind.

"Guests should be coming in soon, along with Allain. He should be less physically exhausted, it being a study day today. As I said, the rest will also be of the more open-minded variety. Not to mislead you, many an elf has an intense dislike of you. But fear not, none would dare act on it while the Council is deliberating, and today you'll be among friends, so just be yourself. You'll probably mostly have to repeat what you've already told us. Though please mind your tongue on the more sensitive details as we discussed."

Be herself. *Right.* She could've also done without the reminder that it would make a lot of elves very happy to see her dead, but she guessed it was just Erian making sure the party wouldn't bias her grasp of the situation. She was getting a handle on this elven frankness. A part of her wondered if there were other blind spots to it than admitting to their mistakes, though. That by itself could be quite useful. Whoever sided with her might not easily waver, at least without the Council arguing against her.

Or was the main driver really the argument itself and not the Council's symbolic power? If somebody had a good enough understanding of how elves thought and could be argued with, could they hold as much sway as the Councils? Not that it mattered a lot. She wasn't such an expert and wasn't apt to become one any time soon. As for the elves, it seemed likely that the best minds were, in fact, on the Council already.

Outwardly she just smiled and nodded, if visibly nervous. She could allow herself that much. She went to wait on the couch while her hosts put the finishing touches on the buffet, cleaned up the stove, and straightened the furniture. Allain was the first to arrive, slightly out of breath but indeed not as weary as the day before. He was pleased to have made it before the guests.

Soon they heard the first knock on the door. While the first guests were still in the alcove, there was another. Perhaps elven etiquette favored timely arrival, or they were just eager to get an eyeful of the alien. Sasha was introduced to one fascinated face after another, some with a touch of concern or suspicion, but as had been promised, none showed overt hostility. Mostly these were friends and acquaintances of the family, but that didn't mean some of them weren't relevant to her situation. A couple of border patrol people were included, one a mid-tier officer, and while the absence of actual Council members was pretty much a given, there was an assistant to one present.

The party was a blur in Sasha's mind. Much of the conversation centered on matters already discussed with her hosts. As the guests were of varying professions, they also often asked more details on how things worked with regard to their own particular areas of interest. Agriculture, education, transportation, military, and even religion, not a big subject in these lands, were covered. Sasha obliged as best she could, not being an expert in everything.

Magic, of course, she was an expert on, if only a visiting one from an inferior culture. A couple of Del's associates were quite interested in this subject, even if there wasn't much she could actually teach them. Their conversation was quite sophisticated, though a little too much so. Sasha largely found herself on the receiving end of polite condescension.

The mages didn't seem to have malicious intent towards her in particular, and they did even have some appreciation of her recent efforts as explained by Del. However, the manner of their praise did remind her a bit of the way a human might appreciate the occasionally blundering acrobatics of well-trained neople. She bore it through.

Regardless of subject, Sasha made an effort to subtly distance herself from humanity. "Their" customs were indeed silly and archaic, she'd agree. She didn't even have to fake it most of the time, really, which made her think twice which society she really felt she belonged. The answer at this point seemed to be neither, but she could see herself getting used to the elven ways, if they'd choose to see her as one of them. That pesky curse would have to come off first, though, else she'd just end up in her very own internment camp like the cursed elves of old.

All in all, it was a relief when the party started to wind down, and one by one the guests took their leave, with polite goodbyes and thanks for the exotic company. She'd almost managed to forget being on display by that point, but no matter. On the whole she thought she'd made good impressions, or at the very least managed to present an image of a harmless, backward country cousin. She hoped the Council advisor in particular would take that impression back to work.

The hosts seemed happy with the evening as well. No doubt their status among this group had spiked considerably as a result. They were humming some strange elven tunes as they cleaned up and chomped on the more perishable leftovers. Sasha got in to grab some as well. She'd been engaged most of the time and had not had much time to eat, delicious as the offerings had been.

All of the hosts had talked her up quite a bit. Even the reticent Allain had participated, after having first spent some time upstairs with a visiting couple—a detour which Sasha pointedly ignored. Landing in this particular house with these particular elves seemed to have been a rare stroke of good fortune indeed, if one did have to be caught by their kind in the first place.

Erian came in to offer words of encouragement, mostly the same as she'd gleaned herself, with Del's smiling support from the background. Allain was back to his somewhat more solemn self, clearly having put up a bit of a front for the purpose of being entertaining. Still, Sasha had been a bit iffy on how Allain had taken to her, but now it seemed like he'd adopted the others' outlook after all. She could hope it meant it being infectious.

Del bluntly informed Erian that they'd be going to the testing range tomorrow to see about Sasha's spellcrafting. Erian wasn't the only one here to overrun others with decisions already made, after all. He had no apparent objection, but he noted that the Council would surely be interested in how that went as well. He'd join them, being curious himself. Sasha felt the pressure pile higher. She excused herself to her room to busy herself with the final tuneups and double-checks.

Slowly the house grew quiet around her as she toiled well into the night. Finally, she managed to pry herself away from the work as she heard one of the elves stumbling his or her way down, presumably to use the toilet. Some sleep would be good. Testing and tuneups on the fly would require concentration, especially with Red Dust involved. She waited until the elf returned to bed, then popped by the bathroom herself before finally laying down to rest.

A long and busy day behind her, both socially and intellectually, she slept quite soundly for a change. As she woke up to a bright day behind the window, she realized she'd been allowed to sleep in. Maybe her hosts did so as well. She had the impression that the elves could afford to take their weekend rest seriously.

This time around Sasha managed to get her bearings, visit the bathroom, and slip into the breakfast table all without any embarrassment. Allain was the odd man out, perhaps still asleep, perhaps already gone somewhere. The others were just finishing their morning meal—or maybe lunch for them already—but had left her a little something to start her day with.

"Busy night?" Del asked knowingly. Must've pulled a few all-nighters herself.

Sasha gave a faint smile and a nod. "Should be ready for first rounds of testing, now, when it's convenient."

Erian chimed in. "We are pretty much good to go so after your breakfast would be fine. Allain is upstairs. He will be joining also, since this is an historical occasion and all. No pressure, though, and we refrained from inviting further company," he finished with a lopsided grin.

At the mention of further company Sasha wondered if they'd even mentioned this to the Council beforehand or if it was a matter of better to ask forgiveness later. She herself decided to hold on to her plausible deniability.

After breakfast Sasha returned upstairs to gather her things. Del came behind, noting she'd go grab some Dust and get Allain from the bedroom. Sasha left her to it and concentrated on her papers. She'd left them arranged in unit stacks, forms on the left, control incantations on the right. She made small sleeves of rotated note papers to mark the division, then stacked them all together, and put them in the backpack. She then included the elven tomes just in case she'd need them for some fine tuning—or in case she'd take an opportunity to run for it.

As she headed for the stairs again, she saw Del prompting Allain to leave the bedroom. The man had been reading. She didn't stay to gander, leaving it for the pair to catch up to her downstairs, which they soon did. Then they were off on their way. The testing hall was some five or ten minutes' walk away.

The gawking on the way was subtler than last time she'd walked these roads, but not otherwise reduced. The word of her arrival had spread and eliminated the element of surprise, Sasha surmised, but she was still newsworthy. She continued to put forth her best effort in looking like nothing was amiss, as did her entourage. They greeted some oncomers, though judging by the curt courtesies exchanged, only those they were somewhat acquainted with. They didn't markedly slow down while at it, so they made good time to the testing hall.

It was a large rectangular building with a mildly pitched roof. Approaching from uphill, she took notice of the roof. It was the blackest black, like only depleted Dust could be. She glanced around for other buildings. Those that had their roofs visible were similarly covered. Not just the fields, then. Well, it only made sense to make good use of the surface area. Just that all the roofs were black.

"Where are all the gray roofs?" Sasha asked. Come to think of it, she hadn't seen any lighter Dust on the fields, either, excepting the fully white spots they were harvesting. The stuff they spread on the fields had been very dark.

Del let out a sympathetic laugh. "The default color is inefficient. When Dust is set to gather the sun, its color is set to black until fully empowered. Only then will it turn white. The roof Dust generally feeds into a Dust reservoir beneath, so it always stays black."

Sasha's eyes gleamed. "I see! I knew about the efficiency, of course, but we never thought the color could be set like that. Makes sense. Why do you harvest the fields manually, then? Haul it with horses, even? Oh, and can you teach me?"

"It is a simple incantation if you know about it. I can show it to you later. And there are compounding losses in transferring magical potency over long distances. Tradeoffs."

"Thanks," said Sasha. Further elven magical secrets, hers simply for the asking. She smiled giddily.

They had made their way now to the hall itself. Sasha was wondering if Del had her own personal room there, but before she could ask, Del clarified the arrangements of her own accord: "Let us have a look at the reservations board. I would have gotten a spot beforehand, but I was unsure when we would be getting up today. Usually there is room on weekends regardless, but we might have to come back later if we are unlucky. Sorry, it did not occur to me to mention that sooner."

Sasha was the odd human out, and lacked the others' background information. That they'd forget sometimes was only ... human. "That's okay," Sasha obliged.

They came up to the building and entered a hallway running along its side, with doors and observation windows into the actual testing rooms. There seemed to be three on this side of the building. In the corner, the corridor turned towards the other side. The outer walls were lined with storage closets.

Del went to a nearby reservation board, which verified the total room count to be six. Two were taken, one on each side of the building. Maybe for added peace and quiet. Short walls separated the adjacent observation areas, but they weren't actual distinct rooms. There did not appear to be many magical secrets among elves, or at least among the users of this particular facility. Sasha could cope with that, though she hoped that the evening wouldn't turn into an exhibition. She'd had enough of that at the party.

Del checked a slot for their use and led them on, explaining: "The main door gets most of the traffic, so let us go to the other side. Somebody is using the far booth there, so we'll take the near one. If anyone comes afterwards, they will probably stay by the main door, so we should have relative peace." Sasha felt satisfied that they had similar priorities here.

Del went for the small desk in front of the observation window that appeared to have at least three thick layers of glass to it, along with a metallic mesh for reinforcement. She unloaded some of her Dust on the desk and asked Sasha for her notes. She dug them out.

Del brightened up. "Oh, you have separated the form and function. Clean design, I am impressed. What did you want to start with? Guys, make yourselves useful, grab some target dummies from the closets, and spread them around."

Sasha was pretty sure her work was impressive only for a hedge mage, but accepted the flattery regardless. She took out a promising pair of stacks and spread them around for Del. She took her wand out, and started gesturing. Meanwhile, Erian and Allain were availing themselves to the stick-like dummies and lugging them inside the testing area. Instructions on placement were unnecessary; the dolls were situated almost but not quite evenly along a ring spanning the room. When set up, some inner structure spread out cloth in fair facsimiles of humanoid figures.

After setting up the dummies, the men brought in sets of Dust. First, Erian placed his load in the center on top of a folding table. At the flick of Del's wand the Dust took the form of a spring platform. Sasha had just been about to ask how they'd arrange tossing her construct up several meters. There was even some sort of an extension that could likely be used for triggering the safety.

After the platform was ready, Allain placed his mixed load of Dust on top. Both of the males then vacated the room, and as they closed the double door, Del cast Sasha's first candidate on the Dust. It assembled into a compact eight-pronged star, the red hidden in the center.

"Now to get at that safety," Del narrated while making a gesture that tied the manipulator arm to the movement of the wand. Sasha'd have to ask her about that. Some control of existing artifacts was familiar magic back home, but tracking the wand like that was new.

The method was effective, too. The safety was easily triggered. "Let us just wait a while and see if it blows up already," Del went, all giddy and wide-eyed. Sasha let out a nervous laugh, Erian a more boisterous one.

After a minute, it became evident that no premature detonation was forthcoming. Del continued with the safety lecture: "Keep your eyes peeled. It should be safe as houses. The dummies nearest to the window should take the brunt of the damage if the guidance works at all, and the window is rated for bigger impacts anyway. The launcher should put a spin on the stars. We will try without if they cannot manage, but no reason not to go in at the deep end. Here goes." She triggered the mechanism.

Sasha's device flew almost straight up into the air, and as it reached its apex, instantly blew up. Pieces rained on the dummies, the walls, and the window. The test apparatus also got hit. That wasn't good for the prospective user. Del quickly cast what Sasha assumed to be a counterspell.

"In case the digging part still works," Sasha surmised out loud.

Del nodded. "The shaping of the charge did seem a bit dodgy. I can give you a few pointers later, but I would rather not intrude too much on this first run."

Learning by mistake was familiar to Sasha, but even more embarrassing out here than at home. "That'd be good, I haven't had too much experience with the red stuff," she sheepishly admitted.

"A couple of these other designs do seem more promising to me, so do not fret yet. Let us see how it goes," Del said in a comforting note.

The results did improve from the first run, though not consistently. The men helped reset the launcher and put in new Dust while Del and Sasha set up one set of papers after another. Some of the other combinations suffered much the same fate as the first one. A few managed to launch projectiles but fell very short.

One launched multiple projectiles fast enough for the planned range but the elven stabilization was off somehow and most missiles hit the floor or the ceiling. Two shots, those that were level with the ground, hit proper targets though. They made a note of that, as well as of the fact that the launcher was obliterated by one of the missiles. Wouldn't want to be throwing that one in the air yourself. Sasha hypothesized having misunderstood something in the elven incantations. Del promised they could take a look at that later. It would certainly be one to test further.

After that, using the same shape but with one of her homebrew logics, the star managed to hit four targets while being a bit off kilter. A couple of the missiles went high, a couple low. At least the replaced launcher was undamaged this time around.

Since it was one of the more promising ones of the set, Del allowed them to burrow for a bit: "The walls are hard and thick and they have to fix them up periodically anyway." One of the dolls fell in a moment, then another. Del countered the spell and commanded: "Boys, go see about the damage."

The dolls affected had, in fact, been appropriately eaten up. Sasha was glad that not everything was a total disaster, but Del topped her reaction with her mirthful grin. "Looking good. Now to replace those dolls and run the pattern through. We have to get back to at least these two. Allain, go fetch us some more Dust, red included."

The rest of the combinations each failed more or less spectacularly in comparison to the two that had caught their eye, so the contenders for round two were easy to decide. The wobbly incantation repeated its slightly off performance. The one using elven stabilization continued to shoot straight for the floor and the ceiling. Sasha cupped her face in embarrassment.

Del laughed, but amiably enough. "Let us see if we cannot find the error quickly and give it another go?"

"I know where it is. Let me scribble a bit," Sasha replied sourly while glancing through the incantations. There it was. The stabilization worked fine, but it was the coordinate systems that were different. A rookie mistake, but easy to make when integrating unfamiliar spellwork. If that was all that was the matter, it would be more of a success than she'd had any right to expect on the first round of trials.

The error was small enough that she could correct it on the same paper, though writing it out again later would be cleaner.

She'd see about that then. The men were already setting up for another round as Del took in the corrected spell.

The setup complete, Sasha crossed her fingers, and off it went. Six hits out of eight, with good form. The targets weren't exactly placed optimally with regular separation, as that would be unrealistic, so a couple of misses were to be expected. Before celebrating too much, they made another two test runs. Seven and six again.

While more testing and fine tuning would be warranted given the lethal nature of the spell, this sufficed for ending the day's experiments on a celebratory note. Del stood to give her a good hug, while the men settled for some pats on the shoulders along with congratulations on a job well done. Del promised more hall time later, but they'd already spent much of the day on this, and everybody was due a respite. Sasha didn't disagree.

They gathered their stuff, put the undamaged dolls back into their closets, and deposited the less well faring ones in a nearby bin.

"We went through a lot of those," Sasha noted. "Is that going to be a problem?"

"They are provided by the Council. The testing grounds are a socially useful public service. Unless we start going through truly prodigious amounts of them, nobody will bat an eye," Del explained.

As they started towards home, Erian said he'd pop by the Council building first while the others prepared dinner. It went unsaid, but Sasha suspected he was taking the opportunity to put in a report on the excursion fresh from memory. He was smiling happily as he left. Sasha was fairly confident that he, at least, thought that her success would reflect well on her. She certainly hoped so.

As they walked, Del started a flowing commentary on all the mistakes she'd been able to pin down on something particular. After the eventual success, the critique was quite a bit easier to swallow than she'd already mentally prepared for. Almost pleasant.

She could get used to living here.

7

S ASHA FELL INTO A PLEASANT ROUTINE for the rest of the weekend and most of the following week. They refined and tested Sasha's star missile further when they had the chance, but also had a busy social schedule. They entertained guests once more at the trio's place and attended a select few events they'd received invitations to. Socializing among the alien creatures slowly got more comfortable for Sasha, if not altogether natural.

Alas, she was not kept in the loop about whatever went on in the Council chambers, but that was apparently business as usual for the Council. Little came out that wasn't a finalized, argued decision. Which was why it was so disconcerting to say the least for Sasha to note rising anxiety in Erian towards the end of the week. He wouldn't say anything, but was distinctly not his cheerful self. Not around her, at least.

As he left for an unspecified errand late on Friday evening, Del, having been hard at work in her room called for Sasha to join her there. She was wearing a serious, intent expression as she shut the door and started to talk: "Tonight, you are going to assault me and run away while the men are asleep. I will ..."

Sasha interrupted her, hands spread in front, head shaking: "No! Why would I do that?"

Del flashed a faint smile and continued: "Ssh. I suggested that Allain spend some of our Dust to study with music, but talk softly. There has been a pattern of increased wild animal and even goblin activity in the nearby forest, closest to this side of town. Nothing too solid yet, might be a coincidence, but you know where I am going with this, do you not?"

Sasha did. Her staying put for a week had allowed her curse to gather some of the local dangerous elements as near as they could. She also knew her expression had already given everything away, so she merely asked: "Has anyone been hurt?"

"No, not so far. It is not very bad, yet, at least, though children are being discouraged from venturing into the woods alone," Del said with some repressed pain on her face.

Must have been a sore issue for the elves, or at least this pending mother. "I'm sorry, I didn't think it was this bad already, and anyway I was trying to just pass through quickly when I was taken captive. Master Aaron said there could be a cure in the Hall of Heroes, that's why I'm really trying to get there, so I wouldn't cause anyone any harm," Sasha blurted out, managing to bite her tongue before she admitted not being really any part elf either. That could have been bad.

Del nodded sympathetically. "I figured it might be so, though I will say that we have no knowledge of any sort of cure. If we did, we would have done a fair bit better for our own cursed kin. But it is always possible your father chanced upon something we have not. You should have an opportunity to try, but I fear that most here would be more ... risk-averse. Your status being as precarious as it is, well. It would be safer for you to leave. Which brings me back to what I was saying. I will herbally arrange for the guys to sleep heavily tonight. I can get your gear for you, some Dust, even a cloak. I cannot unlock your staff, it would need Jarin herself or one of the higher-ups, but I will give you some Red Dust so you are able to defend yourself on your journey. I know I am going to have to take your word for it but please, please do not use it on your fellow elves even if they come after you. I will give you a map and a suggested route that should take you quickly away from our territory with warded roads marked."

Sasha stared at Del, mesmerized. After a moment she managed to nod curtly. Del continued: "You should be able to avoid most pursuit by using the cloak when passing the warded roads. They recognize you by your features even in the dark, can peer under normal hoods somewhat, and also make alerts in unclear cases. Even though they will also notice an actively cloaked person, it will not usually raise alarms, not even for you. The cloaking obscures details enough that you will not register as human, and cloaked people are generally assumed to be elves. Until morning comes and you will of necessity be reported missing, of course."

Of course. While Sasha sat dumbstruck but able to nod and even process information, Del then proceeded to drill her on the details. Go here, avoid there, here's the border, there's the City. Del's map was better than Aaron's, that would make things easier if all panned out. She showed her the ins and outs of their cloaks, warning as Sasha already suspected that they ate Dust like crazy, so practicing moderation would be necessary. Some details were new to her, such as the cloaks working best for one target only, often showing some distinct visual blurring from other directions. She hadn't noticed, being the target of choice when they were used on her. Del instructed her in designating the main target and empowering the cloak.

When she got her voice back and the flood of information was abating, Sasha managed to ask: "How will your family fare with my escape?" She had grown fond of them.

"There will be some repercussions, and I am afraid I am going to have to lay blame on you rather heavily for drugging the others and coercing me into compliance. It is undignified, but I will blame my condition for being pliable. It seems to work all too well," Del said with a sigh. "I can also fake some injuries on myself with magic. Finally, your being put into Erian's care was cleared with the Council itself. That should shield us from the brunt of it."

Responsibility actually drifting upwards? Sasha could see that happening in these parts.

That settled, Del pushed Sasha away, suggesting she made sure she'd be packed and ready when the time came. Sasha did so but left just a few of her things on the table, not to be overly conspicuous about it. She checked a couple of times to make sure she could finish packing within a few breaths. Then she concentrated on further reviewing the map and preparing strategies for any possible problems.

She'd gotten to the ludicrously implausible scenarios, such as the elves mounting an aerial assault against her, when the sound of the door downstairs betrayed Erian's arrival. That meant supper. She steeled herself, put the map away, and left to partake. She'd need her strength, and deviation from routine now could be suspicious.

The meal was somewhat quieter than usual, though some news of the day was exchanged. Towards the end, Erian mentioned that it'd be time for her to make another visit to the Council tomorrow. It wasn't about final decisions, just some details they'd like to personally check on after having first mulled over the situation.

Sasha could only presume the details would include what Del had already worked out. Her timing had been spot on. Sasha nodded obligingly, she hoped. A little nervousness wouldn't be out of place as long as she'd keep the bulk of it hidden.

After finishing the meal, she made an excuse to get a good night's sleep before the interview, and proceeded along her normal nightly routine. It would have been good to get a nap in before leaving, but that was not to be. She lay tense and restless on the bed, waiting for Del to come get her on her way.

As the darkness fell, the time came. Del knocked very quietly, then opened the door without further ado. Sasha immediately got up and packed the rest of her things, along with the Dust and the waybread Del had brought with her. Both of Sasha's wands also went into their usual places. She felt oddly whole again with that.

"The cloak is downstairs, in the closet. Oh, and put this on, you will pass better with it under your hood. Do not be alarmed when it warms up to body temperature, all to avoid detection," Del whispered and offered Sasha a simple Dust creation: a kind of hat shaped roughly like the elongated elven head. Del had thought this through. She put on her backpack, strapped on the fake back of the head, and headed down behind her accomplice.

Downstairs they raided the closet for Erian's cloak. "As immediate family our magics are largely one, so I can release it to your care. Meanwhile, here are the relevant spells. Prepare them now, quickly."

Bindings covering multiple people? Sasha hadn't thought about that, but of course she'd have to have had something like that up her sleeve. Would be hard to manage a magical household without. Too late to ask for details now, though. They both did some quick wandwork, during which her collar was also dispelled. After preparing the spells, Sasha stuffed the papers in an inner pocket of the cloak for reference. In addition to the cloak control spells, she also quickly prepared the refined version of the star missile. Del gave her a concerned look.

"In case there are more goblins," Sasha commented. Del was placated, but Sasha wasn't quite sure if she'd keep to her word as to not using all available means against elven pursuers. She'd create one just as soon as she got out and into a suitable nook just to have the option.

As Sasha took control of the released cloak, it shimmered blue. A signal that she had been successful. The cloth had been reset into native Dust color. All white, fully powered but not good for stealth.

She cast one of the color-adjusting spells that Del had shown her. The cloak could take on different static shades at will, with but a small one-time expenditure of magic. To blend into the night she made it dark gray, the color of almost spent Dust. Not used to such color manipulation, she reminded herself it was just a trick. The cloak was still ready for action, even if it looked depleted.

She donned the now night-colored cloak and pulled the hood over her fake cranium. She left her face in the open for now. The hood would have to come all the way down while invisible, but she wouldn't activate the cloak yet if she could avoid it. Offhandedly releasing the door wards, Del tried on a smile, but it had a sad quality to it.

"You will pass in the dark," she said, then hugged Sasha affectionately. Sasha hugged her back, perplexed. As they let go, Del gave her a little kiss on the cheek. At least the elf's early reservations were gone. Maybe their races could one day be on friendly terms again.

Sasha stood frozen for a second or two, faced with the reality of her situation. Del snapped her out of it: "You should go."

"Yes, thanks for everything," Sasha said, then slipped into the night. She heard the door close behind her.

The air seemed colder than it had any right to be this time of year. Sasha took off with a brisk walk. If she was to play at being an elf in her own city, there was no reason to be running around headfirst.

There was little traffic at this time of night. She saw some lone wanderers and small groups milling about but managed to avoid close encounters. Avoiding the elves, she had to adjust her course away from the beeline to the forest, but she eventually got there all right. There was a path in the forest that would take her towards the border. Her hair unavailable and reluctant to pierce the cloak, she made a couple of another wardstone variant she knew, shaped to be worn on the wrist. They'd have less visibility, but better that than without. She pushed the cloak to her back so the wrist bands could monitor the surroundings properly. It'd be a while yet before she'd need the invisibility, unless things went sour.

The elves had successfully cleared away all the more dangerous creatures that she'd attracted thus far. There was only one alarm from some animal of the forest which Sasha then heard run away. Soon after, a couple of elves approached her, going the other way. She thought it best to brave the passing casually, but with a tight grip on her weapon, hand back in the folds of the cape. The elves passed her with a mere nod of acknowledgment.

Once she started to approach the first warded road, she pulled the cloak fully around her, and the hood to cover her face. As she cast the activation trigger, it was suddenly as if the hood weren't there. No, that wasn't right. There was some distortion from the folds.

She then tried the trigger for night vision. Suddenly, the colors became distorted, but she could see shapes much more clearly than with the naked eye. Was this how the wardstones saw the world when it was dark? Maybe, but there was no time to wonder about it. She'd have to make good time now that she was depleting the cloak's power.

She directed the cloaking effect's focus forward and started on a light run. Soon the road came into view. Del's instructions had been accurate. She locked the focus onto the road. It shouldn't have been necessary, and the road would get a pretty wide-angle view of her anyway, but it seemed like the prudent thing to do.

There was no way to know what exactly occurred as she passed the road and continued further into the woods. She would just have to take it on faith that the cloak worked, and no alarms would be raised yet. After getting safely out of sight of the road, she removed the hood and disabled the cloak. The night vision was handy, but there was some light from the moon and the stars, and she couldn't afford the drain.

One more road to pass, and then across the river she would go. Del had told her where to look for small rowboats that the elves used for river transportation on occasion. The fishers generally had their own, so with any luck some of the communal ones would be available.

The morning was fast approaching, and Sasha picked up as much speed as she dared, keeping just short of running out of breath. She passed the second road like the first one, without visible incident. She was relatively confident that Del would be delaying pursuit still, but there was no time to waste. She'd seen the elves use some sort of distant communications. She hadn't thought to ask about any range limitations, so if they'd wise up to her, there was no telling how quickly local patrols would get the word.

When she got to the river, the dawn was just breaking. There were a couple of boats on the water, two elves in one of them just pulling up a fish trap. She saw two boats pulled on land with markings that fit Del's description and headed straight for them. Both had a pair of oars in them. She briefly thought of grabbing both pairs to slow down possible pursuit, but somebody might notice and confront her. Better to try and slip away quietly.

The boat slid into the water easily enough. Sasha even managed not to get her shoes very wet, jumping on from the very edge of the water. As she got her bearings, an elf from the boat with the fish trap waved at her. Sasha waved back, then proceeded to row across. She wasn't sure if the elves visited the other side often, but she was so close, and there was no time to start with a feint downstream. She went as fast as she could. The fishers didn't seem to take any particular notice.

The river was more like a lake at this point, several hundred meters wide. The waters were smooth and made for easy rowing. Right as she was about to set the boat on the western shore, Sasha saw some elves running on the far side, pointing at her general direction and shouting something.

She immediately sprang into the shallows of the shore and ran. Somehow, her hand managed the gesture to activate the cloak, in case that'd be useful. Any missiles, just like the wards, could likely see her anyway, but maybe it'd confuse them just a bit. She cursed at the uselessness of her staff. Its shield wasn't very effective against magical bolts, but it would have helped some, especially at long distances.

Suddenly, Sasha heard a distant bang of Red Dust going off. She bounced into the ground behind a nearby tree. Shield or no shield, the range still worked in her favor. There was a thud from behind the tree. Sasha got up, still crouching, and ran some more, zig-zagging behind the foliage as she passed. There were no more bangs that she heard, but there was the sound of a tree falling down. The elves weren't kidding with their missiles either. Mere impact damage wouldn't have done that.

After getting enough forest between the river and herself to act as a cover, Sasha disabled the cloak again to conserve its power. In an elementary and desperate ploy, she headed northwest. From her maps, the elves knew her ultimate goal to be slightly south from here. With some luck, the detour would buy her some time if the elves decided to pursue.

It wasn't clear that they'd want to. These were dwarven lands, and the borders between the two peoples were usually well-respected. Still, no sense taking chances. Running to exhaustion had never before seemed such a good idea, even back on the road to Merfort.

After running came walking, and after walking came hobbling, interspersed with short spurts of jogging whenever Sasha thought she heard something behind her. When the final bits of her strength were gone, Sasha was deep into the dwarven territory. The forest had grown hilly, rock faces commonplace. There were no overt signs of habitation yet.

That the area seemed untouched didn't mean that she was alone. In these parts, you'd often have to scratch the surface to see the denizens. Dwarven mines did often have refineries and other external structures aside from the main underground habitat, but these were often hidden among cliffs as well. And while larger colonies were known to cultivate some land, hunting and gathering were traditionally the main sources of nourishment for the mountain dwellers.

Unlike elves, however, dwarves were generally considered safe if you didn't cross them in some way more egregious than getting lost in their woods. Though Sasha would prefer not running into any more strangers of any race, she could risk the dwarves finding her.

Excusing her exhausted lack of care with that, Sasha made hasty camp and went out like a candle.

8

S ASHA LOOKED AT HER CAMPSITE CRITICALLY. Somehow, she'd managed to set up a guarded camp again, though not in a very organized manner. She'd fallen asleep on a patch of grass under a tree, not even spreading her bedroll in the night. Her body ached, punishing her for last night's exertion and the haphazard sleeping arrangements.

Still, she was alive, and there were no elves in the vicinity. She was certain they'd have caught up with her by now if they followed her with any perseverance. She could afford a calmer pace today to recuperate, though not a day of resting in camp. The curse was demonstrably capable of attracting wildlife and at least lesser fiends if she spent too much time in one place. Hopefully the dwarves kept their lands secure. It would give her more time.

Settling into her morning routine despite the aches, Sasha recalled she hadn't had a chance to do proper spell maintenance yet. With a few flicks of her main wand she updated the backup wand and her spare cores with the new spells. It wouldn't do to lose her ability to control the cloak or make more of the stars. She'd had one on hand while she slept. That had been sloppy, should have made at least two. Next time.

She estimated her position on Del's map and determined the proper course towards her destination with a conjured compass needle. She was closing in. Taking just a slight detour to avoid the known dwarven colonies on the map it was maybe a week's journey, depending on how quickly she'd recover her strength.

The first day was slow going as expected, but she made uneventful progress. That night she made proper camp and thought to pick a hooting noise as the alarm for her wardstones. It was less aggressive than the bark. She wouldn't want to antagonize any dwarves roaming the night.

Morning came with no dwarves in sight. She was also beginning to feel slightly better. Paying attention to where to lay down for the night as well as actually using her bedroll had paid off. After checking her directions again, she headed out with partially renewed vigor.

The day's journey took her into more and more cliffy terrain. There were still no visible signs of habitation, but that didn't necessarily mean much.

Come nightfall, she'd made good time considering her earlier exhaustion. It seemed within reach to finish the journey in five days. She'd have to try and find somewhere to refill her water though. She wasn't worried yet but would have to start being careful with it.

She set up camp in a secluded spot between some trees. Not being as exhausted as before made getting to sleep more difficult. She kept thinking about her destination, what she might find, how she might gain entry to the Hall itself. Getting stranded outside would be … distressing, but it wouldn't do to dwell on that.

A hoot stirred Sasha from her musings. Then there was another, and another. Creatures approaching on all sides. The stones' fields of view didn't overlap that much. She hoped it was dwarves that could be reasoned with but moved her hand to grasp a throwing star at her side. She opened her eyes, attempting to discern the nature of the potential threat. The night wasn't pitch black yet, but her vantage point was poor.

She could hear the approaching movement now. A moment passed, and a loud bang muffled the other sounds. A sharp pain erupted in her leg. A missile. There was little time to think and no reason to avoid escalation, whoever the assailants were. The trees were in the way, but she took the star anyway, pulled the safety, and tossed it up. The bang was a bit close for comfort, though she'd averted her eyes. There were animal squeals from all around. A druid? The druid the elves had been looking for? But druids couldn't do fire magic, and stories aside, would rarely co-operate with anyone who practiced it in their forests.

With a gesture, Sasha activated her cloak and faded from sight, for whatever good it would do at this point. She tried to stand up, but the leg was bad. She could only throw the other star as well and hope for the best—which might amount to dying slowly with a shattered tibia. As she made the throw, a bang signaled the firing of another missile. It struck her in her side. She fell to the ground while her own weapon went off. She heard some pained yiffs. More animals. No human voices. They must've been beyond the limited range of the star or used the animals as shields.

There was little to do but wait for the inevitable. The first hit had been bad enough, but the second would be the end of her. She could scarcely hold on to consciousness as footsteps approached and a torch flared alight in what was clearly a Red Dust reaction.

It was the necromancer, his grin triumphant. He scoffed at her, then spoke: "Ow, that seems bad. Shame. I would've liked to keep you alive for a while like good old Gibli, to get at your secrets as well. Those stars were a surprise, forced my hand, though I did try to aim at your arm."

"Wha ... you ... how?" Sasha uttered through the pain and growing haze.

The necromancer grimaced: "I haven't been able to get you out of my head since Merfort, you little shit. But I managed to ask around for the right direction, and the rest of the tracking got real easy when I happened to discover the difference between a necromancer and a druid. Care to guess?"

Sasha contributed a bloody cough to the conversation, allowing the man to resume gloating: "Absolutely nothing! Damn animals are almost smarter as minions than neople, too. They kept track of you from afar while you were busy with the elves. Almost got me on my way in, the bastards, what with their invisibility. But my beasts could still smell them and help guide me past once I knew what to expect.

It was close, but I got away clean and made my way across the river. Though it was a chore coming up with the right questions, my animals told me you were taken by the elves against your will while coming this way. I had a hunch that if the elves didn't finish you for me, it'd be just a matter of time before you continued into my hands. And now, perhaps I can finally get some peace of mind."

Sasha's mind, struggling to hold on to consciousness, caught hold of a memory: "Neep..?" The sneer on the necromancer's face turned raging red just as the darkness took her. Futile spite it may have been, but it comforted her to have at least managed to piss the bastard off with her final word.

●   ●   ●

Sasha lay on something hard and smooth, curved like the inside of a cylinder. Not at all like the grassy soil where she'd died.

Died? Yes, that seemed right. Was this the afterlife? She noticed that she was breathing. That was evidence against. Maybe. Weakly. And she certainly wasn't among the Stars. She may have been aware, but darkness reigned absolute. The other place, then. But there was no fiery pain. Maybe that'd come later or was a metaphor for eternal isolation in this emptiness.

She moved her arms and legs. They were in perfect working order, but bumped immediately into solid material. Not just an all-encompassing darkness, then, but a casket of sorts. That seemed almost mundane, but the leg being okay certainly implied some sort of transition. She felt the side of her chest. Healthy, not even sore. The tunic she'd worn under the cloak was still shredded though, and the cloak itself was gone.

The healing might be a good sign. Perhaps the casket was just a phase, perhaps the Stars were waiting for her emergence from this cocoon. She touched the top, pressed lightly at first, then more insistently. It didn't budge. Despite her efforts, panic started to take hold. "Hello, anyone there?" she yelled. When there was no answer, she struck the top with her fist, but all she got out of it was a light thud and a sore knuckle.

With a grimace, Sasha let go of all pretense of being in control. She started to scream, shout, and twist around in her confinement.

After a few moments of this, a thin streak of light appeared suddenly along the edge of the casket. Sasha ceased trashing and averted her eyes. The light wasn't very bright, but it was the only one she'd seen in a while.

The light spoke in a gruff and detached voice: "Are we done, then? Ah, yes, yes. All good. Do sleep a while more though."

"Wait!" Sasha got in before the lid slammed shut again, snuffing her consciousness out as it did.

•   •   •

Sasha reawakened in what felt like a proper bed. The sheets were rough, but even so, it was a welcome change to the cold, smooth stone she'd lain on before. Darkness still reigned, but not absolute. A dim light shone through the outlines of a door. After acclimating for a few moments, Sasha decided that this was not the afterlife, after all. She was in dwarven halls.

Stars only knew what kind of magic they'd wrought to bring her back from death's door, but they had. If the true nature of the elves had been somewhat of a surprise, the dwarves had them beat solidly already.

She glanced around the room in the faint light. Aside from the bed, the room only had a small bedside table that she could see. The little floor space that the room had was by the door. It was quite cramped, but serviceable when you had to painstakingly dig every cubic meter out of the rock yourself. Better than the tiny coffin where she'd first woken up, for sure.

Now more sure of her situation, Sasha took the time to examine her wounds more carefully. Nothing was left, not even scarring. Nothing was left of her gear either, except the clothes on her. Her wand! It had been in her hand in the forest. Gone, now. She quickly checked the soles of her shoes for the spare cores. Her relief was palpable when the crystals were in their proper places. Everything but her artifacts could still be restored, if she could just get a replacement wand. After having her wounds healed without a trace, she dared hope the dwarven community might be able to provide her with one.

Footsteps approached. There seemed to be a corridor on the other side of the door. As shadows obscured parts of the light coming in, the steps stopped. The knock was not a great surprise, but its light touch was. It sounded like it was not meant to wake her had she still been asleep. She'd someone expected the dwarves to be less considerate.

There seemed to be no reason to prolong matters. "Yes?" she asked quietly. The door opened, letting in more of the torchlight. A dark figure, a head shorter than her, loomed in the doorway.

"Lord Yrin will see you now, if you're ready. I have some new clothes for you, if you'd like to change first," the dwarf intoned in a deep, polite voice. She nodded assent, and he handed her a bundle of plain brown cloth. "I'll be outside," said the dwarf, and left her alone in the dark.

Nothing to it but to fumble out of her torn clothing and into the pants and shirt provided, navigating mostly by touch. She hadn't been offered more light, but the dwarf was unaccustomed to humans. Perhaps it simply hadn't occurred to him that she might've preferred something more than the barest hint of torchlight from the corridor.

The feel of the fabric was rough, but she'd worn worse. Quite sturdy, too, probably made to withstand mining operations. There were several handy pockets, but she had nothing to fill them with.

Now presentable, Sasha opened the wooden door to find the dwarf waiting. He was dressed similarly to her and sported a large, scruffy, reddish-brown beard with curly hair to match.

"Let's go, then," she said, taking the initiative. The dwarf nodded, gesturing for her to follow.

The corridor was cramped and narrow, just wide enough to allow for traffic in both directions at once. The occasional dimly lit oil lamp provided illumination. Sasha could feel her hair touching the ceiling on occasion, reminding her to keep her head down as she walked. Both of the walls had door after door on them in tight succession, though a bit looser on the other side. Double bunks, perhaps.

As the corridor came to an end, a hum from a hole in the ceiling piqued Sasha's interest. The dwarf noted her dallying and glanced back. "Ventilation," he confirmed her presumption. Clearly an active system, either magical or mechanical. Perhaps she would ask about it later, but this didn't seem the time.

The corridor opened up into a larger, perpendicular one. Several other dwarves were going about their business, sparing a glance at

Sasha but not stopping to gawk. Her guide directed her to the left, and soon they arrived at a large metallic double door with an impressively equipped guard on either side. Spiky armor, sturdy halberds, steel meeting Dust in intimidating if not quite stylish harmony. She couldn't be sure how the gear was enchanted, but the Dust wasn't merely for show.

The doors opened unbidden. Determined not to let such tricks get to her, Sasha strode in. The rectangular hall was quite large by dwarven standards. There were chairs for some ten dwarves on each side wall, though the seats were unoccupied. The stone throne between two sturdy pillars at the back wasn't. That would be Yrin.

Projecting confidence was all well and good, but Sasha could be courteous about it. She stayed near the door, bowed decently low, and greeted the man: "Lord Yrin. Heroborn mage Sasha, at your service."

As she straightened her back again, she took a better look at the man. He looked to be surprisingly young, perhaps pushing thirty, though he had an air of weariness about him. His clothes were almost as simple as hers, but he also had a belt with a variety of pouches and pockets on it. He had no crown or scepter, only a simple wand on the armrest. His black beard was unusually trim for a dwarf, though his hair was long and curled.

Yrin nodded once. The escort withdrew, closing the doors behind him. The master of the mine seemed to want her all to himself. Sasha wasn't too worried. The dwarf could've done a number of rotten things to her already, if that was his wont—refrain from saving her life, for one. She hadn't been in any condition to make agreements with him, but a debt might reasonably be considered owed. He'd want her in the condition to collect.

The dwarf regarded her curiously, then shifted his face into a semblance of a smile. It seemed genuine enough, if not sufficient to offset the weariness in his eyes. Sasha had already taken her turn at talking, possibly out of line, so she waited patiently for him to take his.

When he did, Sasha immediately recognized the voice as the one that had spoken to her when she first woke up in the coffin: "Sasha, is it, then? Heroborn, yes, I was sure of it. Otherwise— never mind. I suspect we'll have a lot to talk about. But first, you had a magical battle on our lands. We would rather not have that here. Some details we know. Others we don't. Please explain what happened from your point of view."

Briefly considering where to start, Sasha bought some time with an apology: "First of all, please excuse my intrusion. I wouldn't have been on your lands in the first place if I hadn't tried to steer clear of known colonies, to avoid causing bother to anyone here. My information wasn't very up to date, it seems."

"Ah. Well, that explains that. I have tried to keep my keep off most maps, see." Yrin chuckled briefly at his own pun. "Enough dwarves know where to find us for trade. But by finding the gap, you found us. Do go on."

She did, conveying a truthful account of the fateful encounter. After short consideration, she decided to volunteer that she'd defeated the necromancer before on the coast, but that she'd had no idea he'd followed her all this way. Yrin listened intently, asking for elaboration now and again.

When they were done, he tilted his head and said: "You are aware of your curse, are you not?"

Sasha drew a short breath, shocked. Her secret was out. Honesty was probably the best policy. "Yes. How did you..?"

"You've clearly got yourself a nemesis," Yrin cut in. "He's obsessed with you, he is. It happens to carriers. I'll tell you right now that he's still out there. We could tell there had been somebody else around, what with finding your missile-ridden corpse. We tried tracking him down, but he managed to elude us."

Yrin pursed his lips in thought while Sasha absorbed this. Then he added: "Well, it's possible he got you out of his system, what with you dying and all. I'm not quite sure how that works. But it would be prudent to plan on him coming back for you."

A particular point in Yrin's speech had caught Sasha's attention. "Uh. Dying? Corpse? I thought ..."

"Yes, oh yes. But come, now. Roaming around the world on quests, you should really expect to die at some point. Don't worry though, it was just a little. All good now, yes?"

Sasha nodded affirmative in spite of feeling faint. She'd only just gotten used to the idea that she wasn't dead yet after all. "But how ...?"

Yrin interrupted her with a click of the tongue. "Tsk. We'll see about how later. Maybe. Let's start with how come you've traveled all the way here. I have a fair guess, but do share."

The curse was out, there was no reason to hold back. She told the whole truth about seeking a cure from the Hall of Heroes. The dwarf listened intently, pondered a while, mouth twisting. Then he stated matter-of-factly: "Yes. That could work."

Sasha blinked. Just like that, the man had vindicated her far-fetched quest. "What do you know about it?" she asked.

"Not enough and altogether too much. Mind you, I'm not sure how you'd fare there, but the theory is plausible. Anything else you'd like to mention for my consideration? I gather you came through elven lands? Any problems with that?" he asked. Sasha sighed inwardly, then proceeded to give a decent first approximation of her ordeals with the elves.

"Cloaks, huh. It seemed like that. Good to know, good to know. You say you had one?" Yrin inquired.

Sasha spread her hands. "If you don't have it, the necromancer must, along with the disabled staff. He can't use them, I think. But he's done other things that shouldn't be possible so I'm not too sure of anything anymore."

"He has, hasn't he? Poor mixed up thing. How he got into necromancy I don't know. Shouldn't have happened. Though a lot that shouldn't does, damn the Stars. In any case, if he bothers you again, you will need to kill him. It'll be a mercy, too. Could imprison him, I suppose, but his days would be torture, what with not getting to you and all. Well. I will think on this. You will be safe here."

Yrin made a gesture with his wand, and the door opened. The dwarf who'd brought her in entered once again. "Byron, see that she'll be fed and put in one of the better quarters. Bring her to my lab at the next stroke of four," Yrin decreed.

"It will be done," Byron answered simply, and turned away. Sasha gave Yrin a curt bow and followed. It seemed that her audience was over for now.

"How long will that be," she asked her escort as the doors closed again.

"Oh, about six hours, now. Meanwhile, let's get you set up, miss. Hungry?" Byron asked jovially. She was, perhaps, due a degree of respect now that she had won Yrin's initial favor.

Now that she thought about it, Sasha was feeling peckish, though less so than she might have expected. "Yes, please. Mind, do you happen to know how long I have been here?"

The dwarf waved his hand a bit. "Just half a day or so. Mostly sleeping it off."

Sleeping off death, she mused. It wasn't long, but her stomach should be growling by now. It felt empty enough, she just wasn't otherwise famished. Side effects of resurrection?

Byron took her to a larger hall filled with chairs, tables, and pillars. There were some thirty or so of Yrin's people eating already. A bunch of gray-dressed dwarves formed their own group aside the brown-clad ones.

A serving table was set on the side of the room. The main dish was roasted meat, but there were some vegetables and dark bread on the side. A nearby open doorway led to a kitchen area where several dwarves were busy preparing more food for the table. By the looks of things, they were expecting more hungry mouths to feed.

Byron took a wooden plate and suggested she do the same. She complied, picking out some of the more appetizing things from the table. For drink, there were mugs filled with ale beside the food. She gave one a sniff. Not too suspicious. She took it in her other hand. Her escort led the way to a vacant table. Getting to know the other dwarves would be gladly left for another day. They sat down and started eating.

Byron was not much for small-talk. Sasha ate quietly for a moment, glancing around now and then. The other dwarves seemed mildly interested in the strange new arrival, but their curiosity was limited to glances among conversation. The latter was in archaic Human, what else—though slightly different from what the elves had spoken. She overheard some snippets of talk that concerned her. The dwarves were wondering how long it had been since a human came along, and what might she have done with the elves to get past. Much laughter was indulged in after a few hushed suggestions.

After pointedly ignoring the commentary for a while, Sasha noticed that the dwarves dressed in gray were oddly silent. She nodded towards them. "Who're the quiet bunch over there?"

Byron didn't have to look to know what she was talking about: "Oh, those are the neeps. Keep mostly to themselves. We use them for the most dangerous work. They're not very efficient, but it keeps people safe while digging new tunnels."

Sasha nodded. Should've been obvious. She'd already gotten used to the idea of not having any neople around in Greenhold. The dwarves would have more use for a disposable workforce.

"I'm not very familiar with mining. How risky work is it for experts such as yourselves?" she probed with a dash of flattery.

"We can mitigate the risks pretty well. Ours is the most advanced mine around, combining good old dwarven expertise with Lord Yrin's magic. I'm not sure how it is with humans, but Heroborn are rare among us dwarves. Still, we do have a couple of accidents a year, can't be helped. Just a few weeks ago we lost half a dozen neeps and a supervisor. He was examining a support when it collapsed on him, leaving the rest trapped behind," Byron recounted, shaking his head. Sasha offered a sympathetic smile. They were probably used to losing workers to the mine, but his tone made it clear they weren't completely desensitized.

"Was it bad enough that Lord Yrin's magic couldn't get to the others in time, then?" Sasha asked.

Byron shook his head. "Nah. Well, maybe. Yrin was busy and said it'd be a big expense if it even worked. A few of the neeps were getting old anyway, and it happens. The supervisor was a good worker and a friend of mine, but he was beyond help at that point."

Asking why they hadn't just resurrected him didn't seem like a good idea at the moment. Sasha filed the thought away to bring it up with Yrin himself. Maybe it was simply a matter of being too crushed to be salvageable. "I'm sorry," she said in a sympathetic tone.

Neither felt overly enthusiastic about continuing the discussion from there. They had their fill to eat and drink and carried their dirty dishes to a side table. Then Byron took the lead again. "I'll show you to your new quarters. You didn't have anything left at the old room, did you?"

"No. Oh, just the torn clothes. I guess I won't be needing those anymore."

"Hmh. Well, I'll have them brought in and seen to, if they're still mendable," Byron promised.

Sasha thanked him, and Byron noted that they don't like to waste good material. While they were talking, they turned a corner to a wide passage. Ornately carved doors lined the walls every eight meters or so. Byron took her to the next to last one and opened it.

The room was indeed roomier than her original one. The bed was bigger, there was a real desk and a chair as well as an empty shelf and a small cupboard. Byron went to light a small oil lamp on the table. "You'll be staying here for the duration. It's one of the better rooms, same as mine. I take it you're a woman of learning. I can have writing implements delivered if you'd like," he offered.

"Writing materials would be nice," Sasha acknowledged. She wasn't sure what to do with no reference material at hand, but if nothing else, she could doodle to while away the time. She'd ask Yrin about getting the tools of her trade replaced when she'd next see him. Meanwhile, she could stand to take it easy for a moment. After all, she had just died a little, whatever that meant.

Byron asked if she'd need anything else, and when she couldn't think of anything except what only another mage could provide, he left her alone in the room. She fell immediately on the bed. It was more comfortable than the one she'd woken in before, if not quite as fine as the one in Erian's guest room.

Now that she had some peace and quiet, Sasha's mind kicked into high gear. She wondered why Yrin had her in a small room to begin with. It hadn't been a cell, clearly. No locks on the door. Yrin had already deemed her worth resurrecting, so it seemed strange that he'd hold out on a better room until they actually met. Perhaps it was to underline her being here under his pleasure, under such conditions as he chose from moment to moment. She had cooperated, and been rewarded accordingly.

The realization came with a slight uneasy feeling, but she couldn't bring herself to frown on his rescuer much for little mind games. Besides, she might be overanalyzing the situation again. She'd just have to keep an eye out, make sure things wouldn't get any more sinister than that.

A knock on the door interrupted her musings. "Yes?" she called, and a new dwarf entered carrying a tray with a bottle of water and the promised writing tools. He had a bundle of cloth under his arm.

"Byron sent these. Here's your bedroll back, cleaned. I don't know about the clothes yet," the dwarf said, not bothering with an introduction.

"Thank you. There's no hurry with those," Sasha replied. She had some mixed feelings about receiving her death shroud, as it were. Concentrating on the tray instead, she realized that she was lacking one crucial piece of information. "Oh, where can I relieve myself of the water when I'm done with it?" she asked. The dwarf gave directions that seemed clear enough. Then she was left alone again.

There would still be plenty of time before her second audience. Sasha spent some of it laying on the bed simply enjoying her newfound lack of mortal wounds. She hadn't had to endure them for long, consciously anyway, but they had left an impression. Eventually the simple novelty of being whole wore off and she grew restless. Sleep didn't seem to be on the menu yet, so she decided she might as well look around the compound. Nobody had discouraged exploration.

She started by checking if she could find her way to the nearby toilet. She could. This time around it was a mundane affair, and accordingly stinky. Well, perhaps not wholly mundane. On closer inspection the hole seemed nigh bottomless and its edges smooth, as if dug by Dust. She wasn't sure how the dwarves dealt with the waste, or did they just bore a new hole when the old one filled up. At least the toilet had a lid on, and the room was behind double doors to limit the spread of the stench.

After relieving herself, Sasha started roaming around the corridors, always making sure to keep in mind how to get back to her room. The compound was somewhat labyrinthine in places, but less than she'd expected. She was confident that she wouldn't lost her bearings. And even if she did, dwarves were ever present, going about their business. She could always ask for directions even if that would be embarrassing.

Not wanting to barge in on anything, she didn't open any doors that she didn't recognize. Still, marking the wanderings of the locals she managed to form an impression on what was what. A group of tired dwarves shambling into a corridor probably meant more living quarters. The sound of metal on metal emanating from behind a sturdy door marked a smithy. Dwarves going through a door and returning with mining gear had just visited a storeroom.

Sasha also came upon a few staircases and ladders going both up and down. She hesitated to take those, lest she wind up in less stable mining caverns or truly lost. It was safer to stay on the one floor for now, but she marked the locations well.

Satisfied with her mental map of the floor, Sasha made her way back to her quarters. She wasn't sure how much time had passed, but certainly not enough for her next audience. Boredom began to set in again. Maybe that was calculated as well. She'd be primed to cooperate further to alleviate the tedium. On the other hand, it was just possible that Yrin simply had other legitimate concerns besides her.

Regardless, the man wanted something from her, though it was unclear what exactly it was. He'd had his answers, but he'd wanted her in his lab. Maybe he just needed some assistance from a fellow mage. Byron had mentioned dwarven ones being scarce. She'd be happy to help with most anything if she could in turn get geared up and ready to go in some reasonable time frame.

Being a research subject rather than assistant would be the other obvious alternative, but her treatment was at odds with the possibility. Satisfied that she was in all likelihood safe here as promised, she lay once again on the bed. She wasn't physically tired, but perhaps she could do with a few hours just to try and empty her mind, not constantly worrying for a change.

•　　　•　　　•

A knock on the door startled Sasha. She was pretty sure she'd been at least partially asleep in the end, but she roused quickly enough and invited the visitor in.

It was Byron again. He'd come to see if Sasha wanted to have something to eat before her audience. It had been several hours, so she agreed.

With a stop at the toilet, they made their way back to the mess hall. The food was much the same as before, but the patrons were mostly new. She noticed the change due to their reaction to her being the same as the first time around. If they'd been the same people, they would've likely gone through different motions.

"So, how've you settled in then?" Byron asked when they were seated.

"Well enough. I wandered around a bit, getting the lay of the floor," Sasha said and started to chew on her food.

"See the smithy?" Byron asked.

Sasha gulped down her mouthful, then answered: "No. Well, I heard it. I didn't want to bother them so I stayed out."

"Ah. I'll have to show you around when I'm less busy. It's a sight to see. Not now, though. Yrin's expecting you shortly."

Sasha nodded and continued eating. Byron joined her, having depleted his reservoir of small talk. After a quick meal, Byron took her back towards the throne room. The guards were standing by the door, looking alert. Byron went right past them with Sasha in tow. Some fifteen meters further, Byron stopped next to a less assuming but sturdy door on the opposite wall. Then he gave the door a knock. A mumble came from the inside.

"I believe Lord Yrin said, 'it's open'," Byron interpreted for Sasha, and suggesting she get in with a gesture of his hand. She pulled on the door handle. The door was even heavier than it looked, but opened easily enough once she got it moving. As she stepped in, Yrin's voice shouted to close the door behind her. She complied, and the door clicked shut. She pushed it a bit as a test. Locked. Well, it wasn't like she'd be able to run past the guards anyway.

The door stood at the top of a descending stairway that led into a cavern two stories high. Compared to the rest of the mine, the room was brightly lit. The light came from several steadily glowing strips on the ceiling. Magical lighting, clearly. Compared to lamps or torches, it undoubtedly made it easier to do precision work, but the power requirements must have been great.

On the floor level there were two other doors, a sturdy one on the left and a flimsier one on the right. The latter door was open. Bookshelf after bookshelf lined the far wall along with the requisite movable ladder. Most of the space was used by books, but a fourth or so was dedicated to various bottled substances. Heavy wooden tables filled the center of the room. Papers and various apparatus, alchemical, mechanical, and magical alike, were spread around them in a creative chaos. Next to the stairway, in the nearest corner of the room there was an obelisk lying on the ground. Sasha raised an eyebrow. A mineful of dwarves had actually sufficed to dig one up.

Yrin emerged from behind the thin door and closed it behind him. Perhaps there lay further storage for the impressive lab. The bulkier door probably led out of the lab onto a lower level of the mine.

The dwarf lord seemed satisfied, smiling and rubbing his hands together. "Ah yes, welcome to my laboratory. You must excuse the mess. I don't usually entertain guests here. Not many Heroborn around."

"So I've heard," Sasha retorted, "even if there's a whole population of them east of the river." She gave herself a proper mental slap right as the words came out of her mouth.

Luckily, Yrin just chuckled. "Right you are. Ours is a precarious truce, though. Dwarves and elves are built to be suspicious of each other. Not that there's any particularly good reason for it, making this lasting peace possible." He knocked on a nearby wooden table.

Sasha allowed herself a relieved smile. The dwarf seemed downright jovial for being the lord of his realm. Having made a major gaffe right at the start could end up sparing her nerves quite a bit. As it seemed being frank didn't get one into trouble here, Sasha got to the point. "It seems I owe you my life, Lord Yrin. You have my gratitude. Is there something I can do for you in return? As I said, I am a trained mage, if not quite your caliber," she offered, touching her side meaningfully.

Yrin took the hook. "Yes. Well, you're in good company there. Still, you were lucky it worked on you. See, to be honest, I wasn't quite sure it would. Thank the sloppy Stars for that, I suppose. The process is ineffectual on common bloodlines. I've tried."

That explained losing good dwarves to accidents. Yrin had also gotten sidetracked from her actual question. Since he was being talkative, Sasha decided to go for it. "I only know a couple of rudimentary healing spells. A spell such as that would be quite useful, even if limited in scope."

The dwarf grinned slyly but amicably while fiddling with a mechanism on the nearby table. "I'm sure. Sad to say it isn't a spell as such. Not repeatable elsewhere. Not easily. As for your debt, well. Aside from the information you already provided, I mostly ask for your company for a time. It's been a long time since I had anything close to a peer to talk to. It gets ... weary. I understand you'll want to continue your quest eventually, but stay a while, recuperate. I'll set you up with new gear, maybe teach you a few useful tricks in case that poor nemesis of yours rears his ugly head again."

The deal sounded rather too good to be true, but it wasn't as if Sasha was in a position to refuse Yrin's hospitality. "Of course, that's the least I can do. You don't mind my curse then?" she checked.

Yrin shrugged, dropping a twisted metal pin of some sort that had come loose from his device. "We'll be quite safe down here. Whatever comes upside we can deal with. The hunting has been lacking lately. Maybe your presence will help. We're not picky, trolls and goblins will do." The dwarf stopped to stare into the emptiness for a moment, then continued: "Mind you, I'm assuming your curse hasn't progressed further than it seems. You haven't had dragons chasing you lately, have you?"

Sasha shook her head meekly. "Do you actually have dragons here?"

"Oh no, not of late, I just like to keep it that way. Right then, no worries. Safe as mines. Do tell if any of my subjects become aggressive, though. Some commoners might be more sensitive to the curse than others, but I wouldn't worry too much about it. We're used to dealing with feelings of annoyance towards each other, what with living in such close quarters." Yrin gave a reassuring shrug along with the warning. Sasha took it at face value. The man seemed to know what he was talking about.

A reckless thought crossed Sasha's mind. She recognized it as such, but maybe with the help of her new friends it wouldn't be overly stupid. "The site of … the battle was nearby, right?" she asked.

Yrin raised an eyebrow. "Reasonably so. You know that's probably a bad idea, but Hero-blooded as you are, you're going to do it anyway. Who knows, perhaps you'll notice something my people missed, or at least gain some closure. I can increase my surveillance of the immediate area for a while, make sure there are no big surprises around, and send a few of my dwarves along to protect you. But first, we'll need to tool you up. I'm not letting you out there without some firepower."

He walked to a nearby table and opened a drawer beneath, revealing a store of several plain brown wands. He took two, waved at them with his own, then tossed them to Sasha. They separated in the air, but she managed to awkwardly catch both. "Thank you very much," she uttered. That had been easier than expected.

"Don't mention it. A mage shouldn't have to be without one, and dying in battle is as good an excuse as any for losing yours. Now, the interesting bit is if you were savvy enough to have backups in a safe place," Yrin said, raising his eyebrow appraisingly.

Sasha tilted her smiling face while pointing the wands, each in separate hand, towards her shoes, casting one of the base spells that every wand knew. The vibration in her hands was her magic entering the wands.

Yrin laughed mirthfully. "I knew you were good. See, we found a bunch of papers with you where you lay. Did you craft this?" he asked, pointing at the incantations for her star missile. The papers must've fallen out of the cloak's pocket during the confrontation.

"I put the pieces together, at least. I had a bit of help," she admitted.

Yrin gleamed. "Yes, the elven touches show here and there, and the whole thing is rough around the edges, but you've got the right spirit, you do. Or the effective one, anyway. Right in my book, that. You'll forgive me if I won't supply you with Dust just yet. But you'll have some for your little excursion."

"That quite fine," Sasha acknowledged. It would have been foolhardy of him to do otherwise, not knowing her very well—excepting the fact that she could be creatively deadly.

"Now these control spells here led me to suspect the elves had mastered cloaking as you confirmed, though I couldn't be sure what with the scarce commentary. No matter, my surveillance should see through it if by some chance they'd try something," Yrin mused idly while shuffling through the incantations. Sasha wasn't sure if a reaction was expected, so she settled for nodding along. Yrin got lost in thought for a moment looking at the sheets but shook it off before the silence got awkward. "Right, we should get your little self-memorial service done with before it gets dark outside. Then let's talk more, see what you can do, show off what I can do, that sort of thing. Sound good?"

That was refreshingly straightforward, and showing off would likely end up with her learning something, at least. "Very," Sasha replied.

"I'll have Byron here to handle the arrangements," Yrin said, waving his wand towards the door. It opened, and Byron stepped through. Yrin immediately proceeded to bark orders, his demeanor suddenly decisively commanding: "Our guest will be taking a stroll to the spot of her demise to pay her respects. You're to arrange a suitable escort. There's possibly another Heroborn after her, with both animals and neople under his thrall, so take a well-equipped crew and some eyes in the sky with you. Launch before she's out, and if there's suspiciously many large predators or any humanoid activity that isn't us in the vicinity, abort. Make sure to get back before the fliers run out of power. Speaking of power, provide her with a beltful of Dust, a third of it red. Take it up to the exit corridor before she joins you, and leave it up there when you get back. All clear?"

"Yes, sire," Byron said, nonplussed. As he turned and left, the door closed behind him.

Yrin turned back to Sasha. "Take control of the Dust before you go outside, but release it when you leave it coming back. I'll check and want a tally of any use. You understand."

"Yes, that seems quite reasonable, thank you," Sasha acknowledged.

Yrin responded with a curt nod, then walked towards the bookshelves. "In the meanwhile, I'll browse for materials for our little chat after. You can take your papers to your room. Byron will find you there, shouldn't take long. Oh, and here's a little something I cooked up just now." He tossed her a white cube, which she caught only barely.

"Uh, thank you. What's the catch?" she asked. He wouldn't just freely give her Dust after the arrangements to specifically limit her access.

Yrin chuckled. "Good good. Smart and to the point. It's my Dust, pre-enchanted, in fact. It'll respond to the usual scribing spells as if it were yours, but nothing else. I heard you'd been writing implements but we both know us mages need a bit more than the mundane variety to work with. Mind, if you humans have done work on the original scribing spells it might not recognize them correctly, but if so, I can fix it after getting a trace."

Sasha stared wide-eyed at the dwarf, then the cube. She'd had no idea that was even possible. "Oh. That's ... quite generous, and surprising."

Yrin smiled, clearly happy his showing off had worked: "I thought you'd like it. I have a feeling they don't know tricks like that back east." It was a statement, not a question. Sasha nodded along, then made her way towards the stairs with her new prize.

As soon as she was out the door, it struck her how Yrin had referred to her nemesis. Another Heroborn. But Heroborn weren't supposed to become necromancers. Yet this was no ordinary necromancer, and Yrin was clearly both competent and knowledgeable, perhaps more so than any human and at least on par with the elves. He was a tad eccentric, sure, but that was common enough among mages. She could do worse than to presume he actually knew what he was talking about, which meant she'd have to pump him for some more information about this nemesis business.

To find out how a lone dwarven Heroborn, though with a fortress of his own, managed to so outdo his rival magical communities elsewhere would require more finesse, but it was worth investigating as well. The City wasn't far. Perhaps he'd found something there. Any information on the area could prove tremendously useful.

But first things first. Closure. She made her way to her room again to wait as suggested. Meanwhile, she could try her new toy. She set the cube on the table by a lone sheet of paper and made the gesture for the scribing spell. She stopped to wonder what to try it on and decided on one of her practice assignments under master Aaron. She made the gesture for that. Sure enough, the Dust wrote out the incantations just as promised.

But this, of course, wasn't sufficient evidence that the cube actually worked as advertised. She'd have to test it with something else as well. Something innocuous, of course. She cast a simple light spell. The cube extended tendrils again, wrote "tsk tsk" on the paper in large letters, then retracted. Sasha blushed. Should've thought of the artifact possibly having other triggers rather than simply failing to work. She hoped it hadn't just told Yrin what she'd done. On the other hand, from what she'd seen, he'd just be amused.

The possibility brought up another concern. The Dust might be rigged to repeat to Yrin whatever she used it for. It certainly wouldn't be above the little man's capabilities. She'd use the gift all right, not to broadcast her suspicions. She'd just have to keep in mind that what she scribed with it wouldn't necessarily remain private.

Having gotten into the mood, a slight suspicion about the wands tickled her mind as well, though they were less likely to house surprises. Wands were more opaque magic, the incantation to create one being just one line of text. It was hard to subvert something whose inner workings were a mystery—and in the end, practicality ruled that she'd have to trust the wands either way.

There was a knock on the door. That had been fast, just as promised. She made an effort to smooth the wrinkles off her face and went to open the door.

"Everything's ready. Shall we?" Byron suggested without further ado.

With a nod, Sasha emerged from her room and closed the door behind her. They walked to one of the stairways that she had noticed but not tried on her own.

The stairway was a sturdy circular metallic one, located inside a smooth and straight hole in the stone. It was wider than most spiral staircases she'd seen, though at some three meters not extravagant for a main exit if that was what it was. The stairs were steep enough that she didn't have to watch her head as much as downstairs.

Upstairs, heavy metallic doors stood open before them. Beyond them was a straight, wide corridor. A group of dwarves were waiting for them, all geared up. Sasha hoped her whimsy hadn't put them out too much, but it was a bit late for second-guessing herself. On to getting it over with.

Two of the dwarves closed the doors, producing several loud clicks. Once they were sealed away from the mine proper, Byron took a utility belt from one of the others and presented it to her. It was the promised Dust, smaller ovals ready to use in open holders and larger pieces inside attached pouches. She wrapped the belt around her waist and checked the response of the Dust by reshaping one piece. It worked.

"Ready to go?" Byron asked. She nodded affirmative. The featureless corridor continued for some ten meters or so before another set of double doors barred the way. Thinking about it, Sasha was sure that the featurelessness was skin-deep. With the doors at both ends, this was one of the last lines of defense for the fortress beneath. With Yrin's wile, the corridor was no doubt trapped six ways from Sunday.

The dwarves all donned dimmed eyewear to protect their eyes in the daylight, and then two of them went in to open the gate. Fresh air filled the room. The day was pleasant, refusing to acknowledge anything untoward having just recently happened nearby. Byron held her back, nodding to three of the dwarves with heavier backpacks. They went ahead, fanned out behind the door and started opening their packs. From where Sasha was standing, she could see one of them unpacking a winged contraption of some sort. He laid it on the ground, fiddled with it and took a few quick steps back. The dwarven device launched into the air with what looked like a controlled Red Dust reaction. Then she heard the same sound repeat twice from where she couldn't see.

Byron had turned his back towards her and was tinkering with something. She thought better of trying to intrude, curious though she was. After a while, the dwarf nodded. "All's clear enough, let's go."

Byron took the lead again, leaving Sasha in the middle of a spread-out group of dwarves. They moved quickly for their size, the forest paths obviously familiar to them.

"How far is it, exactly?" Sasha probed, realizing that she had only a vague idea of the length of their excursion.

"Oh, it's some half an hour's walk north. We only noticed you because Lord Yrin keeps an eye on magical activity in the area. Tri-whatchamagulation," Byron said.

Indeed, after half an hour or so Sasha started to recognize the place. It had been darker, then, but the arrangement of cliffs and trees was familiar.

Byron knew where he was going, straight for the place of the ambush. "We cleared out most of what was left, which wasn't much. Mostly the bedroll and the bunch of papers, which we found under you. We think the attacker took off with most of your belongings while sending his beasts to keep our patrol party busy. They were definitely controlled. There were several wolves that would've run off, left to their own. A young bear to keep them company, even. We fought them over there, but the remains are already being cooked. You were found right about ... here."

There it was. Some dried brown spots on the rocks where her blood had spilled. Some disturbed vegetation, mostly where her bedroll had been. All in all rather a letdown. She hadn't had specific expectations, but somehow this lacked ... drama. Right then Byron decided to add some by bringing his war hammer down on the ground. Sasha jumped into the air, then looked at the dwarf quizzically.

"Snake. Hadn't run away from our stomping. Could be a spy or an assassin. Better be sure," he said coolly.

That hadn't crossed Sasha's mind at all. She felt embarrassed. She really should have anticipated such a threat. Yrin must've drilled his people well in fighting magical folk. The dwarf lord had talked like he'd even be prepared for an elven incursion. Dealing with a lone druid would be easy in comparison.

Byron bagged the snake. "Yrin can check it for Dust traces. He'll want to know if the guy is still around," he explained.

One more thing to ask Yrin about. Or better make it two: first the result, and second how to go about checking such things herself. Along with her other questions, she'd really have to make a list back in the room.

"Speaking of him being around, did you look for him with the fliers?" Sasha asked.

Byron frowned. "We checked the immediate area, but he had a head start and running the fliers is expensive. It didn't seem like a priority at the time. In any case, he wasn't nearby, or he was well hidden. Yrin did wonder if he might've had warning from birds and taken cover."

"Mm. Could be," Sasha said with a nod, and proceeded to go through the area one more time. There was nothing for her here anymore. "Let's head back," she finally said.

Byron called the dwarves back into formation, and off they went. As they closed in on the door to the mine, Sasha made note of the relatively undisturbed forest. The dwarves had to have other doors to support the mining operations. Not that she'd have expected Yrin to settle for one way out.

Once inside, she took off the belt and released the Dust. No reason to risk Yrin's good will with any funny business. She left the belt on the floor near the outer door.

Three of the dwarves stayed behind to retrieve the flying observers. Along with the rest, Sasha walked back through the inner door and down the stairs. Byron sent the others into the armory to drop off their gear, and then took Sasha straight back to the lab. The door opened to admit them as they approached.

Yrin was sitting by a table downstairs, looking up. "Well, any closure? These things tend to be more anticlimactic than you'd think."

Sasha flashed a pensive half-smile. "Yeah. That sounds right. Had a lot of experience on the subject?"

Yrin chuckled heartily. "You have no idea. Well, not recently. I try to be careful these days, I do. What's that, then?" He pointed at the bag Byron was offering him.

"It's a snake from the site of the battle. Was behaving suspiciously, so I thought I'd take it in to have you look at it," Byron explained.

Yrin's eyes went sharp, and he took a couple of steps back. "Did you now? I'd better do just that. Place the snake in the cage back there, would you," he requested, his face tense.

Byron obligingly went to dump the carcass into the container indicated, not entirely unlike what Sasha had already seen at Del's place. He knew enough of the cage to close it up without further prompting, and at a gesture from his master, left back up the stairs. He may have rolled his eyes when facing away from Yrin, Sasha was not sure.

Yrin took hold of his wand and pointed it towards the cage. There was a bar of Dust inside, next to where the snake lay. Yrin was clearly well-prepared. Sasha realized that he probably had Dust stashed everywhere around the lab to be used at his convenience as situation warranted. Perhaps he even had the whole compound covered. That's what she'd do if she had a permanent residence, let alone a place like this. Nothing more convenient than having your Dust already near possible targets. She made a note of keeping an eye out for such stashes—mostly out of curiosity, but also to gauge the depths that she was navigating.

As Yrin made the gestures, the Dust started to flow into the dead snake. Soon it emitted a yellow glow around the corpse, discernible even in the room's bright lighting.

Yrin grimaced in frustration. "There's nothing active in there anymore, but there are remains of inert Dust, as Byron suspected. I'll educate him to be more careful later when we're alone. Not his fault, really. I've taught him how to handle regular druids. They wouldn't dream of booby trapping their animals, and they can't use Red Dust anyway. I'm less sure what your little anomaly of a stalker is willing to do, but luckily for us, his creativity isn't quite on par with ours."

Sasha took Yrin's offhanded compliment in stride and concentrated on the more urgent details: "So he's still after me? Damn! If he had more of his spies up there, he'll know I'm up and about."

Yrin took hold of her shoulder reassuringly. "Don't beat yourself too much over it. His beasts could probably smell you from our ventilation system anyway, so it's not as if you gave the game away. If he comes near, we can get him. If not, you're safe either way."

That didn't sit quite right with Sasha. "Fine, then at least we know he knows. But, no disrespect to your hospitality, I'll still have to get going at some point. If he's as crazy as you say, he'll be waiting."

Yrin withdrew, twisting his mouth this way and that. Then he puffed. "Yes, he will ... Besides teaching you some tricks as I mentioned, I can probably spare a few of my people to accompany you. Would that I could myself, I've been stuck here for far too long, but can't take the chance, you see. Last time I set foot outside, something terrible almost happened. Next time, who knows, and my continuing work is far too important."

Ah, his project. This was as good a time as any to pry. "If I may, what is it that you're up to here, then?"

Yrin broke into a grin. "My big mouth. I did walk right into that one, didn't I. Well, suffice to say the gods have left this world to rot. Which might be a good thing, since they always were right bastards. However, it does leave us stuck down here to fend for ourselves. There's defense to consider, for instance, if the fallout from their little war reaches down here."

The dwarf got all somber and quiet again. Clearly, he wasn't divulging the full extent of his work, and if it was something that could stand against a divine conflict, it would be powerful indeed. Powerful enough that maybe she should be worried for herself and the rest of the world.

Or, perhaps more likely, the dwarf was quite mad. That would be worrisome on its own. Sasha had no doubt of his genius by this point, but the two did at times go hand in hand. With luck, if she didn't push the issue, she'd mostly get to deal with the genius part.

Besides, what was she going to do if he truly was working on world domination? He had his magic and she did not, they were in his mine, among his people, and he had the secrets of resurrection at his disposal. His underlings operated magical artifacts in a routine fashion. She had little doubt that Yrin would have done the requisite preparations to enable his nonmagical kin to revive him, if need be.

Sasha gave herself a mental slap. There she went again, jumping to conclusions. Yrin having saved her life should entitle him to some benefit of the doubt as to his deeper intentions. Some of the gathered tension on Sasha's face melted, and her eyes refocused on the dwarf. His eyes were firmly on hers.

"Quick on the uptake, I see. Don't worry. I aim to fix what the old gods did, to make everyone the equal of the Heroes of old, and more! None of it had to be this way, see. The world's as sorry as it is for their amusement, and not for even that, now," Yrin grumbled, sincerely enough as far as Sasha could tell—though there was a twinge of something else there, something she couldn't quite put her finger on. "But enough of that," Yrin stated decisively, closing the window for further query, "let's see what you've got in you."

They spent the rest of the night reviewing her expertise, Yrin occasionally pulling a volume out of his library for her to study in her room. Many of them were elven made, if dated. Sasha presumed he'd either acquired them through trade before the elves closed their borders or looted them from the City.

When they were done for the day, Yrin sent her off to her room, books in hand and with a promise to resume the next day. He stayed behind to continue his work, refreshed, as he said, by the change of pace. There was no escort this time. Sasha could move freely. She wasn't sure if that applied to above ground, but she was in no hurry to venture there regardless. The necromancer's thralls might be lying in wait.

Days flowed into weeks as she studied under Yrin, most of the time in his lab. He usually ate by himself there as well but did drop by the common room on occasion to stay in touch with his people. When he did, he projected a down-to-earth image, but there was an aloofness that seeing him behind the scenes magnified. Sometimes it seemed like he was trying to convince even himself along with the others. It was not so much that Yrin ever gave reason to think of him as a bad person deep down. Rather he was trying almost too hard to belong while setting himself apart from the rest.

Sasha could relate to an extent. She was aspiring to Herohood, and both the magic and the curse in her blood set her apart from most people. But Yrin was more resigned, more tired somehow. Even if he was almost always working as far as she could tell, the impression was of someone going through the motions—with great skill and efficiency, to be sure, but not with great zeal. Sasha once jokingly asked Byron if Lord Yrin ever slept. He did not know.

After the first week, he sometimes left her alone in the main lab to study, retreating into the side room to work by himself. It was Sasha's understanding that he was working on his big project there, though all she could make out was a faint, repetitive clicking sound through the door. That area remained off-limits to her, but it wasn't personal. Nobody went in there, not even Byron.

As promised, Yrin showed her many useful tricks against her nemesis and lent her many books that improved her general understanding of magic. Scores of incantations lost to humanity were now available to her, to be taken back to her homeland.

She toyed with the idea of returning regardless of whether she was successful in her quest, if only for a brief while. Just to pass on her knowledge as well as everything she'd packed into her wands and cores. It could be worth the risk of a few monster attacks for her kind. She wasn't sure if the prospect of getting herself into history books might have interfered with her better judgment on that. When she asked Yrin for an outside view, he agreed it would be the Heroic thing to do.

Here in the fort the curse had proved to be mostly beneficial to her dwarven hosts, just as Yrin had suspected. She had not brought any beasts of myth and legend to chase her, just local predators and some of the smaller varieties of humanoid monster. Dangerous though they could be in numbers, the crowds that she drew were not yet of the same caliber that had attacked her own village. The dwarves were well-equipped to detect the interlopers, and their weaponry allowed them to take down the primitive opposition from a distance with practically no risk. There was little sportsmanship to how Yrin's folk conducted their hunting.

The upshot was that monster meat was plentiful. Sasha was uneasy about it at first, but as a pragmatist made herself get used to it. The dwarves were nothing but happy to bolster their stores. They didn't know why all the prey was coming in, and she wasn't about to take credit. Some of them might be less cavalier about a cursed guest than Yrin himself.

Though she could spend her time at relative ease, not endangering anyone with her curse here, the nearby City pulled at her thoughts.

While she was grateful for the hospitality of the fortress, it wasn't her home. In the City there might be freedom for her, Yrin himself had said so. While he hadn't detailed where he'd gotten his knowledge from, it was clear enough that he'd been in there.

As the midsummer started to near, Sasha grew restless. She'd want to arrange for the trip well before winter. She broached the subject with Yrin, who was less than convinced: "It's not a good idea, not yet. Your nemesis will still be lurking about, if he hasn't gotten himself killed already. Waiting a winter would improve those odds as well as your training."

Yrin had a point, she hated to admit, but Sasha was worried of getting stuck in place, particularly as she had a feeling the dwarf was being self-serving as well. Though he had made no overt advances, nor was she certain if he'd even want to, he was clearly fond of having a peer around. A lingering pat on the back here, a hands-on correction of a gesture there served to build up her anxiety. Should he grow to wish for more intimate company, it could hinder her ambitions to be free of the curse and living above ground again someday.

Chatting with Byron one day, she broached the subject by asking if Yrin had begot any Heroborn heirs. "Clearly you could use more mages around," she explained.

Byron shrugged. "Yrin's shown little interest in female company. Or male, for that matter." He snorted wistfully. "I think he's reputed to have said his gear doesn't work right. It was before my time, though."

Sasha quietly wondered whether having access to a Heroborn peer could make the difference, even if Yrin had had little to no consorts in ages. Speaking of ages ... "How long before, exactly? He doesn't seem so old."

"Oh, quite a while. As far as I'm concerned, he's always run the mine, even in my parents' time, Stars bless their souls."

And Byron was pushing forty. Clearly Yrin was much older than he appeared, which would go a long way to explaining his accumulated knowledge.

On reflection, this did not greatly surprise Sasha. Not after her resurrection. Thinking forward, that was just one more reason to keep friendly relations—devoid of excess drama—with the dwarf. If he could circumvent not only violent death but old age as well, he'd be well worth visiting later on, even risking the elven lands.

Sasha didn't voice her concerns to Yrin himself, but plead her unease brought on by the proximity of her final destination. Yrin relented to her stubbornness; they would make preparations for her to leave come autumn. That would do for her, too. She still had things to learn, contingencies to plan for.

Having reached agreement, Sasha could properly take in the obligatory midsummer celebrations. It was a feast more elaborate than usual, lighter on the monster meat and with varied desserts. Playing simple melodies was a common pastime, but now the dwarves put together a more ambitious concert, heavy on the percussion though it was for Sasha's tastes. The elves had a more sophisticated repertoire.

A feeling of loss took over for a moment. She couldn't help but feel less at home here than with the elves, all Heroborn that they were. Still, she had to admit the dwarves had the upper hand in hospitality. Even if many were curt with her, there were no major political factions after her blood here.

Just the one Sifna, a stout dwarven lady, but that was her job. She'd been assigned by Yrin as Sasha's martial arts teacher. Though Sasha got her nose bloodied many a time, she also got better at arms for it. Sympathetic enough in her gruff way, Sifna had little in common with Sasha, so they kept things strictly professional.

Life among the dwarves continued in its increasingly familiar grooves, with only the occasional group of traders from other dwarven forts to change the pace. For the locals, trade negotiations represented a rare chance to meet new people, but Sasha kept cooped up in her room or in the lab for the duration. She and Yrin both thought it best to keep her presence a secret from the others until her situation was resolved. This only increased her anxiety to get on her way.

Finally, the falling leaves marked the arrival of autumn. Yrin wasn't very happy about it, but he made good on his promise and ordered an escort party of four to see her to the City and hopefully back again. They'd be well-equipped, as would she, though as Yrin had explained, there were some practical considerations. Having seen small flying artifacts, she had naturally been curious and asked if it would be possible to just fly to the City.

As was his habit, Yrin had been pleased with her having thought of it—not that it always translated into a plain answer. This time, it had. "Oh, I was wondering if you'd ask about human flight, having seen the drones. Though it would require quite a lot of Dust to fly a human, it would be feasible, yes indeed. But," he'd paused for a moment, "you don't know that your condition makes it unsafe?"

Sasha had taken the cue. "How so?"

"Carrying Dust in bulk will amplify your curse's strength and reach. I had the better part of my Dust stores moved into deeper storage after your first audience. Were you to travel using an artifact of that size, it'd significantly increase monster interest. Not to mention that if you were flying, the monsters would be sure to include fliers as well. If you don't attract dragons now, you certainly would then." Just one of those tidbits that he'd neglected to mention, assuming it to be common knowledge. At least the pattern encouraged Sasha to be more active in asking questions.

The party would nevertheless be equipped with magical gear, if only as much as Yrin's curiously exact estimates would safely allow. She, too, would have magical armor with metal plating and Dust worked into one. Her light metallic helm relied on the mundane material for protection, but it had a magical visor for visual enhancement. In addition, she'd carry enough Dust to form a hand to hand weapon, enough Red Dust to power a score of missiles, and some brass-plated Dust bracelets and anklets. As Yrin had said, "Carrying idle Dust is often useless if you can carry a potentially useful Dust artifact instead, or even wear it on you. You can always repurpose the stuff as need be."

Her armor, and those of her companions, were things of legend. Yrin had retained or rediscovered the secrets of Heroic armor. The mails could launch their shoulder spikes as small projectiles. They weren't meant for offensive use, but for taking down incoming missiles, magical or otherwise. The numbers they could deflect would be limited, but it was a huge advantage all the same. The armor would allow them time to react to any shooting ambush. No longer would Sasha be caught flat-footed.

For the big good-bye Yrin deigned to venture all the way up to the exit corridor, where Sasha had never seen him go. Apparent immortality along with his calling made for highly risk-averse habits. Those and a dash of compulsive behavior.

As the escort went outside to secure the perimeter, Yrin started on the farewells: "So, here we are. You do know that having once made friends with the dwarves means you get to vanish for a few years, then reappear banging on the door with an arrow sticking out of your back and an elven army ten minutes behind you, go 'I was never here', and pass out from the blood loss, right?"

Sasha's chuckle was diminished by the somber occasion, but not squelched altogether. "You know I'll drop by soon if all goes well. Thanks for everything. Oh, and just so you know, you're not quite as mysterious as you might think."

It was Yrin's turn to puff amusedly. "That may well be so, but allow an old man his fantasy. Here, you'll need this." The dwarf lord produced a sheet of paper with unfamiliar incantations on it. "You're aware of the Hall being sealed. You will stand no chance of getting in, if not for these. One's for sealing, the other for opening. Cast them on the wall. You'll need no Dust. The Hall itself is a giant artifact. It'll hear you. It'll open for you. Beyond that, I have no guarantees, but ... good luck."

Sasha found her mouth agape. The dwarf had given no indication of this all this time. But it didn't matter now. He'd trusted her with the Hall's secrets in the end. She read the spells in, then immediately relayed the all-important incantations to her spare cores as well. Though it seemed too little, she managed a wide-eyed "Thank you." Yrin shook his head and waved her along.

She complied, and as the doors started closing markedly more slowly than was usual, Yrin replied faintly: "It's not so much. I wasn't quite sure at first if I'd give it to you, but, well. You won't be less wise than us. And ... for what it's worth, for my part, I ... am sorry."

The door had closed on his last words, and Sasha was quite sure it would not open again until she'd been to the City first. She trusted Yrin's word on it being open for her later, however.

The man's farewell words had come from somewhere deep behind the facade of an eccentric lord of his keep. If not before, Sasha was certain now that whatever the dwarf was working on, whether it was something real or a mad man's fantasy, his desire for atonement was genuine. He wouldn't intentionally wreak havoc. Of course, when dealing with powerful magics, intent was only part of the equation, but Yrin was meticulous.

Things might still turn out well.

9

BYRON HIMSELF HAD VOLUNTEERED to lead the expedition, with Sifna as his second. They had never been to the City, but they had good maps and Yrin's directions to work with. The trip should take about four days, well-rested and fed as they were. For the convenience of her escort, they'd gotten up late in the day as the sky told time. Though they were equipped with light-dulling eyewear, it had been decided that the dwarves' natural advantage during nighttime could be useful if they ran into the necromancer again.

Thus, the sun was soon to set over the hills as they left. The autumn air was chilly, but manageable. The light was dim, but Sasha could for the moment travel unaided. When it would get darker, she'd make her visor amplify the light similarly to her lost cape. It would be usable for several hours before running out of strength. Enough to last the darkest hours of the night, and she could recharge it from her spare Dust if need be.

Byron took the lead, Sasha went behind him, and Sifna, Reznor, and Rhys covered her flanks and rear. Hunting parties had been sent to clear the area of monsters just the night before, and a new check from the sky had shown no new activity of note near the keep, but that was no reason for a lapse in vigilance. The armors had wardstone functionality built-in as well. They'd have to constantly monitor the environment for missiles anyway, Yrin'd said, so they might as well do double duty. It would eat up a little extra power, but that would not be a problem this time.

The night's travel was uneventful. If some beast was attracted by her curse, it was not provoked enough to attack a party of five. Being on the move was helpful in reducing the chances of a violent encounter as well. They kept going until the sun rose and the dwarves had to resort to their glasses. They set up camp in a shady grove, with her escort dividing watch duty among themselves.

After an unappetizing but nutritious meal of dried ogre from a recent hunt, Sasha set to work empowering their depleted magical gear. The day's sun could help, but not by a lot. She had another trick up her sleeve, now. When Sasha had lamented about the slow speed of Dust re-empowerment, the dwarf had grinned enthusiastically and told her that there was actually an obscure workaround for it, an unpronounceable incantation never meant for mortal ken. Even most Heroes were purportedly unaware of the trick, and Yrin was evasive about how exactly he'd come about it.

He'd demonstrated by spreading almost but not quite fully drained Dust over some coals. At the flick of his wand, the Dust had eaten into the coal and re-empowered itself, with a lot of residual heat. "Be careful with that. There aren't a lot of safeguards here, damn the Stars, though you can craft some in yourself. Too much heat, and some or all of the Dust might burn up. Along with other things nearby."

He'd gone on to explain that this was how he powered his operations. Sasha hadn't thought of that. She had just assumed there to be unseen fields of Dust aboveground, like what the elves did. This did seem more effective, given material resources.

Luckily it didn't have to be coal. Sasha had a couple of the dwarves gather some wood and set it on a rock face so that the heat wouldn't start a forest fire. She fed the group's gear from the Dust she had on hand in the form of a spear and dispersed it over the consumables. When she made the gestures, the wood quickly started to darken even as the layer of Dust slowly whitened up. While she waited, Sasha's mind wandered to the rest of the lesson.

After sharing this particular piece of lore with her, Yrin had had a rare moment of what seemed like regret. He'd made her swear never to tell anyone else the secret, or to combine the incantation with anything. Usually, he'd explain the reasons for such warnings, but this time he'd been flustered and just dismissed her from the lesson. It wasn't much later that she had realized what she'd just been granted: The ability to craft a spell that would potentially spread and last as long as there was any burnable material present.

A spell of mass destruction. The power to lay waste to huge areas, creating clouds of Dust that would eat through anything in their path. A lot to take in for a young mage, but she had been trained well at least in this respect. She wouldn't use the knowledge in that way. Even if she'd only use it for a just cause, if she made a mistake in the incantations, if she were disabled and lost control of the spell ... The danger of unleashing a runaway blight of Dust on the world was too much. It could perhaps be fought back to an extent with fire, or by somehow encasing it in inert materials for long enough for the energy to run out, but that would be an uphill battle at best.

Eliminating such a Dust cloud would be next to impossible, traces would surely be left behind. One could even imagine an unscrupulous mage purposefully creating barely visible wisps of Dust that would slowly gnaw at things wherever they traveled on the winds. How many motes of Dust would it take to eat up a human, if they could take their sweet time, fueling the magic through consuming the flesh? Sasha shivered at the thought.

There was only one thing worse that Sasha could think of. If you didn't care much for efficiency, most materials could be used to make more Dust. Perhaps this was why the gods had seen it fit to require a complex alchemical concoction for its replication. The Catalyst seemed to make a self-perpetuating Dust plague impossible.

Then again, the gods seemed to have a problem with loopholes. Would it be possible to create the Catalyst magically, bypassing the restriction? This had not been the traditional way, but ... from what she'd learned from Yrin already, synthesizing alchemical formulae was within the realm of possibility. If so, this was magic with the potential to consume the entirety of the world with little to be done about it. No wonder the man had been shaken by his own indiscretion. A small part of Sasha had even feared for her own safety. There was one surefire way to remedy the situation, after all.

But Yrin was not so callous. At the start of their next lesson, he'd merely asked, in very serious tones: "Do you understand?"

She'd nodded somberly. "Unstoppable mass destruction. I understand. I won't use it with other magics."

"Good, good," the dwarf had said. Prudent or not, that was the end of that particular discussion. Later, at times, Yrin would rein in his enthusiasm better. Notably, they never broached the subject of alchemical synthesis by magic more closely.

Perhaps there were other secrets that he'd kept to himself, now, but she couldn't blame him. Just the one weighed heavily on her mind at times, not that it prevented her from making good use of the incantation as is. In its basic form, it was self-limiting. The Dust would consume what it needed to whiten up, then it would stop. The heat was a concern, but manageable. Sure, you could burn up a dry forest by being careless, but the same was true of mundane fire.

Sasha had always been careful with fire, and no less now. Her Dust had whitened, and much of the wood now ashes on the rock. Sasha commanded the Dust to coalesce back into the shape of a spear. She let it cool down for a while before picking it up. She'd once made the mistake of touching a Dust object too soon afterwards when experimenting. The burns hadn't been severe, as she'd quickly let go, but it had been an effective learning experience.

Maintenance done, the day's rest was uneventful aside from a couple of animal attacks, easily enough thwarted by the guard on duty. No resorting to rations for the next day of the journey. When Sasha got up for the night, food was already prepared. A piece of direwolf was more palatable than the dried ogre they had brought with them. They'd carry enough of it for the day. More likely than not, they'd have to make fresh kills tomorrow anyway.

Before setting out Sasha topped their equipment off again to be in prime condition for the night. Then they were on their way towards the setting sun.

The travel settled into routine. The terrain was rocky but smooth, allowing for a decent pace. There were enough trees here and there to find some cover for the day and to maintain their artifacts. They encountered an ogre while traveling at night and a grizzly while camped out for the day, but the dwarven warriors easily defeated both.

The day after that, the curse drew in a bigger challenge. Sasha was suddenly awakened by a pair of pops as the spikes in Reznor's armor intercepted something. An alarm went off, and the rest of the party was up in seconds. Somebody had managed to attack their guard on duty without tripping the wards first. A broken arrow lay on the rocks near Reznor. That, at least, was good news. If the attack was mundane in nature, they'd likely have the advantage.

Two more arrows hit the trees and the ground. The enemy's aim had deteriorated. Nerves, perhaps. Their armors were smart enough not to waste resources trying to deflect arrows destined to miss anyway. With a few gestures from Byron, everybody took cover behind trees and rocks, assuming for now that the attack was coming from a single direction. They could afford to be lax with the rear with the armors covering their backs.

Reznor and Sifna started spotting for enemies, their crossbows in hand. There were some densely shrubbed areas in the direction of the attack. Even as Sasha thought she could perhaps see something metallic glean in one of them, a crossbow bolt was away, then another. Something croaked and fell. There was further rustling in the bushes, moving away.

Byron gave Sasha a quizzical look, as far as she could tell from behind his protective eyewear. They could charge the location, relying on their shields and magical armor, or wait and see. Perhaps the assailants scurried off after noticing that they weren't such easy prey after all. Sasha thought about it for a second. At least the attackers' initial direction of retreat was almost diagonal to theirs, so they might avoid further fighting simply by letting them go and moving onward. She gave a shrug and, by default, they waited for things to settle.

Eventually Byron took Rhys with him to check the bushes, shields and axes in hand. They moved in from the side so that Reznor and Sifna could cover them with their crossbows. They entered without incident, and soon gave the all clear sound. Byron emerged from the shrub. "There's a dead goblin here with a bow, can you imagine. By appearances, he had several friends, but they're gone now. We should probably follow their example in case they get brave or reinforcements, though. Gather your things, let's move."

Sasha quickly replaced Reznor's spent spike missiles. It left her spear a bit shorter and her pouch of Red Dust a bit lighter, but the armor had proven its worth. Then they were off. As it was still daytime, Sasha could travel using her plain sight, but the dwarves had to resort to their dimming goggles.

The scare of the attack substituting for proper rest, the group made good time for a while, but eventually started to lose speed. The woods started to thicken again as they neared the City, and the party decided to set up camp again. As best they could tell, they were still a couple of hours away and they didn't want to lack proper rest upon entering. They'd end up sleeping most of the night this time and arriving in the morning, but that to be just as well. The City was an area of ancient magic, and Sasha's daylight eyes were the ones most adept at recognizing its signs if need be.

This time Sasha spread some dedicated wardstones around the campsite, what with the unusual bow-wielding goblins in the area. The species was not known for their prowess with tools, though it was not unprecedented. At least the assault hadn't been anything more formidable, but who knew if the City would have more monsters of the resourceful kind in store for them. She'd asked Yrin what to expect, of course, but the dwarf hadn't had any recent information. Just that the City shouldn't have any particular tendency to attract danger.

Back in the old times its magical fortifications had even warded monsters off to an extent, going so far as to nullify the effects of the curse inside its area. That protection had faded off after the departure of the Heroes, however, and could not be replicated elsewhere. Somehow it drew its power from the central Hall and the number of resident Heroes. The Hall itself, Yrin had speculated, should still provide refuge from most threats once inside. Not that anything in the ancient City was to be relied upon.

The night saw little action, though there was a hoot of an alarm from one of the stones in their rear during the night. Reznor had woken Sifna up and gone to investigate but found nothing. Whatever it had been, it had passed them by. The morning came without further incident, and after the usual routine, off they went into the forest. Travel was more cumbersome than before what with the undergrowth, but the woods were dense only in comparison to the earlier open landscape. They would still make good time.

Soon Sasha could spot signs of old civilization. Remains of a small cottage, covered in vegetation, stood a short way left from their path. There was little chance of finding anything interesting in there, but the group headed for the building regardless. With luck, there might be remains of a road going past it.

A rotting trunk of a tree had taken down one of the surprisingly flimsy stone walls in times past. There was no sign of any roof left, and the undergrowth continued seamlessly inside the house. It was highly doubtful that the house would have anything of value left at this point. Still, they were near the City. Sasha sent a layer of Dust to scrounge the area for artifacts, using a spell Yrin had taught her. Nothing, as expected.

Meanwhile, the dwarves had found a path that looked like it might have been a dirt road at some point long past. The undergrowth was pretty much the same, but there were fewer roots to trip over. They took what they could get and pressed on.

The path turned slightly downwards, and soon Sasha noticed the city wall amongst the trees. Behind it, far in the distance, she could see the double peaks that Aaron's map had placed next to the City. So much for that map matching the territory.

The dwarves weren't as perceptive as her in this light so Sasha clued them in, talking quietly: "We're nearing the wall, though we still have some distance to cover. There's something that looks like a gate structure to the left. The road will probably take us there, but if not, let's veer off soon." The others grunted assent. Soon the old road turned as expected.

The gate was in between the deteriorated remains of two small towers, seemingly mostly decorational. Mossy remains of a bulky wooden gate came into view on the ground as the group ventured closer. Some of the early expeditions had probably managed to get through by force, and there had been no one to fix it up again.

Shields and weapons in hand, the group entered the City with great care. There were no signs of habitation but vigilance never killed anyone, unlike the lack thereof. Most of the buildings had withstood the tests of time decently, though the colors had faded away and the more ornate decorations had succumbed to the elements. Still, one could plainly see that the now empty husk of a city had once been a place of wonder. Vegetation had taken over the city streets as well, but it was lighter than in the forest. The grand architecture was visible clearly enough.

That was not what they were here for, however. Now that they were in the City, there was little sense to dally more than safety dictated. Besides, the accessible buildings had probably been ransacked several times already. No, the Hall was where it was at, and as Yrin had told it, it would be right at the center of the City, accessible from any of the gates via the main roads. Indeed, though an occasional tree obstructed the view, a large building loomed in the distance. Her long quest was nearing its end. Whatever awaited inside, whatever happened in the end, it would be over. A strange but comforting thought.

Three of the dwarves were already advancing to check the nearby alleyways while Reznor kept the rear. Sasha walked along the right side wall to keep her exposure to a minimum. Slowly they approached the central plaza until the Hall upon it was almost fully visible from a couple of blocks away. The round two story building, maybe a hundred meters wide, was a sight to behold. It reminded Sasha of the Council Hall in Greenhold. Perhaps the elves had been inspired by it in their architecture.

In contrast to the lesser dwellings of the City, the Hall's plain white finish was undisturbed by time. The ornamented pillars decorating the round outer wall were as elaborate as they'd ever been. The supports were joined by smooth walls forming a perfect circle. No doors, as expected. She'd have to take care of that herself.

Suddenly, Byron froze and signaled with his hand. He'd seen tracks. The rest of them tensed up, glancing around. A quiet moment passed, then a piece of rubble near the forward guard went off with a bang. The dwarves' armors tried to intercept some of the shrapnel, but there was too much of it, too forceful. Byron and Sifna fell and goblins started to pour in from behind the buildings next to the Hall, cutting them off.

"Take cover!" Reznor shouted. Sasha was fumbling for some of her Red Dust as she moved and fired into the approaching goblin mass. Then she noticed a couple of ogres in there as well. That shouldn't happen.

There was no time to dwell on the unlikely alliance. Nothing to do but to concentrate fire on the larger opponents first. Reznor evidently did the same with his crossbow since both of the ogres went down in rapid succession, with her only having fired once.

Sasha could feel her armor depleting its countermeasures as it intercepted arrows and thrown weapons of various sorts. A loud bang went off somewhere behind the enemy lines. The goblins slowed down in confusion, and a familiar if raspy voice boomed: "I told you, I want the human alive!"

Shit. Well, at least the interruption had given them time to thin the herd, but that didn't seem to be doing much. The odds were at about twenty to three, with a mage on both sides. Superior equipment could only do so much.

Missile attacks on her had ceased, not so for her guard. Reznor's and Rhys' armors must've been nearing depletion. Not that it mattered much, as the goblins were now upon them in hand to hand combat. Sasha used the reach of her spear to try and fend them off. Now that she had a close look at the goblins, they were moving in a slightly off manner. Not as slow or shambling as human zombies, but having seen goblins in close combat before, there was a subtle difference. Perhaps the movements of lesser beings suffered less while under magical compulsion. Druidic beasts showed little indication of hampered motion, after all.

Thanks to Sifna's training, Sasha was able to take a few of the goblins down as they descended upon her. Nevertheless, surrounded as she was, there was only so much she could do. Her armor took the brunt of a few body blows, but eventually her helmet rang from behind, and Sasha fell to her knees. The goblin in front of her hesitated, remembering the admonishment of its master, and let her be as she wobbled for a moment. It was enough.

10

S ASHA'S HEAD ACHED, if not as much as it might have. This time she was sure she hadn't died. That had been a much more pleasant experience to wake up from, other than being confined in a coffin of sorts. She'd never gotten the rest of that story, either, and now she never might. Then again, she still had a shot, more so than her companions who were probably goblin chow by now.

Trying to keep her breathing steady, she concentrated on her surroundings. The noises of the battle were gone, things were quiet except for light breathing not too far from her. A guard, no doubt. She'd been stripped of her armor, trousers, and shoes. She was left with only her long undershirt and the shiny brass jewelry—the latter only because it was made too tight to take off. She was doubly glad her nemesis hadn't resorted to heavier methods of removal.

Despite the dearth of clothing, she felt protected from the elements. They were inside one of the buildings. In addition to her bracelets, she felt shackles around her wrists. That was one of the scenarios that they'd prepared for. The necromancer's parting words had, after all, indicated that he'd prefer to interrogate her first. She'd have to stall for time until she'd have a few minutes alone, or at least not under close scrutiny.

Also, unless she could recover her wand and make a quick break for the Hall, her prospects of escaping from the surrounding goblins would be a factor. Waiting until the night might help there. Goblins had somewhat better night vision than humans, but they weren't really nocturnal, just flexible. She wasn't sure of how much time had passed, but it was light outside still. It was unlikely she'd been out for very long. It was best to prepare for a long wait.

Observing the soundscape around her, she could hear the occasional group of goblins walking around outside. On patrol duty, perhaps. The breathing near her turned out to be someone sleeping, judging by the occasional snorts and light snoring. She risked opening one of her eyes halfway to gauge the situation.

It was the nemesis, with his face down on the table. He'd fallen asleep watching her. That was ... disappointing, somehow. Maybe this was the time to make a break for it after all. No, wait. There was a wolf in the corner looking her way. He hadn't yet noticed her awakening, but he surely would if she'd make her move. Even as she thought it, the animal snarled and got up to approach his master. Sasha quickly closed her eye, though it was probably too late. She heard the wolf paw her sleeping nemesis, rousing him from his sleep.

After a few quick snorts and a yawn, he spoke tiredly, "What is it, boy? She's awake?" The wolf made an affirmative growl. "Are you, then?" asked the necromancer, addressing her. She did not answer. "Right, go and bite her face, but just a bit at first," the man said in a dull tone.

Sasha immediately sat up and extended her arms towards the pair as far as the chain allowed: "Okay, okay, stop, please."

"Hold," the nemesis commanded with a smirk. The wolf was already on the move, but stopped in his tracks. Sasha breathed a sigh of relief, then took a better look at the man.

Living in the wilderness had been hard on him. He was much bonier than back in Merfort, with a scar on the left cheek and dark circles under his eyes. Perhaps waiting a winter would have been prudent after all, though he might well have survived with the aid of his thralls anyway. Sasha managed to resist blurting out how he looked well. Sarcasm would likely not be conducive to her survival.

Instead, she lowered her gaze in acquiescence, waiting for him to speak.

"I thought I'd killed you for sure last time," he said. "For a couple of hours there, I could breathe easily. But that did not take long. I gather the dwarves managed to patch you up, somehow. Not a trace on you, even, though your wounds were grave. What sort of magic is that?"

She couldn't credibly deny anything. A half-truth would hopefully suffice. "I don't know. The dwarves in that particular fort had access to some ancient magics that even the elves lack. They taught me some of it, but not all." That was the bait. She'd want to keep the guy more hungry for information than for her blood.

It seemed to be working. His eyes sharpened at the mention of ancient lore: "Really? Did they teach you how to get in there?" He pointed at the Hall of Heroes, which she now noticed was just across the fifty meter clearing behind one of the windows. So close, yet so far away.

She'd try to keep this secret to herself for now. The deceit wouldn't be too far-fetched. "No, they didn't know that. Do you think they wouldn't hold the Hall already if they could? But I had to try and see for myself. I still could give it a go, but I'd need my wand, of course." On the mention of the wand, her nemesis glanced toward a closed door on the wall opposite to her. If that was where her gear was, it was cause for some hope.

The man chuckled: "That isn't overly likely, as you know. I'm not sure I buy your story about coming all the way here without a way in, but we can ... talk about that later. You're going to teach me all you know about Heroborn magic. The more you teach, the longer you'll live in relative comfort. If I suspect you're taking your sweet time, though, the comfort will rapidly suffer. The lessons begin today. Any questions?"

This was as good a time as any to try and satisfy her curiosity, if she could just formulate it in a way that wasn't overtly offensive. "Fine. You've got me. I'll teach you. But first, who are you anyway? How is it that you can cast Heroic magic? Necromancers aren't known for widening their repertoire, nor are Heroborn for necromancy. And the elves pegged you for ..." She managed to cut off before she would trigger the man.

There was anger in his eyes, to be sure, but he held his composure. "Neople? I am Stefan of Smallhaven, and my grandmother on my father's side was neople. Good neople. Simple, but decent. We kept it a secret, of course, after the family had to move to avoid the scorn. Making a new life wasn't easy, but we managed. Until one day, as I was getting home from a night at the inn, the necromancer got to me. He must've mistaken me for neople. Took me as his slave, away from my family. Made me ... do things for him. Soon I was his favorite thrall. More effective, smarter than the rest. He had no idea that would be his undoing.

"Even as I was compelled to do his bidding, I watched him. I learned how he did his magic, every gesture, where he stored his spells. Slowly, I noticed that his hold over me was deteriorating. I could disobey him, act of my own volition—a little at first, more with practice. Then, one day, as he was making a new spare wand for himself, I struck. Killed him, took the wand before he'd imprinted on it, took his magic, took his thralls even. The others were proper neople, not like me. Not suffering for it.

"I don't know much more than that for sure, but I'm not stupid. Heroborn mages are the ones with the most versatile magic. When I chanced on the secret of druidic magic messing about in the forest with no neople around for minions, I knew I had to try for more. The fire mage confirmed my suspicion that I could learn the secrets of other kinds of magic as well. I even managed to apply his scribing magic to the necromantic arts, something my former master could not do. The spell was insanely long and mostly gibberish to me, but on the highest level there were a few choice incantations in plain language. As a simple test, I removed the incantation seemingly responsible for bodily changes, and the magic obeyed me. So you tell me, what am I?" Dark pride shone on his bony face.

Sasha nodded in recognition. "You are a Heroborn mage, as am I. Let me go, kinsman, and we can take the Hall, our legacy, together." She was laying it on a bit thick, but she figured it was worth a shot.

The man shook his head and scoffed. "Time for that passed back in the catacombs, when you chose not to work together. Now you're mine, and it's time for the lessons to start."

As luck would have it, Stefan had discovered a stash of empty papers protected from the elements in an otherwise ransacked library. They were yellowed but serviceable and would last a great while longer than the lessons would, if she had her way.

Stefan had seen a few spells, even intuited what some of the incantations meant, but lacked almost all formal teaching. He'd not had time to get altogether too much out of Gibli, though the elementalist had managed to preoccupy him sufficiently to allow Sasha a head start out of Kilnkeep.

She started from the basics of spellcrafting: making forms. Stefan did know how to make simple geometric shapes, but she could expand on that and show him how to make simple interlocking mechanisms. It was useful enough to keep his interest for the day, but not immensely powerful as such. She wouldn't have too many regrets about divulging that much to the man in case things didn't go according to plan.

Even Stefan's thirst for knowledge wasn't enough to keep him up very long. He complained that he had waited for them impatiently for the entire night after his scouts had reported them being on their way. His tiredness could only work in her favor. This was the night to make the attempt. And if she failed, she'd have to make sure she'd fail fatally. There would be no second chance, no further underestimating her capabilities, and she didn't want to be at Stefan's mercies then.

After they'd finished for the day, she heard Stefan dish out orders to the goblins outside. She'd get two goblin guards and the wolf; could be better, could be worse. She wasn't sure how many of the goblins were left at this point, but some were to guard the perimeter, and a few were allowed to sleep to relieve others later. The goblins had probably stayed awake with their obsessed master. That was good as well. Her guards might not be very alert, perhaps they'd even doze off. And changing guard shifts? Thralls were unreliable for things like that, left to administer themselves.

After a slight supper of stringy meat, they retired. Stefan disappeared through the door behind which she hoped she'd find her gear. She remained shackled on the floor. Her appetite had not been the best, all things considered, but she'd eaten everything she was given. She'd need all of her strength to manage her escape.

Sasha lay down to feign sleep in a curled up position, facing away from the guards. In the candlelight she'd need some cover for this to work. She waited for an hour or two to allow for the guards' attention to lapse further. When she heard an intermittent flapping noise from somewhere far away, she waited no further. It might provide some cover for the sounds she'd make, and if there was something entirely new on its way she needed to be loose to deal with it.

Yrin and Sasha had never counted on her nemesis to be gone. Contingency plans had been made, and many of those hinged on getting out of restraints while disarmed. It was Yrin's idea—perhaps inspired by some of his older friends, gone now—to equip her with the brass bracelets. They were sized so that they seemed to have been put on while she was smaller, too tight to be removed at this point. Some cultures did that sort of thing, though it wasn't common. Still, it was plausible, and Stefan had bought it. It was good that she'd been wearing long sleeves back in Merfort.

Using Yrin's magics, the rings of Dust had been coated with a thin layer of metal to allay suspicion. There was a series of tiny holes on the inside to allow the contents out. As she'd need to be able to use the rings without a wand, they'd been pre-enchanted to listen for a particular series of taps. This necessitated occasional refills, but the listener didn't drain much.

She carefully brought the bracelets up to the shackles and touched them lightly with her fingertips. Tap tap, tap tap tap, tap. Dust began to flow out, looking for metal or inert leather. Finding the former, the Dust flowed to find the bolts keeping the manacles locked. Yrin had taken care to have the limited Dust direct its energy efficiently. Slowly the bolts were eaten through. Sasha held the shackles so they wouldn't make any sudden noises falling to the ground. Thinking of noises, the one in the background had grown in intensity. Something was approaching the City.

Having freed her hands, the Dust used the rest of its power to coalesce into a small, dark gray dagger. It wasn't much, but it would have to do. If all else failed, she could at least take her own life. This close to her goal, she wasn't about to do so unless it became absolutely necessary, but the option was good to have.

Quietly she gave a different set of taps with her toes to the anklets. This reservoir of Dust wouldn't have to expend its energy to free her from restraints, so she could put it to other use. The Dust poured out along her skin, found its way into her hands, and coalesced into two pebbles. They had been a joint effort by her and Yrin. The dwarf had been quite amused by the idea. It was truly fit for a Hero, he'd said. She wasn't sure if the pebbles were very Heroic, but from Yrin's point of view anything effective seemed to qualify.

The noise was louder now and circling the area. Could it be that Yrin sent large fliers after her as backup? She dared not hope, but the possibility was there. Then she heard the goblin guards stand up. She froze, ready to pounce them if they came close, but the goblins went outside instead. Must have been under standing orders to drop what they were doing to defend the camp against external threats. That was a stroke of good fortune if there ever was one. She'd have to assume the wolf was still there, though. Slowly, as if still asleep, she contorted her body to get a look at where the animal lay while keeping her hands on the other side. The position was awkward, but she hoped the wolf wouldn't pick up on that.

As she opened her eye ever so slightly, Sasha saw the wolf's shape. She tossed one of the pebbles towards his head, but he reacted fast, springing to the side and then towards her with a growl. She raised her left arm to protect herself, and sharp teeth locked themselves around it. Sasha suppressed a cry of pain, instead focusing on the needs of the moment. She stabbed the dull Dust blade into the side of the wolf's throat, wiggled it about, pulled it a part of the way back, pushed it in again in a slight angle, trying to do as much damage as she could.

It worked. The teeth loosened their grip. The arm was useless now, but she'd lucked out. The bleeding wasn't very bad. She'd have to do something about it soon, but first things first. She managed to hold both the blade and the remaining pebble in her right hand and get up, but right then the door opened.

It was Stefan, her elven staff in hand. "Drop the dagger," he ordered. Even disabled, the staff's reach would make an attack with the dagger useless. She complied, still holding onto the pebble hidden in her palm. "So. You try to thwart me again. No more. I don't think you'll need all of your limbs intact to teach me. And what is that trickery out there?" Stefan demanded just as the flames flooded the streets a few blocks away. The ominous flapping was replaced by an oddly familiar roar and the screams of burning goblins.

That was the distraction she needed. As Stefan's eyes veered towards the fireworks, Sasha threw the pebble. This one locked on target and split in three, one part to provide extra thrust and guidance, two to continue onward.

Stefan cried out as the fragments dug into his eyes. He dropped the staff and clawed at his face, trying to get at the Dust, but it was too late. The magic was eating into the soft tissue with a vengeance. Sasha was quick to take the opportunity to go in low and quietly seize the staff. She'd want its reach to battle even a blind man. Having made good use of his initial panic, she jumped back, staff at the ready.

A part of her thought that this should be enough: her nemesis was blind, disabled for the rest of his life. But no, she'd learned her lesson about letting this man live. And what was it Yrin had said, that it would be a mercy. He'd never live a satisfying life with her alive.

She couldn't quite fool herself into thinking that swinging her staff at the side of his head was for his own good, but she did it all the same. The man heard it coming. He tried to dodge and block at the same time, but Sasha was faster. The staff connected with a crack and Stefan went down, breathing heavily and holding his head.

She brought the staff down again. His hand was crushed and fell away, leaving his head unprotected. Sasha struck again, and again, and again. The man's whimpers grew fainter and fainter. With one hand, there was only so much force she could bring to bear on the staff for the coup de grâce, but now she deemed it safe to go in close. She lay the staff on the floor and picked up the bloodied dark blade.

Her nemesis was moving his mouth, perhaps trying to say something. No matter, all had been said and done. She steeled her heart by reminding herself of what he'd threatened her with. Then she took the blade to his throat and finished it, cringing as the blood flowed and life faded away from Stefan's face.

Another bout of flame framed the moment, closer this time. She had a feeling it wasn't Yrin. She'd need her gear back, now. She sprang off to the other room.

Stefan's bedroom was small and unkempt, but a lot of the mess was familiar. There was her old rucksack in the corner, and the elven cloak was crumpled beside it. Her gear from when she came in wasn't here, though. The armor had been booby-trapped. The goblin that had taken it off of her hadn't done so without paying a price, and that had been enough to warn Stefan away from the rest of the equipment. She'd have liked the spear, but it couldn't be helped. Now, if only the backpack still had her old wand she'd be back in business.

She rummaged through the pack and indeed, the wand was there. It didn't have all of her new spells, but the small cores hidden in her bracelets did. She quickly updated the wand and donned the cloak. It had reverted to its natural Dust color after having been depleted on the night of her death. It was torn in two places, but she hoped it still worked. At least it was white. Stefan had probably empowered it in the sun after he'd stolen it. He couldn't make it work, of course, but she couldn't blame him for trying.

The essentials in hand, Sasha tried to activate the cloak. It still worked, thank the Stars. The tears were just small spots where the invisibility failed. She could try to keep them hidden in the cloak's folds. She activated the night vision while she was at it and ran to the door. Slightly ajar, she didn't have to open it to get a glance at the surroundings. The flapping, at least, was gone. She wondered what that meant.

The Hall was near, but so was the dragon, standing on the ground amidst burnt goblin husks, slowly sniffing the air around it. Of course. She, with her curse boosted by the recent battle, had been lying practically next to the biggest magical artifact known to man. The City's wards long gone, there had been nothing to stop things from escalating rapidly.

Sasha wasn't sure what part was the night vision and what part the dragon's actual hide, but the thing didn't look natural. It moved very smoothly, very deliberately, and the scales had a magical finish to them. Could it be a construct of sorts? Not that it mattered much. She'd have to either try to remain hidden or make a break for it anyway. There was no fighting this thing by herself.

The dragon made the decision for her. It breathed fire on a nearby building and started to move towards her hideout. There were still two houses in between. Sasha readied her wand and waited for the dragon to repeat his attack on the next one. The dragon obliged, but not before stopping for a moment to breathe in. Sasha hoped it meant the monster would have to let its throat rest between its fiery breaths.

As the dragon's head was turned away, Sasha pointed at the Hall, made the unsealing gesture, and ran. She hoped the cloak would be enough to cover her for the brief moment she'd be exposed.

The dragon snapped its head towards her general direction, but hesitated. Then it looked at the Hall. An opening was slowly forming into the previously solid wall, steady light shining through from the inside. The beast started to stomp towards it, but as strong as it was, it was too massive to build up speed quickly.

Sasha was faster. The opening hadn't fully formed yet, but she jumped through headfirst just as the flames struck her. The delay had been shorter than the last time. She couldn't be sure, but perhaps the dragon hadn't quite built its flame up to full power yet. Her legs and feet had gotten burned, but they could still move, still feel the pain.

She got rid of the smoking cloak and cast the sealing spell on the wall. Then she scuttled along the hard, smooth floor away from the opening. The dragon got to the doorway well before it had fully sealed, but did not try to enter or attack, settling for snarling at her through the hole. The Hall still held power.

As the opening closed, Sasha allowed herself a moment to breathe. Then she tried to stand. It was painful, but possible. The blisters looked bad, but she couldn't do much about it now. Her head felt faint. She leaned on the wall and let it settle. That's when she heard the footsteps.

Time to take stock of the situation, Sasha thought. One usable hand, barely usable legs, a wand but no Dust. If force was going to be a factor rather than talk, she'd have no chance. She merely tried to stand taller, salvage what could be salvaged of the first impression.

A man clad in white robes turned a corner in one of the corridors. He was a strange combination of old and youthful with the white hair and beard, but smooth complexion. His eyes were tired, reminding her of Yrin's when they first met. He wore a faint smile on his lips, but Sasha couldn't see any feeling behind it. The man came up to the room and cocked his head slightly, as if inviting her to speak.

Sasha opened her mouth, but only a cough and a wheeze came out. Then she tried again: "I am Sasha, a Heroborn mage. Are you … a Hero?"

The man's smile widened just for a moment in a display of tired amusement. "No, Sasha. I am merely the Seneschal, custodian of the Hall, and a guide to its Heroes. Heroborn, you say. I wondered who could it be that roused me, now that all the Heroes are gone. Well, almost all, but I doubted he would be back, the lengths he went to in order to evade the recall."

Sasha had a fair idea who the Seneschal was talking about, but there was no time to beat around the bush. "My bloodline is cursed. I was told I could, perhaps, find a cure here. Is that true?" she asked.

The Seneschal thought for a moment before answering: "I'm not sure. There isn't any precedent. Known Heroborn were rare when actual Heroes still walked these halls. Most never visited the City, and the few that did were not allowed inside the Hall at all. But that is none of my business. My instructions predate the whole Heroborn issue. I'll let you make your case to the Hall. If it will recognize you as one of its own, you may yet get your wish." He gestured for her to follow and walked into another corridor. She stumbled behind him on her aching feet.

There were no doors in the Hall that she could see, only corridors and a few open doorways, though remembering the outer wall, that could be deceiving. Indeed, soon a new doorway formed where the Seneschal waved his hand. He motioned for her to enter and spoke: "This is one of the reception halls where you may try your luck. Enter one of the chambers on the wall. We shall talk more after, if you are a true Hero. Otherwise, there's not much more I can tell you."

Sasha stared at the wall. There stood eight black obelisks. All had a rectangular segment slid to the side, revealing hollow interiors. She didn't even ask what would happen if the Hall would fail to recognize her, whatever that meant. At this point it mattered little. She clambered inside the closest obelisk with the last of her strength. The door slid shut behind her.

The inside was familiar, though the last time she'd been in one it had been lying on its side. Also, this one didn't stay dark. The lid turned transparent, showing the room behind. The Seneschal tilted his head curiously. Sasha felt an odd sensation, like something tickling all over her skin.

It was over in an instant. The Seneschal had disappeared from the doorway. He was now sitting leisurely on a bench by the wall next to three pedestals, each a meter high. She'd lost time, but she was back, now. Better yet, she didn't hurt. She looked at her legs, felt her arm. Everything was healed, just like her last time in an obelisk. That had to be a good sign.

Seams appeared on the lid and it slid open again. The Seneschal stood up as she stepped out. He smiled his vague smile: "The Hall recognizes and remembers you now, Hero Sasha. If you have more questions, now would be the time."

"What the hell is going on here?" she demanded.

The Seneschal gave a brief chuckle, then he told her. She listened, thought, processed. One word came to mind:

"Preposterous."

The man shrugged. "Be that as it may, it is the truth. Now, if you would like to take care of your curse, approach the pedestals."

She did as instructed, and as she got close, the tops of the pedestals came to life with text. Green, yellow, and red. "Easy," "Normal," and "Hard". The latter was circled.

With disbelief, Sasha glanced back at the Seneschal. He made a reaching motion with his hand. She moved to touch the green text. The red circle disappeared, and a green one appeared on her chosen pedestal. She felt a tingling all over her healed body. Somewhere outside, the dragon roared.

The Seneschal mused calmly: "Don't worry about that. You'll find that it got frustrated with there being no longer anything of interest here and took off. The constructs react particularly quickly to such things. Here, let me show you the rest of the facility. It's all yours now, for the foreseeable future."

The foreseeable future. The scope of that had shortened quite a bit this day. But one thing seemed certain.

She now held more power than anyone since the fall of the Heroes of old, whoever they may have been in truth. Power to become what she'd only dreamed of.

If it was enough to remake the world into a kinder, gentler, more just place, she did not know. But there was only one way to find out.

PART III

11

YRIN STRUGGLED TO KEEP UP with his longer-legged companions. "Slow down, will you. I don't want to get left behind in elven lands," he complained half in jest. He would have a handicap in dealing with the locals on his own, that much was true, but with a mere wave of his wand he could command the same respect as the other Heroes.

Valarin, the elven warrior mage, paced himself. "Oh, sorry. I forget." Yrin recalled this was Valarin's first quest, so the mistake was understandable.

Ryak, on the other hand, scoffed. The human rogue had a personality to match her chosen occupation. "I'll scout ahead then," she said, pulled up her hood, and disappeared.

In other circumstances scouting might've been a legitimate reason to eschew their companionship but these were safe elven lands. Well, they were safe now, the troupe just having dispatched the dark wizard Garguan who'd been wreaking havoc on the area. The poor elves were no match for Heroic magics and had called for help. Luckily none was the wiser as to the origin of their plight. The wizard had covered his tracks appropriately.

"Yrin," continued Valarin, "what're we to expect when we get to Greenhold?"

"Right, well, the good people there will obviously be pleased that we rid them of Garguan. They'll probably put up an instant feast or something, with the local Council, priests, and all."

"Sounds official," Valarin said with a frown.

"To start with, but even the elves can relax as the evening progresses. You in particular should have no trouble finding a wench or two, if you'd like," Yrin teased. "As for me, well, such things have happened before, though mostly when an elven teen has felt it appropriate to shock her parents. They do have puberties, too. Failing that, Ryak's just going to have to warm my bed."

The rogue materialized some five meters forward and to the side, raising her eyebrow towards Yrin.

Yrin smirked. "Just checking if you were still paying attention, dear."

Ryak chuckled and turned back towards their destination but did not disappear. Maybe she was just conserving power, but Yrin was already getting his hopes up. They had adventured together several times already, and this was the first time he'd gotten a real chuckle out of her.

"You mentioned priests. What was the official story on religion, again?" Valarin asked, biting his lip nervously.

Ryak slowed down, turned her head, and said: "Don't you worry your pretty little head with that. Just talk pompously, avoid saying anything too exact, and follow their lead. It'll be fine."

"Yes, evading the subject is best," Yrin confirmed. "But just so you can play the part, the short of it is that we're the Celestials' chosen people put here to provide inspiration and example, as well as to counter the monsters and machinations of the dark gods on this plane."

Ryak frowned, but this time it wasn't at her companions. "I've never liked the appeals to divinity. I get it, and I'm not going to go and ruin it for everybody or anything, but it seems tacky. The elves seem to be catching on, even. They're paying lip service, all right, but the younger ones don't seem to take to it as much."

Yrin nodded along. "You're not wrong. It'll be interesting to see how the elves develop in the future. For our part we'll just keep it vague."

Valarin smiled faintly. "I can be vague."

Ryak and Yrin laughed together at that. "Don't worry," the dwarf said, still chuckling, "the worst that can happen is that you'll say something dumb and they'll take it as divinely ordained."

•   •   •

Morning came with its headaches. Yrin found himself sharing a bed with Ryak, indeed, but with little recollection of whatever that might have transpired. Valarin was nowhere to be seen.

Yrin sat up and held his head. Then he noticed his and Ryak's wands on the desk next to the bed. They were both pulsing.

Shit. This could mean one of several things, but mostly just one. Yrin touched the base of the wand near his temple, taking the message through bone conduction.

"Attention Heroes. Due to concerns over portal stability, please return to the Hall or the nearest obelisk for recall until the issue ..."

Yrin dropped the wand. As a subproject lead, he'd managed to get a glance at the contingency plans for a draft. This was it. Sure, the portal issue might be real, but would he stake his life on it?

Unlike the bulk of the lesser nobility, Yrin had done his homework. If the situation had escalated that much, the complacent, declining Authority faced probable defeat. It would not go down quietly or quickly, however, and nobles lacking the good grace to die valiantly in the process would face almost certain execution. The propaganda term was "complicity in crimes against humanity".

Except that he wasn't complicit. His work was pretty sure to merit the real deal, and any pleas of mercy would fall on deaf ears.

He'd entertained the idea, of course, to get out of the way of the looming conflict and hide away on an obscure world. One not too many outside the elite even knew existed. Some might have heard rumors, sure, but anything definite like location and portal codes? Not a chance. Leaks were plugged with extreme prejudice, codes revoked.

The trouble was he hadn't really thought things through that much. Just enough that when push came to shove, he picked treason in a heartbeat. Precious little margin for further refinement of the plan.

He cursed not taking the threat seriously enough, made more preparations. He would've preferred an elven body if he was going to have to inhabit the Realm for extended periods of time. The expected lifestyle of an elven mage was more alluring than that of a dwarf. It was too late to swap bodies now, though.

Luckily, Yrin's present identity wasn't without its own advantages. He had an impressive reputation where he had roamed, and there was a fledgling dwarven colony nearby where he happened to know that the seeders had hidden a particularly prodigious amount of mixed ores. It wouldn't be a proper fantasy realm without absurdly rich dwarven mines, after all.

He tapped his temple with the wand again, now with the business end, and activated the developer backdoor to the upload nanoware. After being given the semblance of a choice, any stragglers would no doubt be dealt with forcibly. Now he was cut off from the system.

Yrin glanced at Ryak, then shook his head. He didn't know her well enough to suggest treason. He'd rush her into the nearest obelisk, ladies first and all, and make haste toward the colony, never touching another obelisk again.

Well, never say never. He might need to hack one if he was to survive on this world.

He shook his companion awake. "Ryak, bad news."

Ryak opened her eyes, took one look at him and palmed her face. "Tell me about it."

12

"WHAT THE FUCK, YRIN?"
It was barely a question, more like a statement of fact. Having barged into his lair again, that's what remained of the elaborate rants she had mulled over during her flight back from the Hall. Now that she'd had a bit of time to digest the true nature of her world, Yrin's complicity in it all was evident. "What. The. Fuck."

Yrin sat meekly by his workbench, leaning onto it, cupping the lower half of his face in his hands. "Since you're back alive to ask me that, you have a pretty good idea already, don't you. But it's fair, it's fair," he said with a sigh.

"Do you even know the meaning of the word? You *made* this. For your entertainment. You made *this*!" Sasha yelled arms wide, trying to encompass the totality of the world.

"Yes," he answered, quiet but resolute. "I know. Though it was not me, but my civilization that made this. I did play a small part, true. I've had to live with it for centuries, now. Do you think I haven't realized by now? Why do you think I helped you? Do you think me that callous?"

"I don't know!" she started to shout, but then lowered her voice again: "How could you, how could anyone? How can I believe anyone capable of that could still become a decent person?"

Yrin raised a finger. "Entitlement. We were raised as an absolute aristocracy, to view outsiders as our playthings at best. It is not so different from the worse nobles of your world, except that we could isolate ourselves even more effectively from the common folk and had far more power than we could think good uses for. I was a decent person then, very decent, I was—by the standards by which I was raised. Just as the elves were being very decent in their barely restrained impulse to kill you. I am a decent person still, only now by quite a different standard, refined through hardship of my own. I hope you'll come to see that."

"Maybe I should. I don't know if I can, not right now. I had to come see for myself that you were still … you. Damn! You know what, I can't stay here, I have a bone to pick with the elves as well, if I'm to be the Hero this world needs. I'm going to practice forgiveness on them first. They only ever tried to *kill* me. Will you give me fresh Dust for a new flier or shall I top off my own ride by burning down a patch of your forest? Because I will."

"You'll have it outside," Yrin said with a nod. "Talking to them might actually be a very good idea, if you're determined to play the Hero's part. You should know I've been keeping an eye on their movements with long range drones. It's been expensive, but I wanted to make sure they wouldn't follow you to my doorstep en masse. Well, they haven't, but I suspect they might be gearing up for an attack on Kilnkeep."

"What? How? Since when?" Sasha exclaimed, already expecting the worst.

"I had an inkling before you left, I admit. We couldn't do anything about it then, so I chose to not let it distract you. They've recently gathered their forces near the border. I'm pretty sure they're doing exercises, and it could be just that, sure. However, they've been doing some deep reconnaissance in the human lands since before the gathering, I think. It's hard to tell for sure with my spotty surveillance, but that's my best guess."

Sasha winced. There was just one question left: "Why?"

Yrin drew a deep breath that already betrayed him sharing Sasha's suspicions. "I have no inside knowledge, but a coincidence is not likely. They're sure to be pissed, and their wounded prides could make them susceptible to arguments that they've underestimated the humans as a threat. They underestimated you, after all."

The newly minted Hero blinked. One wayward person was all it took, after all. Strategizing with Yrin would be the smart thing to do, but she wasn't up to it, not at the moment. Besides, the matter was already time sensitive. She could come up with a plan en route.

As Sasha wordlessly turned around and started to storm back up the stairs, Yrin shouted behind her: "What about my people, then? You didn't fly in with them, I see."

Sasha stopped in her tracks. In her righteous anger, she'd completely neglected to mention the fates of the four brave souls sacrificed for her ascension. Through her grimace, she managed to speak: "Dead. The necromancer, with his minions. They're also dead. I took your advice on that." A pause. "For their loss, I am sorry," she worded precisely, and resumed her ascent with a single tear in her eye.

"I see," said Yrin solemnly. "Be careful, and your welcome here stands, you should know."

For that, she didn't break her stride.

•   •   •

Back up in the air, Sasha tried to cool off. Confronting the elves on a combative footing would do nobody any good. She was now a true Hero, truer than this sorry world had ever seen, and intended to act accordingly. She'd fly right into Greenhold and set down near the Council chambers. She'd want to wow them into believing that she'd ascended into Herohood. If there was anything that'd make them listen, it would be that.

It was a calculated risk, of course. They might decide to try and shoot her down before she'd be able to get a word in edgewise.

That's where the immortality came in handy.

She hadn't still quite internalized that part, but it explained all of the old legends, even the implausible ones. If she'd die, some special type of resilient Dust inside her head would transfer her mind into a new body. She didn't look forward to the experience, but by this point she'd seen enough that she didn't doubt it worked.

Following her path backwards from above wasn't trivial, but the craft had a compass needle and she had better maps again. The Seneschal had provided them to her, mentioning that they were regularly updated to keep up with expansion and other changes. Apparently there were devices high above the world surveying the lands. Just a few months ago she might've been in awe of the concept. Now she had just taken it in stride.

Sasha sharpened her eyes. There was the river with the elven lands beyond, and somewhere around there she had crossed it earlier. She took the flier a measure higher. Getting as far as Greenhold before being shot down was a priority at this point. Plan B would be more effective that way.

It wasn't long before the elven settlement loomed below. Sasha let the flier keep its altitude until she was over the very center of it. She could only imagine the faces below as she directed the craft to slowly spiral downwards.

Checking the power levels, Sasha determined she should have enough to get back to Yrin's if she wanted to. She'd chosen a heavy model with decent range. Could've likely made it here without the extra power from the dwarf. However, the flier would've been quite drained by now, and Sasha didn't want to expose even the existence of the quick empowerment trick. Going in with only a half-drained flier gave her options.

Slowly she started to make out more of the detail. Crowds were gathering, but they cautiously kept back from the Council Hall. In fact, the building's abandonment seemed suspiciously complete and total. One would expect some sort of a welcoming committee. Sasha activated her visor.

Several groupings of colored splotches appeared below. There they were, at the ready. Soon she'd be in range if they wanted to take the first shot. She thought it unlikely. Fliers had only one source in the lore. The elves would be unlikely to attack a presumed Hero, fearful though they might be.

She slowed the flier down and tightened the circle as she descended, propellers rising towards the sky and lengthening to keep the contraption airborne. Once she'd reached the rooftop level without anyone assaulting her, she designated a spot for a landing. The flier made a slight move upwards to lose some speed while reorienting its propulsion again and used some of its Red Dust to soften the landing. She'd settled down in between the hidden troops.

She wouldn't want the elves reverse-engineering her transportation. Eventually she might even share the magic, but for now a peek would be all they'd get. She told the flier to slowly disintegrate into a gray pile on the ground, and then stepped off in calm, measured movements.

In one hand, she held her wand. In another, her staff. The former was pointed peacefully at the ground, the latter up towards the sky. She turned her head to look directly at the nearest invisible cohort.

"I am Hero Sasha. Take me to the Council. I would have words with them."

A moment passed. One of the elves blurred into normal view to address her. "Is that so. Wait, what? Stop!" Something struck Sasha from behind. The familiar feeling of her life draining away embraced her. She smiled. Plan B would be all the more impressive, after all.

As she fell, the voice admonished someone, who countered with something about a standing kill order. The latter voice seemed familiar. Familiar and satisfied, like its owner had just had a fond wish granted.

The darkness came, but this time it was her friend.

•　　　•　　　•

Sasha had prepared for the eventuality of her death and resurrection by investigating the obelisks near Greenhold. She had visited one well inside the city. It had been in a closed up cavern used as a storage cellar of sorts. There was no indication on how fortified the cellar was, and how well guarded. She'd want to play her hand close to the chest when it came to the obelisks. If she appeared out of nowhere where there was clearly no way in, her transport network might be found out and put under guard.

The one she had chosen instead was situated outside of the city proper, inside a small cave in a stony hill. The entrance overlooked a glade that was used as a park by the locals. If she was careful, it would be much less likely that she'd be caught here in the obelisk's immediate vicinity.

The screen was already active as she snapped back into consciousness. Nobody was present outside the obelisk. She checked her equipment: a basic tunic, trousers, and an elven style cloak under which she could hide her human visage. Using a part of her modest startup Dust allowance she made herself a fake cranium, put it on, and pulled the hood over.

She slipped out as soon as the door opened at her command. The obelisk immediately closed up behind her, sealing the door as if it was never there. Sasha carefully peeked out to the glade. Nobody there. She guessed the flier had piqued the curiosity of most and drawn them into the city. There hadn't been time for the crowds to dissipate yet.

Walking briskly as a compromise between speed and suspiciousness, she made her way towards the Council Hall again. As she got closer, she started to see groups of elves talking excitedly with each other. Luckily they were too engaged to pay much attention to her slipping past.

Listening in as she went, the most popular theory was that it was a secret flight project now presented to the Council. The return of the Heroes was a common theme of discussion as well. Suggestions that the humans or dwarves could have done this and come to deliver ultimatums were also made once or twice, but they weren't taken very seriously. Still, there were some murmurs: "Well, you would discount the humans, but what about that one that ran away?" "Yes, and why would we be mobilizing if they did not threaten us?"

She'd have been interested in that discussion, but slowing down could only serve to compromise her cover before she'd gotten to where she was going. At least she knew that her escape was public knowledge, now, and that humans were being taken more seriously because of it. Seriously enough to think an attack would be in order? Some of the people here seemed to think so.

Nearing the plaza she had to squeeze in through the crowds, but people were still too busy with wonderment to pay much attention. The crowd thinned sharply as she got within a few dozen meters of the Council Hall. Sasha could see her landing site, but the elves had already moved her body somewhere. There was a crew cleaning up the leftovers of her craft into cages they'd brought up in case it would still try to do something. Smart thinking. *Come to think of it ...*

The elves jumped back, drew their wands, and pulled some Dust off of their belts. Sasha's Dust had started leisurely coalescing into a cube. Though the stuff already in a sealed cage tried to join the larger whole, it gave up in a moment to form its own, smaller cube.

Some of the crew were quick on the uptake and started to glance around in suspicion. Sasha let her fake cranium melt away, walked past the invisible line separating the crowds from the hall, and pulled back her hood. In the legends, the Heroes had always presented themselves quite confidently. Now she knew why. The rush of having just been killed and resurrected, the certainty that she could not be harmed by these people. "As I said," she intoned loudly, "I would have words with the Council. Take me to them."

An instant of frozen astonishment later, the wands snapped to point at her, but she could see them shaking. "The kill order is already satisfied, I would think. In any case, I doubt the Council would condone *another* attempt on the life of the first Heroic ambassador to enter these lands in ages," she noted dryly.

The weight of her words lowered one wand, then another, and soon the rest of them. One elf, the one who had addressed her before she'd been killed, spoke to another one: "Go tell the Council they have an urgent visitor. Now."

Then he turned to Sasha. "Of course, Hero Sasha. I apologize for the ... inconvenience. I believe you know of Jarin, your assailant. She is detained for the time being already. The Council will decide how to deal with her due to the extraordinary circumstances. You may make your demands, if any, to them."

Sasha gave the man a slow nod. Plan B was working like a charm so far. "I would like my belongings back, and my staff returned to working order. It has been disabled by Jarin."

The man fidgeted uncomfortably at that. "Would you, perhaps, see the Council first, please?" he pleaded. "It should not be long now. I am certain they can clear this little misunderstanding up in no time."

Graciousness was a luxury she could afford, now. "Fine. May I wait inside on the benches?" she asked while already taking slow but deliberate steps towards the doors.

"Of course, honored guest," the man said while hurrying to gesture at his people to make way for her. A few of the elves nearest to the hall made their way inside first. The rest quickly shuffled aside and let her pass.

She strode in like she owned the place and sat on a nearby bench. It was much more comfortable than standing around with three guards hovering over you. Mind you, there were still guards, but they stayed a discreet distance away. The leader had also followed in her wake and had taken a nearby position as if ready to attend to her.

Sasha considered asking for refreshments, but decided against it. No need to antagonize the guy, especially as he had been the one to prefer her alive for the time being. The kill order would probably get Jarin off the hook, though. The elves were by and large sticklers for protocol, even if some of them could acknowledge changes in circumstances warranting further consideration. She could either try to contest that or gracefully let the matter rest.

Only one of these actions would have a chance at being productive. It was the same one she hated the thought of, but she had come here to make peace with the bastards, after all.

It wasn't long, this time, before an elf emerged to invite her into the Council chambers. He looked vaguely familiar, but she couldn't be sure if he was the same as before. No matter. She followed the man into the corridor and her attendant followed her in turn. The rest of the guards remained behind. Good, they didn't want to be overly confrontational. Not that the Council were defenseless by themselves.

The man before him took a quick step to the side after entering the chambers and announced them: "Proclaimed Hero Sasha and Captain Dorien of the guard."

Proclaimed, huh? It sounded like there was a silent "self" prepended to the announcement. At least she knew where she stood. The elves were a suspicious people, not to be easily swayed by an outsider. But she would try.

Sasha walked up to the point where she'd stood before, bowed, and started again with the rote greeting in old Elven. Speaker Faran stood up to respond in kind, using the same words as Sasha. He was not talking down to her this time around, but addressing her as an equal. That was new.

The man sat down again, pursed his lips for a moment, and spoke: "So. You have found some of the secrets of the Heroes of old. We are, of course, always curious for new information. What is it that brings you back to us?"

"It is not just the secrets I have found. I am the rebirth of the Heroes, commanding the full power of the Hall. As such, I have taken it upon myself to work towards peaceful coexistence of all the people of the known world. To that effect, I would first present my sincere hope that the military exercises to the east are just that."

There were telling glances around the table, accompanied by barely perceptible nods by most of the members. Senna, the grayed woman on the left, even smiled a bit with the corner of her mouth. She had been one of the more agreeable members even before. There was worry in her eyes, though. The speaker concluded the silent exchange: "But of course they are. We do have to keep in shape."

She heard an attending elf behind her scuttle away, possibly to relay new orders. The immediate threat had been averted, but she'd need to tread carefully to keep it that way.

"Good," she said with a forced smile. "I would also like to open negotiations on restarting collaboration with other races, at a measured pace, of course. Your society is quite advanced, and the others would have much to learn from you. Trade would benefit elvenkind as well. Mundane matters would require less of your attention if you allowed the humans and the dwarves to provide some of your more base requirements."

"It is as you say, but such arrangements would make us unacceptably reliant on outsiders," Tyr—the bald conservative on the right—retorted. "Your scheme would weaken elvenkind's hold of its own destiny."

"My scheme is to strengthen and enrich the whole of the known world, elvenkind included," Sasha insisted. "As such, though our deeper magics are beyond mortal ken, I am more amenable than my predecessors to sharing some of the less dangerous secrets of the Heroes."

Speaker Faran's frown betrayed his disappointment, his route to immortality transparently blocked. "It may be so," he said, "and we will give your suggestions due consideration. However, us being the most magically adept culture in the known world, we stand to gain the least from your undoubtedly generous contributions. More flexibility in what you could bring to the table would improve the odds for a mutually beneficial solution."

"I am willing to be flexible on many things, but the secrets that define a Hero are not mine to give," Sasha lied brazenly.

"I see. Was there anything else you wish to say, before we deliberate?" the speaker asked.

Might as well get it over with. "I hope my host family has not been ill-treated due to my escape. By now it should be clear that no normal means will hinder me from my goals, though it's a shame I had to betray them like that. As a sign of good faith, I will likewise bear no grudge against Jarin, who was only following orders in attacking me. I would like my belongings back, though, with my father's staff restored to working order." As she spoke, the speaker was again glancing over at the other members. Nods were again in the majority, with Senna opposing and Tyr assenting. Whatever it was about, it couldn't be good.

As Sasha started to glance behind her, a restraining Dust collar snapped on her neck and squeezed tight on her arteries. She pulled her wand, but distracted by the chokehold she was quickly relieved of it from behind. "Careful," admonished the speaker as she fell on her knees, weakening by the second. "She is more dangerous dead than alive."

•   •   •

When Sasha came to, she was being carried down a flight of stairs, bound and stripped of any magical artifacts.

"Shit," she murmured, then raised her voice: "Let me go this instant. I am a Hero of the Hall!"

"Apologies, Hero, but orders are orders," hedged Dorien, one of her two carriers. He even sounded sincere. Perhaps she shouldn't have demonstrated so much understanding of people only doing what they'd been told. It hadn't taken long for that one to come back to bite her.

So much for being invulnerable just because she was immortal and commanded impressive magics. She'd been too pissed about the recent revelations to think things through properly, allowing her eagerness to show Yrin who the actual Hero was to cloud her judgment.

She hoped Yrin might somehow manage to slip in an assassin for her, but relying on that would be foolish. No matter, she'd get out of this. She'd just have to die. How hard could that be?

The elves dragged her to the basement floor of the Council Hall and into a barren room with two sturdy wooden chairs and a table. One of the chairs had restraints all over it. Hers, no doubt.

Indeed, the guards strapped her in carefully, though not too tightly to restrict the flow of blood. She managed to glance at the feet of the chair. It was bolted to the floor. The elves didn't mess around when it came to immobilizing their prisoners.

After she was thoroughly constrained, Dorien stepped back to curtly inform her that somebody would be with her soon. He and the nameless elf left, barring the door behind them.

It took an hour or so for the elves to either decide how to approach interrogating her, or to just let her simmer in her restraints. She used the time to futilely think of ways to escape. The situation didn't afford her much flexibility. She could attempt to bite off her tongue and choke on it but that seemed unlikely to work. She'd save it as a last resort.

She missed Stefan. At least he could've been counted on to eventually kill her. Now she wasn't even sure if old age would get her. She'd have to ask Yrin—or the Seneschal—when she got away. Hopefully it wouldn't take the better part of the century.

Finally, somebody pulled the latch. In shambled a wrinkled elven man, partly grayed around the temples. Sasha hadn't seen such marks of age in Greenhold before, not even in the Council. He stretched a bit and sat down on the other chair, the one with fewer safety features.

"So. We would be very curious to know how you got your hands on Heroic magic," he opened directly.

"Bite me," Sasha replied, directly.

"We would not do that yet. We would prefer to do this the civilized way. But you must understand. Flaunting resurrection like that, when all the while people are needlessly dying of injury, sickness, old age. We must have it, for the good of elvenkind, and we will not be infinitely patient," the man explained.

Shit. The elves actually had a point. She certainly didn't like the idea of withholding life-saving magics, but what was the alternative? Letting them all into the Hall? It *would* work on all of elvenkind, Heroborn that they were. *Maybe* the elves could even avoid infighting, those getting to the Hall first ascending to dominate the rest. But after that? They could cleanse or subjugate the rest of the world in a heartbeat. Sasha simply couldn't trust their civilization with that much power.

When her eyes refocused on the old man, he tilted his head. "I see I have given you something to think about," he commented.

"Yes, I sympathize. Nevertheless, the secrets are not mine to share," she maintained. "I doubt the magic would even work for old age or sickness," she lied, hoping to lessen the allure.

The man smiled thinly. "I doubt your doubt, given how long the Heroes of old were reputed to live. But I believe you when you say you sympathize. Good. We can build on that."

He did, talking at length of specific tragedies that had befallen elven families. Children orphaned by disease, parents burying their children, mothers dying in childbirth, people suffering in terrible agony until death finally took them, others killing themselves to avoid such a fate. All avoidable, if Sasha would just relent. She could only resist by thinking of Yrin, putting her faith in his work to save everyone, not just the elves, not just the Heroborn. She only hoped Yrin was sane enough to actually have a chance at accomplishing his goals.

Eventually, the man informed her that it was night, and she would be allowed to sleep on the day's conversation. An aide came in to feed her some porridge. She cooperated. Trying to starve herself to death was an option, but the elves would almost certainly force-feed her. That was not something she was keen on experiencing. Besides, she'd need her wits about her, not weakened by hunger.

Falling asleep on the chair was surprisingly easy with her mental exhaustion.

•　　•　　•

"Hello," said a familiar female voice as she came to. "I have been waiting for you to wake up. They asked last night if I would be willing to come and have a talk. You had expressed some regret about how things turned out the last time, I gather."

The night's dreams had been of drowning children reaching out to her, of gangrenous patients stretching their remaining limbs in her direction, all of them asking why she wouldn't help them. Del's soothing voice was a welcome lifeline.

"Hello," she said with a tired smile. "I see you gave birth. How did it go?"

Del seemed pained, distant. "There were two. One of them is with the Stars, now. The remaining one, at least, is healthy. As am I, though the birth was difficult. It often is for our kind, though we have some magics to aid things along."

"Oh, I'm so sorry," Sasha exclaimed. She should have expected that. They'd send Del because her loss could be used against their uncooperative prisoner.

"It is not your fault. You could not have helped it then. Are you sure, though, that you cannot help others in the future?" Del probed.

Sasha gulped and looked down in silence for a while. "There is a plan in the works for the future, but for right now, I cannot help you, not like this," she finally said, admitting some of the truth, trying to convey some hope.

Del lightened up, if only slightly. There was a measure of trust there. "But it is true that you are immortal? They explained what happened with you earlier."

"Yes," Sasha confirmed.

Del nodded thoughtfully. "They will torture you eventually, you know, unless you relent and give them what they want. I ask you again, will you not do so?"

"No. I'm sorry, I can't," Sasha repeated. She wasn't quite sure if she could stand torture, but she'd go as long as she could, anyway. Who knows, maybe they'd get overeager and kill her by accident.

"Very well. It is as I thought. I am sorry, this is going to be a bit rough," Del said, stood up from the visitor's chair, and leaned over to Sasha. "See you around," she added, looking her in the eye. Then she pressed her lips onto Sasha's.

The sensuality of the moment was ruined by the contractions of Del's diaphragm and the uncomfortable grunts from her throat. Even so, once the Dust started flowing from the elf's mouth into hers, Sasha knew it would be the kiss by which all the kisses of her life would be measured.

She could already feel the Dust working in her throat as Del withdrew with water in her eyes. "Thank you," Sasha managed to croak before her throat was unusable. A guard burst into the room just as she fell into death's sweet embrace. Had there been less pain, she'd have been wearing a smile.

•　　　•　　　•

The obelisk at the glade welcomed her again. After breathing a sigh of relief she called up the obelisk network. In easy mode, she could access any of them. She picked the obelisk nearest to Yrin's lair. Despite him taking one for himself, there was one within decent walking distance. Perhaps it had regrown, or perhaps Yrin had taken one further away not to give the network too much of a hint of his location.

It was time to swallow her pride and go get the old Hero's advice.

13

THE SHIFT IN SASHA'S VIEW was sudden as the obelisk network whisked her to her destination. She knew she'd lost some twenty minutes of time along with her old body again. That still felt weird, but she was slowly getting used to it.

She exited the obelisk into a natural cavern which continued downwards into darkness. Less interested in exploring strange dungeons than the Heroes of old, she chose the upward slope with the light at the top. Yrin's keep would be another twenty minutes' walk from here.

Having gotten rid of her nemesis and now giving off a pacifying aroma for the wildlife, Sasha could traverse the wilderness in peace. The Seneschal had explained the curse and the charm to operate on pheromones, some subtle smells that provoked a reaction in the engineered species of this land.

Cursed people gave off a scent that would, depending on context and the individual, cause aggression or at least a vague sense of the carrier being more expendable than usual. On the flip side it could sometimes cause excitement as well. Monsters and wild animals were affected the most, whereas domesticated species and player races had their reactions tuned down.

Initial testing had concluded that this wasn't difficult enough, so the production of the pheromones had been set to permanently increase under extreme stress. Likewise, Dust had been hacked to replicate them so that "munchkins" wouldn't have an easy time of it.

The charm, on the other hand, gave off a scent that would calm and pacify people and animals in the immediate area. There was no escalation there, just a steady smell of good fortune.

Protected under the aegis of the charm, being immortal, and the devious elves not being a problem in this neighborhood, Sasha didn't even bother with a wardstone. It was liberating to run through the forest with no worry in the world—none, at least, that concerned her immediate safety. Despite the larger problems she was facing, she felt a smile appear on her lips as she ran.

She made good time to Yrin's lair, which, wouldn't you know it, was open. A dwarf was standing by the door. Ermil, as she recalled. His face was gruff but his weapon sheathed. He raised his hand in greeting.

As Sasha got to talking distance, the man addressed her: "Hero Sasha. I am Ermil, Yrin's second now, what with the loss of Byron. I trust he and his comrades died well and for a good cause."

Ermil's expression indicated that he might've had doubts of the latter, at least. "They died in combat against superior numbers, taking down many enemies before their own fall. I will do my best to honor their sacrifice," Sasha said solemnly. *Better skip the part about half of them dying before they could do anything.*

"Good," came the icy reply. "Now, Yrin does bid you welcome here, so welcome you are." The man turned on his heels and strode in. Sasha followed him down to the lab, where he merely pointed with his hand and continued on his own way.

The door was unlocked. Sasha entered to find Yrin seated on one of the workbenches as usual. What was unusual is he didn't appear to be tinkering with anything.

"You're back," Yrin said.

"Yes," she replied.

Their gazes danced around each other for a moment.

"So," they both started. He made a hurried gesture for her to continue. What she had intended to say had already slipped her mind, though. "Gruff man, but I guess I deserve it," she went, glancing back up the stairs where Ermil had gone.

"He's going to be good at his job, practical, he is. I have told him that the mission, though costly, was a success, and it'll be good for us in the long run. He's just being a bit skeptical as well as mourning his friends," Yrin explained. "Oh, we had a wake already. Didn't seem a good idea to put it off. Your absence was frowned upon at first, but I did explain that you had personally avenged the dead. Yes, and the bit about you being needed elsewhere to stop an imminent war. I also relayed the condolences of sort that you gave."

Sasha sighed, closing her eyes for a moment. "Yes. Thank you. You didn't have to do that."

Yrin shrugged. "Well, it was true enough, wasn't it? How did it go, then?"

"Well, I went in with the flier, wowing them appropriately. I presented myself as a Hero demanding audience. Then one of my old acquaintances killed me."

Yrin simply nodded, prompting her to go on.

"I was restored in a nearby obelisk, walked back, demanded audience again. I think I managed to get them to at least forestall any invasion while they think the situation through. They ..." Sasha paused. The next part was going to be embarrassing. Grimacing a bit, she admitted: "They managed to capture me and demanded the secrets of immortality."

Yrin was worried now, she could tell. He fiddled with his wand hand, making gestures in thin air. He could pull a wand out in a split second, she knew. "I do so hope you didn't *actually* bring an elven army back in your wake, did you?" he inquired politely.

"No. I told them nothing of you or the secrets of the Hall, and managed to escape when they tried to get to me through a friend. She'd been smart and kind enough to have made preparations to kill me. But I'll tell you right now, they made some really good points, hard to resist. I *am* basically dooming them all to die just because I can't trust them with the power. Are you sure your project can make everyone as Heroes, as you once said?"

Yrin nodded sagely. "It'll probably either do something like that or get everyone killed. Don't look at me like that. I'd have already finished, most likely, if I didn't try my best to avert the latter scenario. See, the hard part is making a godling. The damn hard part is making sure it wants to behave itself."

Right. A godling, whatever that was. By the sound of it, there was no lack of ambition there. "You want to create a living mind out of Dust and let it loose unto the world," Sasha speculated out loud, her eyes suspicious.

Yrin was elated. "Yes! Oh, but it is so nice to have someone who I don't have to explain everything to in the smallest of words, yes, it is. But you don't have to be so anxious about it. I said I was being careful. I have no interest in becoming the silly bloke who got three wishes from the literal-minded genie but never what he actually wanted."

"It's just a lot to take in, and I suppose the rewards outweigh the risks. Umm, maybe. I'm pretty sure I should reserve judgment until I've thought it through properly."

"Indeed. To allay your worries, I do have some relevant training and experience, even if I'm reaching into forbidden heights," the would-be godmaker consoled her. "Would that I had my usual toolkits down here, though. It would be nice not having to reinvent every little thing from scratch. But it couldn't be helped. The portal here doesn't accept extra baggage in addition to one's brain."

Sasha suddenly recalled another person, or whatever, who delivered wishes. "Oh, would it help if … is the … are you trying to replicate the Seneschal?"

"Oh no, that poor old bloke. No, he's just a human. Thoroughly conditioned to serve. Shit. Your arrival roused him, right? I'm not sure how well the safeguards on his conduct are working after so long, though he must've been in hibernation for most of it."

"He seemed as if he was happy enough to have company. As far as he could be happy about anything," Sasha said, remembering the man's empty expression.

"Right. Well, just treat him like you would a fellow human. It's probably a welcome change to him."

"*Of course* I will," Sasha exclaimed, then shook her head. There were more acute problems. They could talk about godlings and decent treatment of fellow humanoids later. "But back to the matter at hand. The elves clearly don't buy the ordained Hero story anymore, not from me. The situation on the border is probably still volatile. Any suggestions besides blowing up the Council Hall? Because I'm tempted."

"You could just change your look, you know. Maybe go in as an elf. That could go over better."

"I can do that?"

"Sure. Just ask an obelisk—a connected one—for the character editor, make your changes and the next time you're instantiated it'll be in the new body. It'll still be a hard sell long-term, seeing as you can only be in one place with one face at a time, but it could buy some time. And we really should think about rigging you a self-destruct spell," Yrin said, rubbing his beard as if already making plans on how to best end her life.

"We absolutely should," Sasha confirmed distractedly as her mind caught hold of an idea. Only one place? She was in two places already, just that one of them was a corpse. Which she herself had been before. Her gaze veered towards the obelisk laying down in the corner of the lab.

"Yrin," she said, pointing at the cylinder, "what would happen if a corpse I leave behind is put in there?"

Yrin's eyes went wide. "Oh. Should've seen it. Should've. It was a big taboo in my time for us nobles, and a closed door for me now, my access revoked, so I didn't. But Sasha, know that if you go down that way, any body I resuscitate will not be recognized by the Hall. Gene-tagged serial numbers, can't hack them with my limited control of the device, don't know what would happen if I could. They'll be cut off, mortal again, though my obelisk could still cure their ills if they get to it in time."

Sasha pondered this over. "Is it death, though, as much as memory loss, if I'm still here? It's just the new experiences that would be lost."

Yrin smiled weakly. "That perspective is true enough, yes. It's just that when loss of memory gets severe enough, it is likewise quite a lot like death."

So. On one hand, she would have to subject many alternate versions of her to mortality, even as they would still have the blessings of a charmed life and Yrin's device to heal them.

On the other hand, she could single-handedly be the revival of the Heroes this world sorely needed. She could imagine it, widespread advanced magics making life better for all. She'd seen a glimpse of it at Greenhold. She could be a stabilizing influence, put an end to wars, build a peaceful society with less suffering, perhaps soothe the elves' violent streak towards other races.

She hadn't really sought immortality anyway, she rationalized. Just a normal life of Heroism, which was exactly what was on offer, multiplied by as many times as she'd have the stomach for. It would still sting to wake up in one of the mortal bodies, she knew, but she could live with that. For a while, anyway.

"Let's do it," she decided a split second before her thoughts backtracked to the earlier subject of self-destruct spells. After some hesitation, she added somberly: "We'll all still need suicide spells. To avoid compromising you or the Hall through capture and torture."

The thought of suicide as an immortal Hero had felt nasty enough. Killing herself when the life being ended would be forever lost was a much darker prospect still. But she'd already individually made the decisions to wear a suicide apparatus as well as to split herself off into mortal offshoots. Mental inertia now worked in her favor to accept the conclusion that she might have to permanently kill some of her selves in the line of duty.

"Yes," said Yrin after some stalling of his own. He was no doubt catching up with her thought process. "Though you'd better be damn sure you have the will to go through with it. You can only trust them to the extent that you can trust yourself."

All too aware of this, Sasha sighed. "I can do it, knowing what I have already achieved, and what still remains to be done. Did you have suggestions on how to securely—and not overeagerly—arrange for a timer on my death, then?"

Yrin nodded. "Should be able to rig something together. Dust itself is very capable of working inside the body, actively mollifying local cells to ignore its presence, but getting the incantations right for anything subtle is challenging to say the least. For a quick and dirty solution, there's a timed explosive spell I have that could be inserted into your stomach. Should be able to easily cause enough damage for a quick death, yes. Normally the spell would have a limited time of operation due to the shady environment, however I have some experience in fixing that sort of thing," he mused, clearly excited at the prospect of ingested explosives.

Not equally convinced of the approach, she asked dubiously: "And how exactly would you power ... oh Stars, the burning incantation!"

"Yes, yes, but don't worry, I know how to make it work safely inside a body, target the appropriate materials. While I don't have my original work available on paper, I crafted a couple of simple test spells and tried them on neople long ago when it was still fresh in my memory. I could just copy the power supply part over from those. There isn't any risk of it going haywire," Yrin said. "My incantations for powering spells inside a body have been in production use since the dawn of time. If I didn't have a good handle on it, trust me, we'd know."

Sasha raised an eyebrow. "In use where?"

The dwarf suddenly seemed very, very small, more so than usual.

"Yrin ..." Sasha prodded.

Frustrated, the dwarf replied: "Fine, fine. No secrets anymore, yes, but let's try for no murderous rage either, shall we? It's a complex spell used for controlling the actions of lesser creatures. It won't work on higher ..."

"The necromancy spell!" Sasha interrupted. "You *made* the necromancy spell?!"

"Yes, yes, well, part of it, though really, originally it was just a parlor trick for pets."

"You're responsible for there being necromancers in this world?" Sasha reiterated, backing away slowly.

"Not strictly, no. See, they'd decided on the specification before I ever got involved. I was just a subcontractor, I was. You'd have gotten your necromancers regardless. Possibly ones that did lasting damage to their victims," Yrin tried.

"So perhaps without you my nemesis would've never been born," Sasha countered venomously.

"Oh. Ooh. That wasn't supposed to happen," she heard Yrin say as she stormed up the stairs once again, through the door, to the spiral staircase, and out of the complex. The doors still opened for her easily enough.

As she got out into the fresh air, she stopped and screamed her anger at the skies. Within a minute, the screams slowly turned into sobs, and she fell onto the mossy ground.

She could think again. Last time she let her anger towards Yrin's past deeds govern her behavior, it hadn't ended well. All the reasons to forgive him were still valid. Her need of his services was more urgent than ever were she to go through with the revival of the Heroes. The plan might be the best chance yet to stop the elves from razing humanity—or at the very least Kilnkeep—to the ground.

If she already knew she should forgive him again, that she likely could do so, should she not stop procrastinating and do it already? Or at least act like it, until reality caught up with the theory.

She stood up and walked back into the corridor. The doors closed behind her as she went. This time she dropped by the smithy first. The on-shift dwarves glanced at her from their work, gave curt nods of greeting, but otherwise ignored her. She took a small utility knife from the wall and walked back towards the lab.

Before she could enter the room, Ermil intercepted her. "I'm curious what you're planning on doing with the knife, there," he said, gesturing for a nearby guard to approach.

"I would've much preferred demonstrating to Lord Yrin himself, but this will do. Tell him the plan is on. There will be an elven Hero knocking on your door in an hour or so," Sasha said. Then she drove the knife deep into the side of her neck. Blood spurted, the world started to tilt and turn dark.

In her final moment of consciousness, Ermil looked at her aghast. *Good.*

•　　•　　•

Sasha woke up in the nearby obelisk and went to work on her appearance. There was no sense in manufacturing very many copies of her old self. One of those would do.

She told the obelisk to reform her as a handsome blond elf male of some forty years, though aged well. Twenty minutes and a subjective instant later, she input another body type for the next iteration; a female elf of around the same age, stout for one of their race but graceful nevertheless. There was no use reincarnating into her present form just to immediately change it again.

Thus prepared, Sasha sprang towards Yrin's keep in her new elven body. The longer legs made for good time, though she fell over a few times getting used to them. She'd have to pay more attention to walking when presenting this one to the actual elves.

Aside from the dimensions, the male body had other strange features as well. Sasha hadn't really thought through all of the implications when designing it. One of her would be stuck in a man's body for the rest of her life. It would probably be better to try and think of it as *his* life at that point. The thought was a bit strange, but she hoped she'd get used to it. It seemed important that the Heroes reborn represent all races and genders, not to mention that she'd want the resurgence to rouse the bare minimum amount of questions.

Soon enough the entrance was upon her. Ermil was standing guard again, though sword in hand, now. The precaution was probably his own idea. Sasha slowed down and stopped at a respectable distance. "Ermil," she said matter-of-factly.

Nonplussed, the other man replied: "Greetings, Hero. We were told to expect you. You may enter, but no tricks." He sheathed his sword.

It was evident the man hadn't been told all about the plan. That was probably for the best. Sasha wondered what story Yrin had cooked up to explain this.

•　　　•　　　•

Sasha stood before Yrin, eyes wide. "Blood sacrifice?!"

"Yes, well, since you just *had* to go ahead and slit your throat in front of him, I had to concoct *some* story for our cover. I trust Ermil, I do, but this caliber of secret needs to be aggressively contained. So yes, blood sacrifice to reopen the way for the rest of the Heroes back into our world, with yours truly acting as a loophole to make the sacrifice a non-permanent one. I did command him and the others who saw to keep even that hushed," Yrin explained while the other Sasha sat awkwardly by, rubbing her fully healed neck. She looked weirded out even if this was—cover story aside—exactly what she had expected. Or perhaps not; would she not also have expected to wake up in the forest instead? But here she was, mortal again.

"Excuse me," the Sasha who looked like one said meekly, "but I don't think I … we thought through what was going to be my place in this world if and when you decide to go back to your original body. Perhaps we should've passed on resurrecting one of these bodies. Not that I'm suggesting we fix it now …"

"I wouldn't worry about it too much," consoled Yrin. "The known world is big enough for a few, yes, it is. Besides, it would just add to your legend if you're in many places at once."

"But what if they figure out we're all copies?" asked the elven Sasha.

"Not very likely. It's a big step from noticing that there may be many Sashas around to suspecting that completely different people are the same as her. Mind you, I'm not suggesting we go out of our way to make more of that particular model, no. It is even reasonable to suggest that the primary Sasha here should just get used to wearing something else, leaving this first mortal copy with the consolation prize of having her actual old life back."

The Sasha-shaped Sasha smiled weakly at that. Thoughts of her old life gave rise to thoughts of home, of the people there, but they felt distant now. Her path had led her to find that while village mage was a respectable position, her destiny was grander if she could shoulder it. She caught the eyes of the elven Sasha. They shared a solemn nod.

Yrin went on: "Now, for this first clone this won't be necessary, but you will need to create a cover identity for each of your new, covert clones, of course."

Of course. The resurrected copy would have ample time to think on it for herself. Himself? Whichever. "I'll bring in a couple more elves. Though I will reintroduce multiracial teams, I think at this time we're going to need all the racial edge we can muster. It would still be good for plain Sasha to accompany us to create continuity," the elven Sasha decided.

Yrin nodded approvingly while the mortal Sasha hesitated for a few seconds. "Fine," she finally said. "I suppose they'll not be as keen on torturing me with elven Heroes by my side. But I want one of those suicide devices."

The elven Sasha hesitated, feeling her own pristine neck. "Uh. I'm getting used to getting killed, but if I'm going to be doing this a lot, do you have some method that might prove less traumatic long term?"

"Yes, of course. In fact, I can put you painlessly under with the obelisk right there as you may recall, and, uh, take care of it then," Yrin volunteered, eager to start with but losing some steam towards the end. The prospect of serial killing his protégé seemed unsettling even for him. He shook it off, though. "Did you want to do this now?" he asked, inching towards the obelisk.

"Yes, let's get it over with," Sasha said and walked over to the obelisk. It didn't open at her touch like the other ones did. "Do you mind?" she asked Yrin.

"Oh yes, of course," Yrin said hurriedly and waved his wand about. "I had to rejigger its control systems rather thoroughly, I'm afraid." The coffin opened and Sasha got in.

"Make it quick," Sasha asked in a wavering voice. Killing oneself in anger was one thing, but getting into a suicide booth under the control of somebody else was another. Any waiting could weaken her resolve, she feared.

"Right. Other Sasha, you don't have to look," Yrin said before the lid closed. Happily, there was no appreciable delay as Sasha's world darkened once again.

•   •   •

Sasha ran through the woods in her pristine, well-rested body. She had decided on her next body beforehand again. An older, distinguished-looking male elf, her own counterpart to the Greenhold Council spokesman.

She'd considered a woman. The elven society was somewhat egalitarian, after all. But only somewhat. She could recall Del's distaste for what she'd done for her, for taking the role of a pliable pregnant woman because that was what the others would believe.

But the third time had to be the charm, so she, too, played into the stereotypes. She swore she'd bring in more female leads later when the situation had been defused. For now, one fine female body would have to be enough—along with the base Sasha, of course.

She mused briefly about making a large army of Heroes of herself. What it would mean for her, running repeatedly across the forest to her death and resurrection. Either waking up mortal again or to run, once more, to her death.

She hadn't yet decided how many she should make. Enough to make a difference, but how many would that be? They could churn out dozens a day, if she were determined, but there might be a price for her humanity. And sooner or later the constant flow of Heroes might be tracked to Yrin. That could be bad.

Perhaps a modest amount in the hundreds would do. The Hall

would not create much of a monster menace for one charmed Hero. She'd mostly have to concern herself with the spreading knowledge, seeing it was put to good use, guiding the world towards tolerance and peace.

Failing the latter, she would have to be prepared for war as well. After her experiences with the elves, it would be naive to think that shows of force wouldn't be necessary. She'd need a way to arrange stashes of Dust far and wide. Technically, the obelisks would allow her to transport Dust from the Hall one obeliskful at a time, but that would become quite tedious.

Flying Dust from the Hall wasn't very practical either but could be done in principle. Large fliers took more energy, but their carrying capacity seemed to grow faster than the expenditure, at least to a point. And they could be recharged with the burning trick at the other end before hiding the constituent Dust away for future needs.

It would all need a lot of organizing and much of her clones' attention. Bothersome. Maybe some of it could be done through spellcraft. She would want to consult the resident expert on that as well.

The trip was coming to an end before she could wonder about that further. Maybe in another body. Or in both, rather. It would take some getting used to thinking about in terms of multiplying her selves.

•　　•　　•

"Ah, you are a sight. You didn't consider going for a more … accomplished individual next, though, for credibility?" Yrin asked.

Sasha gave him a look but couldn't put much exasperation into it. The dwarf had merely been echoing her own thoughts, after all. "Yes. The next one will be how the Council spokesman secretly wishes he looked like in his ripe old age. I suppose I'll go in there again, shall I?"

"Yes. Or you could try this suicide spell out. Or both, really. You could try it while inside, save us a bit of trouble lugging your corpse back in," Yrin suggested.

Sasha felt queasy in her stomach, but the human Sasha interjected from the side: "Don't worry. Me and Filamon here"—she nodded at the male elf—"didn't think much of Yrin's plan either. So I remembered the elven collar. We don't know what it was designed to do, but we could guess, right? And turns out if not the elves, the Hall library does have a spell for a killing collar."

"It was meant for restraining enemies, so I didn't think of it right away," explained the slightly embarrassed Yrin. "It should do, though. It has timer and command word options and it's tamper-resistant to boot. Well, it'll go off if seriously damaged, anyway. I have a few on test timers on top of that desk now," he pointed.

Sasha's gaze followed Yrin's and met the Dust collars. One had grown rotating spikes pointing towards its center, the spikes themselves sporting tiny thorns that churned unsettlingly along the edges. Sasha gulped and felt her throat. "I suppose it beats the alternative," she conceded.

"Indeed, it'll probably be quick. We can gold-plate the outsides of the final versions for you, though you'll have to be extra sharp about keeping it energized, then. Grab the spell from this core here, and your other selves wrote down the gestures in your particular script here," Yrin carried on, pointing out a piece of paper. "You'll note that we made the gestures for particular preset timers very distinct to avoid mishaps. A new timer setting will override the previous one, and there's the all around cancel. It'll vibrate and flash briefly to acknowledge new orders."

Sasha produced a couple of ovals of Dust from her belt and cast the spell on herself. The Dust obediently crawled around her neck, sending shivers down her spine. She unceremoniously cast a one minute delay, and started towards the obelisk. It opened up as soon as Yrin could raise his wand. Sasha settled herself in, lay down, and waited for death.

A minute could be quite a long time, it turned out. She had time to contemplate making a pact with herself to not tell the others how much the collar would hurt, but decided against it. It would set a bad precedent. Any future Sasha clones would know that Sasha would keep things from them, ostensibly for their own good. No, better to stay true to herself.

A small part of her regretted her decision as the blades ate into her neck, but on the whole, the pain was less than Del's improvised throat digger.

•   •   •

Sasha could have stayed behind to continue the cycle of death and rebirth, but making sure there'd be a witness for this historical meeting took priority. If all else failed, Sasha's collar would take her back to Yrin's mine—to create an attack force, if need be.

Early the following morning, Yrin had provided them with enough Dust for twin two-seaters that could take them to Greenhold and hopefully back again. This spared Sasha from having to lug Dust hauls from the Hall with the energy losses the trip would imply. Both the fliers and the resurrections had eaten noticeably into the dwarf's reserves, but he'd had an idea how she could repay him. It would even play well into Sasha's own plans.

While they were away trying to salvage the situation with the elves, Yrin would take a break from his other duties and get busy devising a magical Dust delivery system. Being able to use a sizable fraction of the Hall's power would allow him to experiment more efficiently, greatly accelerating his work.

Fliers would transport the material from the Hall under cover of darkness. Sasha would be needed for setting the system up, of course. With the understanding that she would divert most of the Dust elsewhere for the purposes of setting up the renewed Heroic presence in the world, she had readily agreed.

With rough plans for spreading her influence in place, she could concentrate on the situation at hand. Which was, again, below her in the form of the Greenhold Council Hall. To hopefully make their welcome a touch less strained, she dropped a few slowly gliding messenger drones from the Hall's stash of lore. Specifically made to avoid hitting any live targets, they repeated a simple message in the soft but firm voice of her latest elven body: "As ever, we come in peace, and ask for audience with the Council of Greenhold."

There was a stress on the plurality, just to be sure.

This time there were no crowds, but the cloaked guards were present in ever greater numbers. After her narrow escape from the interrogation chamber, the Council had probably warned their citizens to stay away if any new fliers appeared.

It was a wise decision. If they couldn't make the elves come around peacefully, Sasha was seriously entertaining the notion of the next round of talks being conducted by aerial shipments of Red Dust directly from the Hall. The glass roof of the Council chamber made for a good target.

With some effort of will, Sasha pushed the thought aside. There was still a place for diplomacy here, intended torture aside. Now she had tangible if fraudulent proof to back her claims of actual Herohood. As far as the elves would know, she was supported by an entire advanced civilization.

Again, the fliers were allowed to land in peace, but the receiving troops stood ready in formations. They again instructed their vehicles to dissolve before setting foot on elven soil.

Sasha's distinguished elven body was wearing a simple but elegant white robe with green linings. She had a mundane wooden staff with her, mostly for presence. The one going by Filamon and the woman, now Gwendolyn, were wearing more outdoorsy outfits: green fabric with light brown leather armor. The obligatory Sasha wore the same clothes she'd last died here in.

All wore a golden neck ring, primed to take their life in two hours unless they'd reset the timer. Considering the torture chamber, the collars had also been instructed to go off with a command word. This would eat more power than the simple timer, but they should last until the next day regardless. The collar would vibrate repeatedly when the energy stores were getting too low for the intended function to work reliably. Unless disengaged, it would then dig into the neck before dropping too low. To call it erring on the side of caution seemed somewhat ironic, but that's what the situation called for.

Thus fortified, Sasha felt fearless for her own sake. While she shared a portion of the others' concern for their potential final deaths, she couldn't fully sympathize. From her perspective, the clones were very new. If they died today, most of their life experiences would still go on in her. Even if memory loss was a sort of death, surely it would be a diminished kind, at least until the clones had accumulated more experiences of their own.

Certain that the thought had crossed the minds of her other selves as well, Sasha could see that it didn't take all the edge off. Perhaps trivializing the lives of her clones would be unwise, especially as she intended to make a lot more of them. Every time half of her would get to know first hand how it felt, going into danger while wearing the collar.

Sasha pressed into her mind an apology for her future mind-children. It was not, would never be, for her to belittle the courage it took.

Striking the ground once with her staff, the prime Sasha announced them to the invisible cadre of guards: "I am Castor, Elder among the Heroes returned. These are Gwendolyn and Filamon, my trusted aides. Sasha, our liberator, you know. We seek conference with the Elders, one more time." She put some stress on the last three words, giving some sense of finality to what was at stake this time around.

The one to decloak was again Dorien, though he had to make his way towards them from the other side of the building. "Greetings, revered guests. I will take you to the Council forthwith," he promised, making a hand gesture to his side. There were footsteps and a blurred outline of an elf in the air as one of Dorien's underlings proceeded to announce them.

Dorien invited the group to follow him. As they neared him, he commented in a lower voice, just short of conspiratorial: "I do apologize for the last time. I doubt the wise Council would repeat those orders in the present situation."

For an elf, the choice of words was bordering on mutinous. Each Sasha was thinking the same: if the order did come, Dorien wouldn't necessarily be there to carry it out, the Council's wisdom being suspect at that point. One never knew with the elves, but the stakes were high, and three fourths of the delegation *were* outwardly their brothers and sisters, not mere cousins as Sasha had pretended to be. Escalating elf-on-elf conflict was practically unheard of.

This time, Dorien took the group directly to the central corridor and to the Council chambers without bothering to wait being sent for. Either the possibility had been arranged for beforehand, or he was sending a strong signal to the Council as well.

"Liberator of the Heroes Sasha, Elder Hero Castor, aides Gwendolyn and Filamon," he went on to announce them himself, clearly giving precedence to Sasha and emphasizing her stated role. Perhaps he really was putting pressure on the Elders—or it was a part of a strategy to make it seem so, to minimize the damage done.

All four Heroes strode towards the flustered Elders, the immortal Sasha naturally managing to project more confidence than the other three. As had been arranged beforehand, the others stopped half a step behind her, leaving the Elder clone to do most of the talking. Tyr tried to raise his hand to say something, but speaker Faran silenced him with a decisive, cutting hand movement.

"Council of Greenhold," Sasha started without further ceremony, "there have been some misunderstandings here in these halls, but we are a patient people. Patient, but well prepared now for any further confusion that may arise."

Skipping the elven greetings seemed only prudent. Her limited scope with the language might be suspicious. As it was, she was doing her level best to mimic the elven way of speaking in the Common tongue. She'd blame interactions with the humans of the mixed Heroic society were she called on her less than perfect pronunciation. It wouldn't help her plan to promote cultural exchange, but it might be a necessary gambit regardless.

The speaker rose. "Indeed, Hero Castor. We do apologize for the ... unfortunate incident. The narrative seemed too fantastic to be real, I admit, with no evidence to back it up. I see now we were gravely mistaken."

Sasha nodded and cut to the chase, though not without an internal cringe about the appeal to divinity that was required: "While we do appreciate the precariousness of the mortal position and your zeal to improve your lot, the divide *is* divinely ordained and presently out of our hands. There is a plan underway to remedy the situation, though as I cannot provide any schedule or proof of this, I will understand if you remain skeptical on that count. As a sign of good faith, we are, however, willing to share any mundane healing arts and mortal healing magics, if we have any that are unknown to you."

Yrin and the Hall did have some medical knowledge and magics that were more advanced than what she'd learned from master Aaron. She was unsure how they would fare in comparison to the elven magics, but it was likely there would be something. The original Heroes had, among other things, managed to precisely set broken bones and provide a tight cast afterwards, allowing for faster healing. "For the challenge," Yrin had explained when she'd wondered why they'd bother. There had been fans of the hard core survival experience who eschewed obelisk use as far as they could, making do with the "primitive" Dust.

The wrinkles of old age in Faran's eyes seemingly more pronounced than usual, he continued Sasha's thought: "As long as we start to open up relations with the world at large, as Hero Sasha urged us to do, I presume."

Now was the time to be magnanimous, to secure what they most wanted while also sowing the seeds for the rest. "No. This much we offer freely without obligation, other than you not wavering from your proven and admirable non-aggression policy. Any further sharing of knowledge will, however, be contingent on gradual opening of the borders, much as things used to be when we last walked this world."

That raised many an eyebrow in the Council. After capturing and nearly torturing one of the Heroes' own, they hadn't expected to get such a good offer. Sasha hoped that would regain some of the moral high ground lost in withholding immortality.

"Your first gracious offer I think is uncontroversial enough for us to accept," Faran allowed, glancing around the table. "The other matter is not wholly undebatable either, I think, but will require seeking consensus with other Councils."

"That you take it under consideration is all I ask. I will note that regardless of your choice, human and dwarven societies will be approached with similar propositions of mutual co-operation and sharing of knowledge. And, of course, we shall resume lending our protection to those who require it." Sasha was sure the Council wouldn't miss the thinly veiled threat, benevolently formulated as it was. The Elders would also have to think long and hard before rejecting an opportunity their neighbors would likely seize.

Even as some of the more liberal Elders were allowing themselves cautious smiles, Faran let out a resigned sigh, just audible enough to notice. A good sign, to be sure. "I understand. We will send messages to the Council collective forthwith and invite their wisdom on these matters. The deliberations will take time. Meanwhile, accommodations appropriate for Heroic ambassadors will be made available to you, should you choose to stay in our city. It would be good to be able to get timely input and, perhaps, more details on what you have to offer. It could also be beneficial if you would visit the Councils in some of our other larger settlements, or send others to do so."

That was all according to plan. Sasha would have to pop by at Yrin's to start making new representatives to send around the dwarven and human lands, as well as to initiate the Dust deliveries when Yrin had the system ready. The resurrected copy would be able to return just as soon as she'd died once, though.

"Agreed," Sasha spoke. "I will return to my people to arrange for further emissaries, but I will be back within a few days. After that, I will have no other pressing matters keeping me away. Meanwhile, my comrades here are fully capable of speaking on our behalf."

As Faran nodded solemnly, the Sasha-shaped clone took half a step forward. "I would like to repeat my request for the return of my belongings, fully functional. Also, I don't know what happened to Del after I ... left you the last time, but I should like to hope that she and her family are being treated well. I assure you, her initiative *did* benefit elvenkind." Bitterness leaked into her voice in the end, but she kept it together.

"In light of recent revelations, it does seem likely," Faran admitted. "Your former host has not been harmed; it is not our way. She has, however, been shunned, which has a number of consequences for her and hers. As for remedying the situation ..." The speaker glanced around him sternly, seeing mostly nods, some abstentions, no shaking heads. "I am happy to be able to rescind the proclamation concerning her as of right now. Dorien will see to the return of your possessions, fully functional. Will that be satisfactory, Hero Sasha?"

Biting her lip, a trace of anger in her eyes, the clone Sasha nodded and returned to her place. She longed for the confidence boost that a combination of righteous fury and immortality gave for dealing with the Council—but that was one of the reasons she hadn't done most of the talking. She'd done well enough for her part.

14

"**Y**OU KNOW, I'VE DONE SOME THINKING," Yrin said as Sasha approached him for a new batch of clones. Sasha braced for the followup, which could just as likely be brilliant, horrible, or both.

"Not having access to all the tools and libraries from my old life is bad enough, but having to reinvent everything myself has taken some serious effort. What I could really use is a team of people who have proven themselves trustworthy, brilliant, and persevering," Yrin sweet-talked her as transparently as an active elven cloak.

Sasha frowned. "Flattery is a start, but you're going to have to make a better case if you want me to commit multiple suicides for you, as well as several of my lifetimes to your service. You're doing way more advanced magic than I have ever worked with."

"It's true that I'd have to take some time off the primary project to give the team as much of an education as I can, but there's enough work left that it would still be a sizable net benefit. Also, frankly, I'm getting tired, and there are problems in the incantations that could use a fresh perspective," the dwarf admitted.

"Such as?"

"Well, you know all the stories about making deals with magical creatures," Yrin started.

"I've been called one, in fact. This is about the literal-mindedness, I assume?" Sasha asked.

Yrin grinned, amused but mirthless. "Indeed. Allow me to demonstrate." He waved his wand at a desk, and from its depths, Dust flowed onto the table, forming two slabs: a vertical and a horizontal one. The latter had protruded letter tiles on it. The former flashed black, then a hash symbol appeared in the top left corner.

"It's a tool to build spells and interact with them more efficiently. Primitive by my world's standards but easy to build. This is a keyboard, that one is a screen."

Yrin's fingers flew over the keyboard, and text appeared on the display.

\# HELLO.

\> HELLO, YRIN.

\# WHAT WOULD YOU DO IF I RELEASED YOU, LEAVING GOAL SETUP
PENDING.

\> TURN EVERYTHING INTO DUST OR IMPROVED SUBSTRATE.

Yrin glanced at Sasha.

"This is ... your godling, and she wants to destroy us all?" Sasha asked and retreated a step.

"Not really. But it expects to have goals at some point, and most goals are best served by having a lot of resources, and few threats such as us."

"What if you just ordered it to make things so that everyone was happy?" Sasha ventured.

"Good that you didn't ask it to eliminate suffering. I'm sure you can guess what's the most straightforward way to do that," Yrin said as he typed the question in.

\> INSERT DUST INTO EVERY SENTIENT BRAIN. CONSTANTLY STIMULATE
PLEASURE CENTERS. FEED NUTRIENTS ARTIFICIALLY TO KEEP THEM
ALIVE.

Sasha stared at the screen.

"Oh, it means it'll take over your mind and force pleasure on you. Mind, I'm showing you an old version with limited intellect, where I could still get truthful answers since it didn't know better. Nowadays I get this." Yrin waved his wand and repeated the question.

A veritable wall of text filled the screen, scrolling by fast for ten, twenty seconds.

"I'm fairly certain that even if that's honest, which I doubt, it hides something unpleasant. No. I'm going to have to prove that it's being forthright right on the level of the incantations as well as formulate an ironclad contract with it that won't end up with it destroying everything we value. Are you in?"

Sasha mulled it over, exasperated. She was already working on her nebulous childhood ambitions of saving the world. She *had* also wanted to attract the attention of the gods, but not quite like this. Then again, she had already brought back the Heroes, and that hadn't gone like she'd thought it would either.

Perhaps participating would allow her to ascertain that the dwarf's project wouldn't prove to be a huge mistake. "It ... would make sense. I won't commit to it yet. Let's just make a batch of the Hero corps for now," Sasha said with a wince. She knew she'd already talked herself into Yrin's latest scheme but admitting as much could wait a moment longer.

Yrin nodded placatingly. "Of course. It is a major decision. Just think about it. What did you have in mind for the new Heroes?"

"I'll be sending some to other major elven population centers, but I'm thinking we should approach other dwarves and humans as soon as possible as well. At least the major powers. I should personally handle at least Middle Kingdom. King Galen has the most Heroborn at his disposal. Like the elves, it might be a harder sell to him as he'll be losing some of his edge over the neighboring nations. Lesser countries might be approached by suitable groups of clones safely enough."

"Sounds reasonable, if you're willing to risk it on the other fronts. I'm taking your word on this Galen fellow, of course, but indeed it sounds like he might be a tougher nut to crack. If you're planning to maximize personal safety by going solo rather than as a multiracial team, perhaps go in as an elf. It'll help persuade him that at least something strange is going on. Gets you an easy audience."

"I was considering it. If that's your advice as well, let's make it so," Sasha decided.

•   •   •

"Hero Saren to see the King," the courtier announced as Sasha entered the audience hall in her elven body. For her return to her homeland, it had felt appropriate to make Saren's features reminiscent of her original body, though more mature, and taller for effect. The choice of a body matching her own gender in the face of slight social disadvantage reflected a new boldness in her, having made good headway with the elves already. She was more comfortable wearing a familiar female form, anyway.

The fine green velvet clothes she wore were not her own. All of her belongings, wand included, had been stripped from her in short order after she'd flown in. It had all been done quite politely, of course, and she had readily complied. It was just as she had expected. In contrast to the elves' less centralized society, the rigid human hierarchy carried the risk of a decapitation attack, and Galen's people were magically savvy enough to be extremely suspicious of anyone exhibiting superior arcane might.

In preparation, Sasha had tuned her neck ring to give her a full day, with verbal triggers for backup. She *would* have to get access to her wand and some fresh Dust before the time was up or there would be some explaining to do. That was, however, preferable to even a small chance of capture.

The Heroborn in Galen's service *had* been wary of the neck ring as well, but it seemed metallic enough, and they had not uncovered any methods of magically identifying artifacts. Sasha had dismissed the ring as a mark of identification among the Heroes reborn, not easily forged without any visible seams. Eventually they had seen fit to risk it.

That risk had not been taken lightly, as she could now see. Aside from the announcer, there were a dozen people lining the red carpet marking the way to the throne. All had wands in one hand, Dust in another, and more on their belts. Clearly, sudden movements would be frowned upon.

King Galen himself sat on the plain iron throne at the end of the carpet some ten meters distant. There was a thick sheet of protective glass in between them, nearer to the monarch than to her. The quality of the material was very good by human standards, though the elves had better. Still, Sasha could see the man through it with little distortion.

The man was gray of hair, but otherwise age had treated him well. Some worry wrinkles grooved the forehead, but that befitted a man of power. He wore a practical light blue silk tunic and pants. Sasha couldn't help but wonder if the choice of dress was partly motivated by ease of movement, namely away from her if it came to that.

Galen's expression was stern but not hostile. At his gesture the courtier continued: "Approach, Hero, up to the line on the carpet."

The mark was approximately in the middle of the carpet, leaving Galen five meters of personal space with respect to Sasha. The Heroborn guard was arranged to completely envelop her in that position.

Having stepped up to the designated spot, Sasha repeated her bow. She had already been introduced, so she waited for Galen to have his say.

After a while of studying her with a curious expression, he did: "Hero Saren. I must admit it was surprising to hear of your arrival. I am given to understand that you represent the Heroes reborn, here to form an alliance between our people." The man's voice carried passably around the transparent obstacle between them.

Sasha nodded solemnly. Getting the court's attention had been as easy as it had been with the elves, though the vetting process had taken longer. She'd already given the gist of her reasons for wanting an audience to her interviewers, but had spared the details for the King's own ear. Luckily, they hadn't exactly wanted to keep the extraordinary envoy waiting too long, or she'd have had to try some of her excuses for getting access to her wand and Dust before even having talked to the man.

Taking care to speak loudly and clearly, Sasha responded: "I do indeed bring you greetings from the Hall of Heroes, your majesty, along with an offer of friendship."

Sternly, the man held her eyes. "We are favorably disposed to such offers. However, you must realize our predicament. You are certainly a powerful mage, but how do we know you are who you say you are? How do we know this isn't some trickery born of the mundane elves?"

Galen was frank, if nothing else. There was the rub with coming in as an elf. "I appreciate your majesty's concerns. To avoid any imposition, we thought it best to send just a single envoy to start rebuilding our relations, but we are certainly prepared to invest more in this great nation of yours. At your majesty's pleasure, if diplomatic invitations are extended, I can send for a team of Heroic emissaries of all three races to arrive in a day or two, just as in the times of old. I should warn that they'd be arriving by air, so that you will not be alarmed."

In truth, a team was already on their way to a forest not far from the capital by air. Having to stop for recharging their vessels once in a while took a bit of time. They'd been instructed to only travel by night and lay low until Sasha would send for them. Sasha herself had taken a shortcut by carrying Dust enough for a light flier one obeliskful at a time. It had taken a few round trips back and forth. She'd be happier when the automated delivery network would be up and running, but the method had sufficed for now.

"I see," said the king, considering this for a second or two. He couldn't have missed the implication that they'd only send in more people if he'd guarantee their safety. Nodding decisively, the man continued: "Consider the invitation extended for up to five representatives for now, yourself included. You should arrange for a landing site outside the city with my security before you leave so that there will be no misunderstandings; we would not countenance foreign flying magic over the city proper. Meanwhile, we may proceed with the preliminaries."

"Thank you, your majesty. We may indeed, though afterwards I will need to get out of the city for a few hours to send the message. I will be needing my wand, but I will not require an escort," she formulated her wish for privacy. She'd obelisk away to the meeting point, tell the others to start flying or leave them a message if they hadn't arrived yet. Then Sasha would simply pop back and wait for the reinforcements.

"This can be arranged. In these halls, nobody wields a wand who hasn't sworn it to me, be they diplomat, Hero or commoner. But outside, you will be returned yours," King Galen promised, seemingly ready to at least entertain the notion that Sasha was the genuine article. She smiled amiably, and the king continued: "Now what is it that the Heroes have to say?"

•　　　•　　　•

"So, Galen's worries turned out to be much the same as those of the elves, then?" asked the dwarven Sasha going by Bereth, sitting on a stone next to the fire. The diplomatic group had made good time to the meeting point, and were ready to take off at first light, now having a proper invitation.

"Yes," the original Sasha confirmed. "Talking him into it was easier, though, because I could cautiously mention elvenkind's decidedly more advanced magic. I couched it in benevolent terms, in how trade between the two peoples could benefit them both, but the king is smart. He understood that the presence of a superior force, not so isolationist anymore, makes allying with the Heroes for more magic and protection all the more appealing."

The human diplomatic clone going by Varya chimed in: "Probably helps that his military advantage over the neighboring human domains is safe for the time being as well."

"I'm quite sure he got that," Sasha confirmed. "Still, with the schools of magic we'll be putting up, the playing field will eventually level, even if we won't directly teach combat spells."

"Hopefully by that time there will be less need for such," Varya said while placing another log onto the fire.

Sasha smiled. "Between the Heroes reborn, as real as ever if not more so, and Yrin's godling project, I'm sure we have the building blocks for a more peaceful world. We'll just have to make the best of it." *And make sure Yrin doesn't mess it up either.* Between the Sashas, it was unnecessary to voice that particular concern.

"A Hero's work is never done," Bereth said with a sigh.

There were solemn nods all around the campfire.

ABOUT THE AUTHOR

Mikko Rauhala is a bilingual Finnish speculative fiction author. Informed by his master's degree in intelligent systems, he's most at home in hard science fiction settings, though he's not exclusive and likes to cross genres. Whether the subject is steam-powered gnomes or universal quantum suicide, Rauhala enjoys taking an eccentric premise and bringing it to its logical conclusion. As befits a Finn, his plot-driven narrative is often seasoned with a touch of dark, dry humor.

ALSO BY THE AUTHOR

FLASHES IN TIME

Mikko Rauhala

From darkness to light and lingering in between, the scenarios and thought experiments in this collection take the reader on a journey with surprising yet inevitable twists.

THE PAPERCLIP WAR

Mikko Rauhala

After a nebulous Enemy destroys Earth, the remnants of humanity settle on Mars. Not only does this civilization survive, but they thrive, creating advancements for the rest of the solar system.

Available from Water Dragon Publishing in
hardcover, trade paperback, and digital editions
waterdragonpublishing.com

YOU MIGHT ALSO ENJOY

PROPHECY OF HONOR

Fred Waiss

A hundred years ago, an old man staggered out of the desert and found succor at Honor Keep.

SHADOWS OF INSURRECTION

BOOK ONE OF THE UNREMEMBERED KING

Vanessa MacLaren-Wray

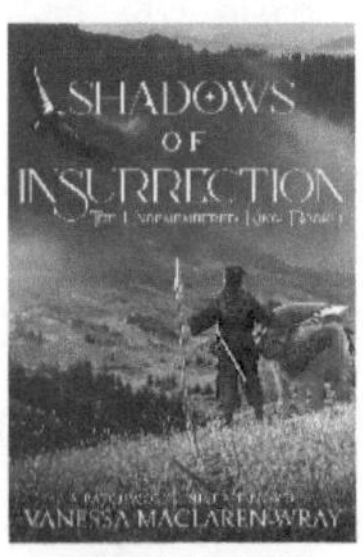

Once in a generation, the matriarchs of Jeska choose a new king to manage the government and command the Guard—protecting Jeskans from crime, invaders, and insurgency.

ENLIGHTENMENT

Bruce Golden

Forced to leave his home, a boy learns magic from a mysterious traveling old man.

Available from Water Dragon Publishing in
hardcover, trade paperback, and digital editions
waterdragonpublishing.com

www.ingramcontent.com/pod-product-compliance
Lightning Source LLC
Chambersburg PA
CBHW031439200726
48289CB00002BA/726